D1607501

PLANET OF THE DATES

PLANET OF THE DATES

A novel by Paul McComas

April '08

For Barb,
See if the lead character's dad
reminds you of anyone. ☺
Thank you for everything
you did for my father.
Fondly,
Paul

THE PERMANENT PRESS
Sag Harbor, New York 11963

For information, address:
    The Permanent Press
    4170 Noyac Road
    Sag Harbor, NY 11963
    www.thepermanentpress.com

Library of Congress Cataloging-in-Publication Data

McComas, Paul
    Planet of the dates : a novel / by Paul McComas.
        p. cm.
    ISBN-13: 978-1-57962-160-5 (alk. paper)
    ISBN-10: 1-57962-160-0 (alk. paper)
        1. Triangles (Interpersonal relations)—Fiction. 2. Milwaukee (Wis.)—Fiction. I. Title.

PS3563.C34345P56 2008
813'.54—dc22   2007043686

Printed in the United States of America.

For Heather—

writer, lover, partner, friend . . .

for everything we've been

to date

and everything yet to be.

ACKNOWLEDGMENTS

An early, shorter version of the Prologue appeared in *The Awakenings Review* Vol. II, No. 2 (Summer 2003). A portion of Chapter 1 appeared in *Peninsula Pulse* Vol. XII, No. 12 (July 2006). Chapter 4 and brief portions of Chapters 3, 5, and 12 appeared as the short story "I Was A Teenage Disco Prince" in the anthology *First Person Imperfect* (iUniverse, 2003).

Thanks to the following for feedback on prior drafts or portions thereof: Leah Barnum, Tim W. Brown, Eric Diekhans, Betsy Doherty, Ben Handelsman, Amy Leonhart, Janet Martin, Hazelyn McComas, Glenda McMiller, Sarah Miller, Nina Newhouser, Teresa Schweigert, Laura Allen Simpson, Greg Starrett, Laurie Starrett, and Tom Tierney.

Deep thanks to Lisa Beth Janis for priceless chapter-by-chapter input; to Lee "Lord of the Facts" Salawitch for invaluable research support; to my publishers, Judy & Marty Shepard, for their belief in and support of this book; to Liz Ridley for personalized promotion; to Susan Ahlquist for deft design; to my mother and, in memoriam, my father, for their unflagging love and encouragement; to my "big" sister Rachel for early (and ongoing) counsel regarding the fairer sex; to Janet Martin, Mark Dintenfass, and Bill Nolan for getting me started as a writer, so many years ago; and, in loving memory, to Julia Sackin for inspiration.

The paragraph in Chapter 15 about the River Styx is adapted from a passage in *Mythology* by Edith Hamilton (Little, Brown & Co., 1942).

FOREWORD

by WILLIAM F. NOLAN,
award-winning author of *Logan's Run*

Remember your teen years?

Remember how you felt, how you looked, how you acted, what wild emotions ran rampant inside your burgeoning young body?

Remember the style of clothes you wore? Remember the music that obsessed you?

Remember how *horny* you were?

Paul McComas remembers all of these things and brings them into vivid focus in *Planet of the Dates*. A peach of a novel (and a strong follow-up to his first, *Unplugged*), *Planet* is a veritable time machine back to the summer of 1980, returning readers to an adolescent world in which sex and rock formed a bizarre intermix of release and raw desire.

Protagonist Philip Corcoran is an emotionally-driven 16-year-old sci-fi fan devising elaborate plans to lose his virginity—and perhaps find true love—by his 17th birthday. He is a bright, creative, industrious young man desperately striving to be cool, racked by desires he's unable to fulfill. There is much humor and pathos in his near-frantic quest. Against all odds, in impossibly frustrating situations, Phil stubbornly plunges onward, convinced that he is drawing close to obtaining his Holy Grail.

It is often difficult for a male writer to create truly believable female characters, but Paul McComas has no problems in this area; he gives us exceptionally strong, engaging young women in Stefanie Slocum, Danielle Payton and Cheryl Jantz. They are depicted as totally different personalities, each one rendered with a prose mastery that brings her to breathing life.

The novel takes a surprising turn in its closing pages, lending a new depth to all that has preceded it. As the final act unfolds, you'll find yourself grinning wide and saying, "Yeah, yeah! Way to go!" And for readers seeking thought-provoking entertainment, a sharply-observed return to their teen years, and a bundle of belly laughs, *Planet of the Dates* is indeed the way to go.

Time for me to step aside and let you dive into this warm, witty, wonderful narrative on your own. So . . . meet Phil Corcoran and company via the magical mind of Paul McComas.

That'll work!

William F. Nolan
Bend, Oregon

PROLOGUE

Journey to the Planet of the Dates

During the summer that our nation turned 200 and I turned 13, the rampant galas and ovations, speeches and celebrations held little interest for either my brother or me. Todd, five years my senior, was far less taken with Tall Ships and parades than with the ship-shape, feathered-blonde coed who regularly paraded past our house in a red-and-white-striped halter top and blue vinyl shorts. Watching her strut her star-spangled stuff as he cut the grass out front, Todd tightened his grip on the handle of our old manual mower till it bent, and though both of his hands were thus occupied, another part of him couldn't help but salute.

Todd's main aspiration for his last summer at home seemed to involve a three-step plan: 1) get to know Ms. Vinyl Shorts, so that he could 2) go out with Ms. Vinyl Shorts, so that he could 3) get into Ms. Vinyl's shorts.

I, with comparatively few hormones thus far in play, was free to operate on a higher plane. Amidst all the Bicentennial blather, destiny beckoned, and I—a budding Super-8 auteur—answered the call. Journey back with me, now, to a sunny June afternoon that found my friend Avery and me kneeling side by side in the sand of Atwater Beach with a tripod, a movie camera and a Prehistoric Scenes model kit.

We were filming my latest Philip Corcoran Production, *Lost Island*, the eight-minute movie through which I explored a question that has tugged at innumerable great minds through the ages: what would happen if an island full of gigantic bears, alligators and woolly mammoths were to dislodge itself from the center of Lake Michigan and drift southward to the Milwaukee shore? (The answer: very bad news for one Midwestern municipality.)

So there I was with my frequent partner in cinematic crime, hunkered down over his foot-long woolly mammoth model. We were preparing to shoot *Lost Island*'s climactic sequence, in which a massive, explosives-induced earthquake buries the last marauding mammoth in several tons of concrete, steel and sand. (The city, at this point in the film, was in ruins anyway, so inducing a 'quake to bring what little was left crashing down upon the attackers seemed to the mayor a reasonable course of action.)

"I don't know about these 'ruins' of yours, Phil." Avery was pawing through the large mixing-bowl full of rocks, tinfoil balls and scraps of corrugated cardboard I'd intended to serve as the remnants of Greater Downtown.

I made an adjustment to the mammoth's trunk, then glanced over. "What do you mean?"

"Well, these pieces here look a lot like . . . aluminum foil."

"So?" I retorted. "Aluminum is a metal. There's metal in buildings. Case closed."

"And this," he continued, holding up one-half of a styrofoam egg carton. "What the hell's *this* supposed to be?"

I stared at it for a moment, then looked him in the eye. "Modular housing."

Female laughter, lilting and light, sounded from behind us and off toward the lake. I turned to see a pretty young brunette sitting perhaps 50 feet away, perched on a jetty with a book in hand. The moment my eyes found the girl, her own eyes returned to the page. She seemed to be about our age but did not look familiar to me.

Avery was eyeing her, too. "You know her?"

"Nope. You?"

"Huh-uh." He paused. "Ya think she was laughing at *you*?"

It pissed me off that he didn't say "at us," but I let it go. "Nah. Prob'ly something she read . . ."

The girl placed a pen to her book—a diary; a journal?—and began intently scribbling away.

"... or wrote," I added.

"I'll bet she's with *Variety*. Prob'ly doing a behind-the-scenes piece on the groundbreaking art direction of *Lost Island*."

"Shut up." I looked at him. "She's not even watching us." I returned my attention to the mammoth . . . but continued to think of the girl. She was cute, all right, with her coltish legs and her lemon-yellow shorts, and her pubescent breasts budding underneath her baby-blue T. And her long, reddish-brown hair falling down her neck and over her shoulders. And . . . what if she *was* watching? Just in case, I decided to show off a bit by shifting into serious-director mode: "All right, Avery, let's do this—let's get the stop-motion sequence. You move the model, and I'll shoot."

"Check." He shifted over to a spot beside the mammoth, positioning himself just out of frame.

I squatted behind the camera. "This scene is *key*. So take your time moving the limbs, and let's get it right!"

He looked at me, perturbed . . . then looked a bit higher.

"How," a sweet yet savvy voice behind me inquired, "would an elephant wind up on a Milwaukee beach?"

I turned all the way around to gaze at the girl, who was, as it happened, even cuter up close. "It's . . . a woolly mammoth," I told her.

"Oh," she said with a wry smile. "Well, *that* explains it."

Our bold interloper lingered for quite a while that day, making small talk and watching us shoot. I was less nervous around her than Avery seemed to be—*and* less nervous than I'd have expected. It helped that she'd met me in a context to which I was accustomed and which, by its nature, imbued me with a certain authority and sense of control. What's more, the girl had a bemused yet affable manner that set me at ease . . . and she seemed to like *me*, too. By the time she wished us luck and ambled off, I had her name, her phone number and, to all appearances, her interest. I also had a burning desire:

To cast her in my next film.

* * *

Stefanie Slocum was my age, but we attended different schools, for while my family lived in a shoreline suburb just north of Milwaukee, hers lived in the city itself—a fact that rendered her both worldly and a tad dangerous. In truth, only 16 blocks separated our addresses . . . but hers had that exotic urban zip code. To my mind, those five numerals conjured a whole string of "Kojak"-worthy images; visiting Stefanie's house at night doubtless would entail walking a gauntlet of street toughs and stoolies, sassy-mouthed hookers and hopped-up junkies, with a siren or two blaring somewhere close by.

Stefanie had a winsome grin and a pair of unusually high-placed eyebrows that gave her a look of perpetual surprise. She was, as luck would have it, an aspiring actress and fellow film buff with a weakness for old musical comedies—not exactly P.C. Productions' stock-in-trade, but as far as she could tell, my little operation was the only game in town. So, yes, I had an "in" with her, and that surely didn't hurt. But as we came to know each other over the weeks that followed, it grew clear that our friendship was based on more than mere "professional" convenience.

One other thing: she addressed me as Philip—never Phil. Though sometimes, when discussing my movies, she called me "P.C.," as if I were some big-time Hollywood honcho. Which, of course, thrilled me to no end.

The first time Stefanie visited my home, I poured us some Hi-C, grabbed some wafer cookies and took her straight to the basement for a screening of the half-dozen P.C. Productions I'd produced up to that time. First came *Snow Kong* (1974, 3 min.), in which a King Kong model kit rampaged (with the aid of oft-visible fishing line) across a backyard snow bank. Taking a page from Orson Welles, I'd shot the action from a low angle in hopes of rendering the snow bank glacial and Kong colossal. But because I was operating Kong-strings and camera simultaneously, each with one outstretched arm, the end result was a rather odd meditation on the cloud-filled January sky—with a blurry plastic gorilla head popping sporadically into view at the bottom of the frame.

"It *was*," I reminded her, "my rookie effort."

"Pretty avant-garde," Stefanie quipped, "whether you meant to be or not!"

Next came a supernatural-horror trilogy: *Werewolf!* (1974, 5 min.), *Death of the Werewolf* (1975, 4 min.) and *The Werewolf Lives Again!* (1975, 5 min.). As I pointed out to my guest, each of these entries added another key component to the P.C. Productions repertoire: in the first case, live human performers; in the second, a tripod; and in the third, a script.

Affirmed Stefanie: "All wise additions, P.C."

The next film, *Were-Bear of Oshkosh* (1976, 6 min.), had been shot on location during a Christmas-week visit at my grandparents'. Its high point was a stunning shot of the full moon rising eerily over Lake Winnebago, followed by the dramatic battle between the bell-bottomed Were-Bear (a masked and moderately inebriated Todd) and a six-foot-long, taxidermied sturgeon.

"Not a fair fight!" Stef objected.

"Why, 'cause they're on land?"

"Yeah," she nodded. "Talk about 'home-field advantage'!"

And then, at last, I proudly screened the just-completed *Lost Island*. The stop-motion-animation sequence that Stefanie had watched me film was rudimentary and herky-jerky—but it was still animation and, thus, a kind of magic: the mammoth appeared to stride across the beach of its own accord. Stef was genuinely impressed . . . at least, until the tinfoil and egg cartons.

"O-o-o-oh," she giggled, "look at that cool modular housing!"

Before she departed, I clued her in on the plans for my next film: an action-packed epic entitled *Prehistoric Planet of the Apes*. "It may have come to me in a dream," I mused aloud, "or maybe not. All I know is that one morning last week, I woke up asking myself this question: 'What if the Forbidden Zone on the Planet of the Apes contained the secrets not only of Man's past, but also of Earth's?' I mean, picture it, Stefanie. . . ."

And by God, from the look on her face . . . she was!

"Ape scientists," I continued, "staring in awe at living, breathing dinosaurs. . . !"

"Gorilla soldiers," she cut in, "doing battle with . . . saber-toothed tigers!"

"Yeah!" I nodded emphatically. "And primitive cavemen, meeting up with . . . with. . . ."

". . . with . . . *other* primitive cavemen?"

I threw out my hands. "The possibilities are endless."

I didn't cast her that day; I was, as yet, only halfway done with the script. Finishing it proved to be a monumental task, for this time around I was working on a much bigger canvas, scripting a movie that would clock in at just under half an hour—as long as all of my other films combined (and, in case the networks were interested, a suitable length for TV).

Of course, with Stefanie on the scene, *Prehistoric Planet of the Apes* would prove pioneering in another way as well. Though not the first of my movies with a female cast member—my older cousin, Barb, had appeared in *The Werewolf Lives Again!*, incongruously towering over her lycanthropic attacker—it *would* be the first to feature an actress who wasn't related to me.

When I finally phoned to offer her the female lead, Stefanie was elated; you'd have thought the call had come from Twentieth Century-Fox. I decided to wait until later to go into any detail about the part, which was, I said, "still in development."

Just as I hung up, Todd grabbed the cast list out of my hand and gave it a look. "A chimp? You're makin' your girlfriend play a *chimp*?"

"She's not my girlfriend," I said, "and Dr. Zira is not just any chimp."

He dropped the sheet into my lap. "Right." Then, under his breath: "Douche bag."

Such was the extent of a typical brotherly conversation during the Summer of '76, for we harbored disparate ambitions that had little to do with one another. Nor was I the only one whose efforts were meeting with success. Todd, by mid-July, had accomplished Step 1—her name was Vicki; she'd just finished her freshman year at UWM; she liked "tennis, Peter Frampton, and cats"—and he'd even succeeded in setting up Step 2: a date. In fact, they were to go out the same Saturday that *Prehistoric* was scheduled to begin shooting.

That day found me ensconced in the cellar, mulling over the synchronicity of it all while using liquid latex to attach brown crepe hair and facial "ape-pliances" to the delicate features of my visibly disappointed leading lady. I was quite proud of these appendages—a lower muzzle, upper muzzle, nose piece and brow—which I'd fashioned from a sheet of foam rubber. (When the first reel came back from Fotomat, Stefanie did appear convincingly simian—as long as she looked toward the camera. But when she turned to either side, the attachments flattened out, and she resembled less a kindly chimp psychologist than a somewhat forlorn 13-year-old girl with great slabs of packing material inexplicably epoxied to her face.)

"You know, Philip," she said as I affixed a huge, sloping brow to her own small, currently knotted one, "this wasn't exactly what I had in mind. I mean, as an actress. . . ."

"Stef, you have all the best lines."

"I know. But no one'll see my face as I'm speaking them!"

"Do you know what Kim Hunter said?"

She scrutinized me with cool blue eyes. "Kim. . . ?"

"She played Dr. Zira in the first three *Apes* films, and she considered that portrayal to be the . . . the crowning achievement of her career. She said that acting with the makeup—*through* the makeup—was more challenging than anything else she'd done. Including Shakespeare. And *that*," I concluded, adding a final tuft to Stefanie's beard, "is why I . . . I had no choice but to give the role to *you*."

"I see." Behind her muzzle, there surfaced a smile. "Nice speech . . . P.C."

* * *

Stefanie appeared in only two more of my films; her school's drama club offered acting opportunities—and a thespian community—with which I simply couldn't compete. But P.C. Productions marched on without her, resolutely cranking out superfluous re-hashes of other people's horror and sci-fi premises for the next 31 months.

By 1980, though, something had changed. A peripheral concern became primary; what had been latent took on laser-like intensity. Three months shy of 17, I found myself tossing and turning through more nights than not, wrestling my sweaty sheets into submission, my head filled with visions not of werewolves but of women. And as for mammoths, well . . . there *was* something woolly I very much wanted, but it was fairly small—and didn't have a trunk.

Todd, by now, made his home several states away, yet in a sense he lived on in my room, my bed, my own feverish head. Thinking back one sleepless early-June night, I grasped at last his fixation with the lithe and lovely Vicki in all her vivacious, vinyl-cheeked glory. I thought about Stefanie Slocum as well: a smart, sweet, pretty girl who had liked me, listened to me, made time for me . . . and whom I, in return, had made into a chimp.

Switching on the bedside lamp, I squinted out across the room; as my eyes adjusted, they fell upon the dresser-top Zira, Cornelius and Dr. Zaius action figures staring back at me in dusty silence. I grabbed my pillow and hurled it at the trio, knocking two of them—Zira and Zaius—to the floor. They landed, as if to taunt me, one atop the other in a rough approximation of "69."

"Damn you," I muttered, Heston-like, through gritted teeth. "God damn you all to *hell!*"

I wanted a woman. A human woman. I wanted to hold her hand—then everything else. I wanted to stroll with and roll with her, amuse and arouse her, dine with and devour her. I wanted to put away the *Playboys* and the paperbacks and find out for myself what "supple" and "dewy" really meant. And I wanted it today. For, like an astronaut plunged through a time warp, I'd crash-landed in an upside-down world where apes were insignificant . . . and dates ruled.

CHAPTER 1

Gainful Employment on the

Planet of the Dates

I'd spent much of the summer of '79 constructing tinfoil-and-Tupperware UFOs for my 16-minute sequel to *Close Encounters of the Third Kind*. A year later, though, I had close encounters of *another* kind in mind—but precious little capital with which to fund my quest. This was at a time when the male half of the couple was expected to pick up the dinner check, purchase the movie tickets, buy the popcorn and pop, pay for the bowling alley and the shoe rental and, in general, shoulder any expenses that came up in the course of a date. It was the girl's option, though not her obligation, to offer assistance—which the boy was to decline. If the girl repeated the offer, then the boy was permitted, grudgingly, to accept. How I'd come into possession of these precepts is a mystery to me; still, I never saw fit to question them.

I needed money, which meant I needed a summer job. So on the June afternoon following my late-night action-figure attack, I drove my Mom's AMC Pacer all over the North Shore, filling out applications for the usual suspects—pharmacies and supermarkets, Baskin-Robbins and IHOP—though I skipped the fast-food joints. I was concerned about the impact on my complexion of daily proximity to a deep fryer, for the volcanic eruptions on the Planet of the Dates took place, all too often, on one's face.

That night after dinner, my father, who was unaware of my day's activities, called me into his study for "a little chat." I always associated these chats with the smell of tobacco. A prominent cardiologist, my father had read the writing on the wall (or, more accurately, in the *New England Journal of Medicine*) and given up pipe smoking a year before, yet the smoke by then had so saturated his study's carpeting, book shelves and walls that its scent would end up lingering late into the Reagan Administration. He'd thrown away every pipe but one—his favorite—which now sat, oddly enough, atop his desk in a Lucite box like some exhibit in the Museum of Upper-Middle-Class Vices.

In days past, he would gesture with his pipe when he spoke, my eyes automatically following the sweeping trail of smoke. Sitting down opposite him now, I found myself staring, by force of habit, at the stationary pipe in its display case. "I realize," my father began, his tone a bit grave, "that you've put a great deal of time and effort over the past few years into producing your little . . . movies. And there's nothing wrong with that. But you're older now, you only have the one year of high school left, and it seems to me that *this* summer, your time might be better invested. . . . Son, are you listening to me?"

I looked up. "Sorry."

He glanced down at the pipe-in-the-box, and his eyes darkened. "Awful habit. Don't ever start."

"I won't. You were saying. . . ?"

"Phil, I think it's time you got a job."

"I think you're right."

My father said nothing; I listened to the ticking of the wall clock. "Oh," he finally managed.

"I applied at a bunch of places today," I told him, then listed a few.

"I see." He folded his hands on the dark, polished wood of his desk, and I had the distinct impression that, though pleased with where this chat had led, he'd rather have steered it there himself. The wall clock chimed; my father emerged from his reverie. "That's fine, son. That's just fine. In addition, there *is* an opening at the building where I work."

"Doing what?"

"The position is, well, custodial in nature. But it's a start. And as a union job, I imagine it would pay quite a bit better than bagging groceries or. . . ."

"I'll take it!" I all but shouted, fearful that someone else might slip in and claim the job—*my* job—before he'd finished describing it. "When do I start?"

* * *

Milwaukee back then was much as it is today: a mid-sized Midwestern city with a lush lakefront, a small but thriving arts scene, and a food- and beverage-heavy industrial base that included Usinger Sausages, Ambrosia Chocolate and a bevy of breweries. (Throw in one of the cheese factories just north of town, and *presto*: the Wisconsin Diet!) In addition, Milwaukee long has boasted more bars and taverns per block than anywhere else in the USA. As if in atonement, the city also houses a multitude of churches: old European-style near-cathedrals with huge, working clocks mounted on all four sides of their multiple steeples. These ubiquitous steeple-clocks date back to the time before wristwatches and were installed, I once theorized, to help the citizenry keep track of how much time remained till the taverns opened.

The Meigs-Childress Professional Building was located downtown, just west of the lake. A block and a half away loomed the 40-story First Wisconsin Bank Building, the closest thing to a skyscraper our fair city has ever had. Meigs-Childress stood, literally, in the First Wisconsin's shadow and, at 12 stories, seemed rather small . . . until you'd been told to empty its 490 wastebaskets or mop its 26 bathroom floors.

My father had pulled some strings to land me this job; that was clear from the day I donned sport coat and tie and went in to apply. Bud Puckett, the manager of building services—a stocky black man of about 50—read perhaps one line of my completed application form before dropping it onto a pile of desktop paperwork. He eased back into his chair, a canny smile playing below his salt-and-pepper mustache, and spoke as if sharing with himself a droll joke: "Welcome aboard . . . Dr. Corcoran's son."

This took me aback. "I . . . uh, you . . . can call me Phil."

"You start Monday. It's a five-hour shift: 5 to 10 PM. Get here early the first day—a quarter till. And you'll want to dress down. Jeans and a T-shirt. No shorts. Wear shoes with some traction; sneakers are fine." Mr. Puckett reached into a drawer and pulled out a thick pamphlet: "Here." He handed it across his desk. "About the union."

I took it, looked at it. "OK. . . ."

"You'll pay a one-time membership fee—I think it's 90 bucks— plus monthly dues. Of course, at $6.10 an hour, you'll make all that back in your first week, and the rest is cake."

I reached for my wallet, knowing that it contained, oh, maybe $6.10. "Do I pay the membership fee now?"

Mr. Puckett regarded me for a moment, then said a bit sharply, "It'll be deducted from your first check." He scooped my application off the pile. "This your first job?"

I considered alluding to *Snow Kong* and *Son of Spock* and the 20-odd films in between, then thought the better of it. "Yes, sir."

Perusing the form, he squinted. "Hold up. Says here you're . . . 16?"

"I . . . yeah. But only for the next two months. Is that a problem?"

"Is for the union: you're one year too young."

I saw my dream job dematerialize like an *Enterprise* crewman beaming down to a distant world—or beaming, rather, into the cold void of space. It suddenly appeared I was to spend the first summer of this bold new decade not on the Planet of the Dates but far outside its atmosphere, penniless, horny and alone.

Yet in the next moment, Mr. Puckett commandeered Transporter Control—specifically, by picking up a ballpoint and altering my date of birth. My boss-to-be then leaned back in his chair and smiled to himself as before. "Happy birthday . . . Dr. Corcoran's son."

I left his office awash in mixed emotions: grateful for Mr. Puckett's intervention, resentful of his attitude, relieved to have secured the position—and very much hoping I wouldn't have to face a *third* stern authority figure from across an imposing desk any time soon.

Driving home, I found myself reflecting on my father's motives. He'd gone out of his way to find me a position that paid twice as much as the ones I'd pursued on my own but which was, at the same time, the antithesis of a "glamour job." It was as if he wanted me to gain some real-life, blue-collar experience down in the city—but to earn, for my efforts, North Shore bucks. I turned into our driveway with a new appreciation for being "Dr. Corcoran's son."

And, perhaps, for Dr. Corcoran.

*   *   *

That evening after dinner, I rode my Schwinn Suburban over to the high school to shoot some hoops on the outdoor court; a decent pick-up game or 30 could be found there more nights than not. I was a player of middling ability, having come somewhat late to basketball and later still to height. By age 16, though, I was finally starting to feel good about my body; all I needed now was some girl to feel good about it *with* me.

Though the court was unlit—the village never saw fit to accommodate us in that department—the June sun took its sweet time setting; what's more, we tended to linger long after dark, playing past the point of safety. In fact, nobody ever seemed to so much as think about heading home until one of us had sustained a darkness-related injury.

"Shit!" the casualty would gripe, hobbling off the court. "Too goddamn *dark* out's the problem. We shoulda quit an hour ago."

The rest of us would mumble our assent . . . then come back the next evening and take it from the top.

On the night in question, there were only two players on the court when I arrived—older guys I'd played with maybe twice—and they were in the midst of a heated game of one-on-one, so I opted to circumnavigate the school in hopes of returning to a bigger crowd. I only made it halfway around, though, because seated there on the concrete stairs, leaning back against the building's locked Door 3 with a Marlboro in hand, was Cheryl Jantz.

Cheryl Jantz smoked; Cheryl Jantz drank; Cheryl Jantz had toked her way through uncounted acres of weed and was reputed to have sampled myriad other substances as well. She was, in the parlance of the day, a burnout. During the school year, she and her burnout buddies—"the Door 3 Crowd"—congregated daily in this same spot, first over lunch hour and then at day's end, to hang out and smoke and listen to WQFM Less Talk More Rock and discuss how much they'd had to drink and where they might be able to get some drugs.

Cheryl Jantz was, I'd always thought, the cutest of the burnout girls, with her elfin features, jet-black hair, smallish breasts and too-big army jacket, and the way she looked not so much at you as toward you through glazed gray eyes, asking questions that didn't sound like questions at all: "Hey. How goes it." "Hey. What's up." Bringing my bike to a stop in front of her, I couldn't help but marvel to find her stationed outside Door 3 even now, a week into Summer Break, like some pot-addled homing pigeon. "Hey, Cheryl."

She took a drag. "What's the good word."

She was wearing torn denim shorts, cut off to two different lengths, and a black Cheap Trick concert T. "Like your shirt," I said.

Her head tilted down so that she could refresh her memory; she nodded in recognition. "Dream Police, man. Dream fuckin' Police."

I nodded back. "I think they're on tour this summer. Probably coming here."

"Right on." She took another drag. "So, what's new in Philsville."

"Just landed a job."

"Whereabouts."

"Some office building downtown."

"Doin' what."

"Building services and property management."

Cheryl looked toward me and blinked twice; I might as well have been speaking Sanskrit. "What's it pay."

"'Bout six an hour."

She closed her eyes and nodded. "Right on."

I spun one pedal idly with my foot, then took a breath and went for it. "So, Cheryl, ya wanna maybe catch a movie some time, or somethin'." (Though not a burnout myself, I was fluent in the idiom.)

The question surprised her. I suspect it never had occurred to her to go out with a straight arrow like me. Cheryl pursed her lips, blew one quavering smoke ring—"Likely"— then another. "Sure, what the fuck."

"How's this weekend?"

She shook her head. "Goin' to Madison, man, gonna score some primo shit." She motioned me toward her and, as I leaned closer, grabbed my wrist; I nearly fell off my bike, and for one electric instant I thought she might be blowing her next ring around my tongue. Instead, she took a scuzzy black Magic Marker out of her hip pocket, uncapped it with her teeth and scrawled her phone number—along with a frowny face—on my forearm. She spoke through the narrow space between pen cap and cigarette: "Caw me neksh week."

Retracting my arm, I nodded—"Right on"—then turned my bike and, heart racing, rode away.

Back at the court, three more guys had arrived, so the six of us split up for three-on-three. Inspired by my recent rendez-vous and impending date, I played the most aggressive hoops of my young life. Then, just after 10, while diving to keep the ball in bounds, I plowed head-first into an unseen post and sustained a cut that, an hour later, would require eight stitches at the Columbia Hospital E.R.

"Shit!" I hollered, palm pressed to my sticky, swimming head, trying to stanch the flow. "Too goddamn *dark* out's the problem."

* * *

The handful of times I had visited my father at work, I'd headed straight for his suite on the 11th floor, paying little attention to any of the other presumably clinical offices below. Yet Meigs-Childress was, I now discovered, a veritable jack-of-all-buildings. In addition to the expected medical and dental practices, it housed several CPAs, a counseling center, two design firms, an ad agency, the administrative offices of a nearby City College, a photo lab, a hair salon and even a dance studio, plus a cafeteria in the basement. There were

51 separate business concerns in all, and by summer's end I knew
the precise location of each.

Every afternoon at 5, as the rest of the building's work force
departed, my colleagues and I checked in with Mr. Puckett to get
our assignments for the night. These ran the gamut from the mun-
dane (vacuuming the hallways; polishing the baseboards; mopping
the front lobby's vast, marble floor) to the loathsome (scrubbing
grease-spatter off the cafeteria ovens; scrubbing other spatter off
the urinals and johns). Everyone dreaded restroom duty, but when
it came to *favorite* tasks, we each had our own. For my part, I had
two preferred duties—both of which involved taking out the trash.

We were given special instructions for discarding medical and
dental waste, a process that fueled my imagination. I pretended that
I was the heroic safety specialist from *The Andromeda Strain,* and
that if I didn't dispose of a certain pouch or vial in time, all humanity
would pay the price. Donning the compulsory gloves, I'd count down
from 20 and follow the protocol with grim determination, the pace
of my work quickening as "zero" neared. It's a minor miracle that I
never sustained a needle-stick—or spilt a single specimen.

My favorite chore, though, was emptying the wastebaskets in
the second-floor photo lab. That may not sound enthralling, but
again, I brought to the task a cinematic sensibility . . . and a predilection for suspense. You see, the lab handled the processing needs
of many of the building's own businesses, among other commercial clients, and each night, the darkroom wastebasket was rife with
slightly under- and overexposed 8×10s ripe for the taking. Sadly,
the subject matter never even skimmed the surface of erotica;
we're talking ribbon cuttings, ground breakings, awards ceremony
grip-and-grins and other p.r. pap, as well as a plethora of middle-
aged-white-guy head shots. But the way *I* saw them, these photos
revealed shocking state secrets . . . and called for espionage of the
highest order.

While overturning the basket into the trash cart, I slipped
the photos out. Then I closed the door with my foot and, by the
glow of the room's single red bulb, eyeballed the goods. Satisfied, I
hitched up one leg of my jeans, wrapped the prints around my calf,

stretched my tube sock up over them and pulled the pants leg back into position. There the photos remained till my 7:30 break, when I was able to secure them inside my state-of-the-art safe box (to all appearances a common lunch box, right down to the sandwiches). Once the evidence was transferred to my bedroom, my mission would be complete—at least, for that night.

Lest you get the wrong idea, I worked hard at Meigs-Childress. I never loafed around, but neither did I rush through my chores: I took the time to do things right. I performed every task without complaint—nor did I hear a complaint all summer from Mr. Puckett. But between the isolation, the tedium and the pervasive silence, I did end up improvising frequent sci-fi and spy-film scenarios, mini-movies with a cast of one, P.C. Productions that no one was shooting . . . and no one would ever see.

At the end of the week, I stopped by the boss' office to pick up my first-ever paycheck. Immersed in paperwork, he handed me my envelope without looking up: "Week one, all done."

"Yup," I replied, apparently having used up all my creativity on the job.

Mr. Puckett made a notation, crossed something out. "How're you liking it so far?"

"A lot. I'm really glad to be here."

"Glad to have you here, Phil. Have a good weekend."

"You, too," I said, brimming with pride simply to have been called not by my father's name but by my own.

On the bus ride home, I tore open the envelope and took out my check. The gross total on the attached statement looked impressive, especially to a not-quite-17-year-old in 1980. The net—after deductions from the state, the feds, Social Security and the union—looked one-third as impressive. But it was enough. The checks that followed would be larger . . . and in the meantime, there seemed no end to the things that I could do—that Cheryl Jantz and I could do—with 61 bucks. "Right on," I murmured, then let my thoughts wander where they would. . . .

An upside-down world it may have been, but the Planet of the Dates was looking more hospitable all the time.

CHAPTER 2

Trial and Error on the

Planet of the Dates

I suppose it was inevitable that I would dream that night of Cheryl Jantz.

Earlier in the week, we'd spoken on the phone and made plans for Saturday evening, now a mere day away. Consequently, after setting aside my *Starlog* magazine and turning off the lamp, I spent a good two hours wide awake, my body embedding abstract patterns into the mattress. I hadn't been quite so worked-up since that watershed moment at Bayshore Mall—the day back in March when I'd discovered that Chapman's department store, without warning or proclamation, had replaced its previous collection of female mannequins with a glorious new "nippled" line.

Now, three months later, with a potentially hot (*and* fully animate) date imminent, my mind reeled with images and intimations, long-sought scenarios and longed-for sensations. Naturally, when sleep at last took hold, these thoughts persisted—with a twist:

Cheryl was now *with* me in bed . . . yet we were at school, smack in the middle of the wide-open Door 3, our blanketed lower halves inside the building and our uncovered top halves out. Classmates filed past in both directions, visibly annoyed by the obstacle. Cheryl, cigarette hanging from her lips, was up on one elbow stroking my chest, tugging provocatively at the six or seven hairs she'd located there, and as she peered at me through sleepy eyes, I saw that she was wearing a lacy black bra embroidered with two words: CHEAP on one cup, TRICK on the other. She slid her fingers under the top sheet, whose tented fabric betrayed the presence of an erection far larger than anything I could produce in real life. What's more, it seemed to be making noise, a kind of bubbling sound. Cheryl grabbed the covers and peeled them back, revealing the source of my sizable, sonorous endowment. There between my legs where should have stood a dong was, instead, a bong: lit, loaded and raring to go.

Cheryl's eyes opened wide. She yanked the Marlboro from her mouth and flicked it away; licking her upper lip, she moved in close. "Right on."

Then the school bell sounded, and I awoke.

I lay there for a moment, bathed in the rays of the midmorning sun, then peeked beneath the sheet: hard, yes, but all me. I was vaguely disappointed; the extra size, I wouldn't have minded. I sat up, pulled on my gym shorts and, softening, stumbled down the hall into the den. I turned on the TV—Channel 4, "Land of the Lost"—but killed the sound, then collapsed atop our squeaky tan sofa and reached for the phone.

My buddy Avery—owner, you'll recall, of the woolly mammoth model kit—answered on the second ring. "Hello?"

"It's Phil," I said, eyes on the TV.

"Hey."

"I just had the weirdest dream about Cheryl Jantz."

"You dreamt she agreed to go out with you."

"Bite me, Thompson. As you know, we *are* going out. Tonight."

"All right, so tell me."

I did. Somehow, the narrative seemed even stranger in the recounting, thanks perhaps to the none-too-convincing claymated dinosaurs and even less convincing child actors silently pursuing each other across the screen in front of me.

When I finished, Avery just said, "Man."

"Yeah."

"Not very realistic, is it?"

"I guess not."

"Cheryl Jantz in lingerie? Like that girl even *needs* a bra."

"No complaints here."

"What do you make of the words on there?"

"On the bra?" I yawned. "Easy. She's a huge Cheap Trick fan."

"Yeah, but was it a reference to the band . . . or to you?"

"Excuse me, asshole, that's my girlfriend-to-be you're talking about."

"So, you'll be registering for wedding gifts at some head shop on Brady?"

"Avery, have a good time tonight with that *ménage à trois*: you, the Jergen's bottle and your right hand."

"Bite me, Corcor—"

I hung up. Avery Thompson, incidentally, was my best friend.

I glanced at my mom's wall-mounted cat clock: 10:10 AM. I watched the clock's tail swing left, right, left, right, as the eyes above did the same. Soon it was 10:11—60 seconds closer to my 6:30 date. With effort, I did the math in my head: one minute down, 499 to go.

I filled up the day as best I could. First, I pulled on my socks, sneakers and Brewers cap, stepped out into the muggy morning and dragged our old lawnmower out of the garage. Having knocked off the back yard the previous afternoon, I now marched the mower out to the front. Pushing it back and forth under the beating sun, I kept an eye, as always, on the sidewalk. The odds were slim, but a part of me clung to the hope that some day, some way, Vicki Vinyl Shorts would make an encore appearance.

That morning as always, the gorgeous Ghost of Summer Past failed to materialize. But I didn't mind—not today. Soon, Summer Present would offer up a worthy vision of its own.

After mowing, I returned to my room, closed the door, turned on the stereo and, to the accompaniment of Steely Dan's "Pretzel Logic," turned my attention to the small but growing stack of 8×10 glossies cached away in my bottom desk drawer. I picked out four: a ribbon cutting, an awards-banquet winners' circle, a head shot of some smug CEO-type and (my favorite) an "action shot" of a matronly dental patient expectorating into a high-tech spit sink, the Cuspimax 2000. I slid the shots into a manila envelope—no return address; no explanatory text—and addressed it to my pen pal, Craig Starling, in Hammond, Indiana.

How, you ask, did I come to have a pen pal in Hammond, Indiana? At age 12, I wrote, drew and Xeroxed the 33-page "Wolfman Referance [sic] Book," which I advertised in the Classifieds section of *Famous Monsters of Filmland* Magazine. Among the 20-odd readers to send in their $1.25 was Craig, who was my own age—and a fellow filmmaker, to boot! We struck up a correspondence, and eventually, with our parents' permission, I visited his home. Predictably, Craig and I hit it off . . . despite some bewilderment at each other's taste in music. (They rock hard in Hammond.) We bonded in all the usual ways—assembling and painting Aurora-brand monster models; passionately debating which "Star Trek" alien could beat the others; and portraying villains in each other's films: he, the human-hating gorilla commandant, General Urko, in *Prehistoric Planet of the Apes*; I, the nefarious, radioactive Dr. Nagasaki in *Sayonara, Mr. Bond* (Craig's film being neither a P.C. Production nor, in retrospect, a very p.c. production).

Another interest we long had shared was the playing of pranks on each other. Receiving those photos was bound to baffle him, and I looked forward to his response. So I pulled on a T-shirt, grabbed $2 off my dresser top and biked to the post office, wishing I could be there to see the look on Craig's face when my "message" arrived.

My postal mission accomplished, I took a different way home, opting for the route that runs by the Fotomat—but the Fotomat was . . . *gone*? I hit the brakes, brought my Schwinn to a screeching halt. How could this be? The yellow kiosk in the middle of the strip-mall parking lot; the humble hut to which I'd taken roll upon roll of exposed movie film and from which I'd retrieved reel upon reel of screenable Super-8 . . . it had been razed. And what was in its place? For what lofty purpose had this travesty been perpetrated? For six additional parking spaces!

I got off my bike, flipped down the kick stand and walked across the asphalt to the spot where the Fotomat had stood. I glanced around—no one seemed to be watching—removed my baseball cap and placed it over my heart. I cleared my throat. *"Snow Kong,"* I said under my breath. *"Werewolf! Death of the Werewolf. The*

Werewolf Lives Again! . . ." A minute or so later, the roll call complete, I replaced my cap, returned to my bike and, without looking back, rode from that spot for what I vowed would be the final time. Others might park in that lot, denigrate and debase that sacred place. But not I.

Seeking solace, I headed for my "birth tree," a stalwart Norwegian maple the village had planted—according to a plaque on the adjacent boulder—in my own birth month of August 1963. When I'd first come across the tree at age six, I'd wondered if it had been planted in my honor, the circular patch of grass around it set aside just for me. Thereafter, I'd brought the tree a thermos full of water on many a hot summer day; once, on my/our birthday, I had tied a blue ribbon around its trunk. From time to time I'd bike over and sit in the maple's shade, reading a Marvel comic or rewriting a script or just gazing up into its boughs, serenely bonding with my leafy twin. There beneath my birth tree, I always felt at peace.

But as I neared the spot that Saturday, I felt queasy. The new decade had ushered new priorities into my life: I hadn't patronized the Fotomat in quite some time—or stopped by the tree in a while, either. Was I somehow responsible for the Fotomat's obliteration? And if so, then what of my maple? My throat tightened; I bent forward and pedaled faster.

It was with great relief that I caught sight of the uppermost branches. Drawing nearer, I ceased pedaling and coasted up alongside the tree; I stopped, pressed my palm against the rough and sturdy bark. Times were changing, and so was I. And though I'd have blushed to admit it—too mushy!—deep down, I knew there were parts of my life that should stay rooted in solid ground.

"Take care," I said aloud, and if anyone heard me, then they heard me. I gave the trunk a pair of pats. "And, oh—wish me luck. Tonight could be big."

* * *

I had been to Cheryl Jantz's home once before, when we were lab partners in Bio; she had missed a week of school for unspecified reasons, and I'd biked over to show her "our" Lake Michigan water-quality report. Now as then, she lived in a cluttered, two-bedroom rental townhouse with her painfully shy kid sister, Gabby; their seldom-seen mother, Annette—a chain-smoking divorcée with a different last name—and a golden retriever named Scout who looked like he'd wandered out of the Cleaver or Brady household, become disoriented and ended up here by default.

I hadn't noticed it during my earlier visit, but Cheryl did not care for the dog. When I rang the bell, much barking ensued, followed by this odd response from my date: "Shut the fuck up! You wanna be astute?" The front door opened, and Cheryl glanced through the screen. "Hey." Her hair was in a state of anarchy, but it suited her; in fact, she was looking fine in frayed flair jeans, plus an army jacket with the sleeves ripped off and an iron-on marijuana-leaf patch on its pocket—a little something from the Stoner Summerwear line.

"Hey," I replied. "Why'd you ask your dog that?"

"What."

"If it wanted to be astute?"

"A *stew*," she said, and reached for the door handle.

"Oh." I led the way to the curb. "Speaking of which . . . you hungry?"

On the way to dinner, Cheryl drummed her hands loudly on the dash, keeping time not to the music on WKTI but, apparently, to some other music in her head. I turned off the radio. "Pacer," she said, still drumming. "This your car, man."

"I wish! It's my mom's."

"Ya like it."

"Yeah, I do. I dig its look, kind of . . . futuristic." I hesitated, loath to come off as the sci-fi dorkus that, well, I was. But then I went ahead: "It reminds me of the maze cars in *Logan's Run*. Ever see that movie?"

She stopped drumming, closed her eyes. "The future," Cheryl said slowly, "as a . . . a huge, sterile shopping mall populated by look-alike, dress-alike drones . . . people so blinded by the . . . the comfort of conformity, they'd sooner fuckin' die at 30 than dare to think for themselves." She took out a pack of Marlboros and a lighter. "Real stretch, huh."

I was impressed. It was the most insightful sentence I'd heard her speak—not to mention the longest. What's more, I agreed. "The guy who wrote it must've studied our school."

"Likely." She lit up; my Mom would *kill* me if she knew, but I didn't care. "So, Phil. How goes it at the workplace."

"Not bad. I like working nights. Leaves my days wide open."

"Right on."

"You workin' this summer, Cheryl?"

"Yeah, some."

"What's the job?"

"Sales." She rolled down her window. "Been workin' with a guy in Madison."

"Hey, how was that trip of yours?"

She turned away, blew smoke into the evening air. "Productive."

We drove to Dos Banditos, a mid-range Mexican joint on the city's quasi-bohemian east side. The hostess placed us at a candle-lit table next to a slightly elevated stage, upon which sat a lively *mariachi* trio. Cheryl was seated beside the swarthy guitarist, and I across from my date, facing the band; the music was loud, but we managed to talk over it. For some reason—perhaps it affected his playing—the guitarist had removed his gold wrist watch and placed it beside his thigh, right there on the seat of his chair. Leaning toward me, Cheryl gestured back with her head. "Good way to lose a watch."

I laughed. "Someone could just reach over and grab it!"

"Yeah." She pulled out a cigarette—"Someone"—and lit it from our candle. Taking a drag, she scrutinized my hairline; I'd told her of my accident over the phone. "Stitches, huh."

"Can you see 'em?"

"Not enough."

I reached up, parted my hair. "Now?"

She nodded. "Wicked."

I felt, for an instant, exposed, as if she'd caught a glimpse of me naked. I liked it.

Cheryl leaned closer, inspecting. "They hurt."

"No; they itch." I let my hair fall back in place. "But they come out next week."

"Right on."

"Cheryl, there's something I've been wondering."

She blew a smoke ring in my general direction. "What's that."

"Outside Door 3, when you wrote your phone number on my arm . . . what was the deal with the frowny face?"

"Whatcha think."

"I don't know. I hoped it wasn't a . . . a warning about tonight. Or a prediction!"

A waitress appeared, bearing menus, salsa and chips. She introduced herself as Carlotta and asked us, "Something to drink?"

"Yeah," Cheryl answered, "margarita on the rocks." She looked toward me. "Hey, man, wanna get a pitcher."

"Miss," Carlotta said, "I'll need to see proof of age." (In Wisconsin at that time, we only had to be 18. But we weren't.)

Cheryl dug into her pocket and produced her fake ID, which appeared to pass muster. I had one, too—a covert Christmas gift from Todd—but had left it at home and so, with some chagrin, ordered a Fresca. Carlotta stepped away, and as I turned back to Cheryl, I blanked. "Sorry . . . *what* were we talking about?"

She dipped a finger into the salsa and drew a red frowny face on the table.

"Oh; right."

"Nothin' to do with you, Phil. Not a prediction. Just kind of a . . . antidote."

"To what?"

She tilted her head to one side. "All our rah-rah cutie-pie cheerleader pals, Tammi with an *i*, Kandy with a *K* . . . smiley faces, hearts 'n' flowers, have a nice day."

Her answer struck me as verse, a sort of Beat poem. "You should write that down. You could get it published."

Cheryl shrugged—"Unlikely"—and swiped her palm across the salsa frown, wiping it away, and it was then I saw the flash of gold upon her wrist.

"*Jesus!*" I glanced up at the guitarist's chair—occupied, now, solely by the guitarist—then leaned in close. "Cheryl, you've got to put it back!"

"*I* know," she said as our drinks arrived. She picked up her margarita, raising it—and, thus, the watch—toward me. "But first. . . ."

I lifted my glass hastily.

Cheryl pulled hers back. "Hold up, man. What're we drinkin' to."

"Whatever. You name it. To you, to me; to . . . Door 3."

"Door 3," Cheryl repeated, then clinked her glass against mine and took a sip. She handed me her margarita; as I drank, eyeing her over the salted rim, she removed the watch from her wrist and tucked it back onto the man's chair. Then she picked up her menu, opened it and began to read. "What the fuck's a 'chimichanga'?"

* * *

After dinner we had planned to see *The Shining*, but by the time we got to the theater, the late show had sold out. The assistant manager assured us, however, that there were "plenty of seats left for *Xanadu*." Perhaps we should have asked ourselves why.

Xanadu stars Olivia Newton-John as Kira, an immortal, roller-skate-clad Greek Muse (with an Australian accent) sent by her father, the god Zeus, to Hollywood. Her assignment is to inspire Sonny Malone (Michael Beck), a frustrated young artist, to quit his job—painting wall-sized promotional reproductions of pop album covers—and hook up with Danny McGuire (Gene Kelly in the role that likely killed him), a tap-dancing, clarinet-playing septuagenarian who shares Sonny's lifelong dream: to transform an abandoned L.A. gymnasium into a lavish, multi-level roller-disco that they will christen "Xanadu." I am not making any of this up.

By the five-minute mark, it was clear that we were in for some rough going. Determined to make the best of things, I leaned toward Cheryl and said, "Maybe it'll be one of those movies that's so bad, it's good."

"Or maybe," she replied, "it'll just suck."

And suck *Xanadu* did, aggressively and unremittingly, for the next 83 minutes. Halfway through, during a musical montage in which the Gene Kelly character tries on a variety of hipster threads and models them for his young friends, I heard Cheryl utter a low, drawn-out moan, and I told her, "We can go."

"Nah, get your money's worth." She stood. "Be right back."

She returned 15 minutes later in an altered state. Sitting bolt upright, eyes riveted on the screen, Cheryl knocked her knees together, tore into our popcorn bag with renewed fervor and greeted each of the film's faltering jokes with a peculiar laugh— "Ha-HUH, HUH, huh. Ha-HUH, HUH, huh"—though at no point did I see her smile.

Whatever drug or drugs she'd ingested, through whichever facial cavity or cavities, the effect, though potent, was short-lived; by the closing production number Cheryl was slumped in her seat, emitting, again, the low moan that represents the normal, healthy response to *Xanadu*. I considered slipping an arm around her, but I didn't want her associating my touch with what we'd just endured. As the closing credits began to roll, she mumbled "I'm outta here" and bolted for the door.

Back in the car, silence predominated. Cheryl didn't drum on the dashboard as before—just sat there taking drags from her cigarette, turning her head to blow the smoke out her window. I tried to engage her, to draw her out, but her responses were even more curt than usual—with a cursory quality I hadn't heard before. This change filled me with the same gnawing desperation I'd felt earlier that day, when I'd wondered whether my birth tree was still standing. It was a desperation I now struggled to mask. "I, uh, notice you've got a cassette there. In your jacket pocket?"

"Yeah."

"Wanna give it a play?"

She handed over the tape, and I stuck it into the deck: out came the unmistakable sound of Cheryl's own palms pounding away on some dashboard or table-top. She did not drum along.

"Sounds good."

No reply.

"We could stop by Doctor's Park," I said, "see if anyone's around."

"Unlikely."

"We could head down to Big Bay: go wading, hang out on the pier. . . ."

"Pass."

I was feeling about as in-demand as a Fotomat. "Well, what *do* you wanna. . . ?"

"I'm *tired*," she cut in. "I want to take a shower, and I want to go to bed." These were statements, simple declarations. By no means were they invitations.

"You've got it," I muttered, and stepped on the gas.

When we pulled up outside her home, I half-expected Cheryl to flee the car as abruptly as she had the theater. But she didn't. I cut the engine; crickets chirped outside. I ejected her tape and handed it back. "Thanks," she said.

"Cheryl. . . ."

". . . for tonight." She tossed her cigarette out the window.

"Did I . . . do something, say something to. . . ?"

"Nah. We're just . . . real different is all. But, what the fuck—it was worth a shot." She leaned toward me—"No tongue; I've got a cold"—and gave me a quick kiss on the lips. I reached to hold her, but by then she was gone. "Stay cool, man. And, hey. . . ." She started toward her house. "Maybe I'll look ya up some time."

Reaching her house, she turned the key and stepped inside. I could hear Scout barking, then Cheryl once more, five sharp words as she slammed the door: "Shut up! Shut the fuck—"

CHAPTER 3

Trauma and Recovery on the

Planet of the Dates

I didn't love Cheryl Jantz. Hell, I barely knew her . . . and what I did know made for a decidedly mixed bag. But if what I felt while watching her disappear into that townhouse wasn't quite heart-break, then it was—at the very least—heart-hairline-fracture.

I somehow had the presence of mind to head for a 24-hour convenience mart. There I bought a can of air freshener, selecting the scent with the most neutral-sounding name. I sprayed the bejeezus out of the seats, floor, ceiling and dash, using up half the can right there in the Open Pantry lot. When I was through, not a trace of tobacco odor remained; rather, the Pacer now smelled as if it had been submerged for days in some second-rate perfume factory's "Reject" vat.

All but gagging, I drove with the windows down onto the nearest freeway entrance. I merged, then accelerated, letting the air sweep through the speeding car in hopes that a steady summer wind might displace the all-too-potent Summer Breeze. Perhaps that same rousing blast would likewise banish the foulness in *me*.

"What happened?" I asked aloud, the wind flinging my hair to and fro. "What the hell went wrong?" We had seemed to be con-necting . . . till the movie. Why the change? Was it the drugs—or something deeper, inherent? And what was I to make of that good-bye? Speeding right past the exit to my home, I revisited Cheryl's final statements:

- "Thanks for tonight." Well, that was all right.
- "We're real different is all." Wasn't that part of the attraction? Besides, in our antipathy toward our school's social order, hadn't we found common ground?
- "What the fuck—it was worth a shot." Yeah—more of one than *she* had given.
- "No tongue; I've got a cold." Cheryl hadn't so much as sneezed all night. And little wonder: no lowly rhinovirus could have survived among the menagerie of toxins and narcotics in that girl's throat.
- "Maybe I'll look ya up some time." As in, "Don't call us; we'll call you." But would she? The prospect seemed, in a word, "unlikely."

By now I found myself nearing Good Hope Road—though not a car-length closer to a good hope of my own. I'd have settled for a clue about what had gone wrong. I'd have settled for some inkling of *why*.

I exited, crossed over, got back on the freeway and drove home.

*   *   *

Sometimes one needs to *stop* thinking to figure things out. Comprehension came to me not as I pulled into the garage, not as I climbed the stairs, not as I yanked off my clothes, crawled into bed and then lay there, brooding and shaking my head. No: it came to me in sleep. For when I awoke Sunday morning, I knew what had gone wrong. It wasn't my fault, and it wasn't Cheryl's, either. The blame lay squarely with Olivia Newton-John.

I'd always liked Olivia: her smile, her singing voice, her. . . . All right: her body. She doubtless marked the genesis of my lifelong attraction to women with hyphenate surnames. But this time, she'd dropped the ball. Granted, Olivia had neither written nor directed the previous night's movie, had simply sung, danced and (I'll be charitable) acted in it. But surely she must have realized, during the course of production, how atrocious it would be. Surely she had the star power needed to secure emergency treatment . . . or, better yet, pull the plug, putting the patient out of its misery—and sparing moviegoers worldwide the same.

Am I overstating? Consider: the film includes an animated sequence in which the romantic leads are magically transformed into a frolicking pair of cartoon *goldfish*. If the studio had deliberately set out to produce a movie that would alienate teenagers and sabotage their dates, it could not have done better than *Xanadu*.

None of this, of course, would bring Cheryl back—not unless she came to the same rather novel realization that I had. Which seemed a stretch.

Sliding out of bed, I spotted the can of Summer Breeze lying on the floor. I stooped to pick it up, trying to decide whether to toss or keep it—a decision that seemed laden with significance. I chewed my lip, considering. If Cheryl's blow-off turned out to be permanent, the very sight of the can would mock me . . . but wouldn't throwing it away signal surrender?

For lack of a hope chest, I tucked the can into my top dresser drawer, in between the sweat socks and jock straps where, I supposed, it would feel needed. Realistically, I didn't foresee myself having occasion to use the stuff again. But I was willing to be proven wrong.

In the kitchen, my mom scooped scrambled eggs onto my plate, just the way I liked them. Her tone was jaunty: "Nice 'n' runny for my honey."

"Thanks."

She returned the pan to the burner—"By the time your father comes down, the rest should be ready for him"—then leaned back against the counter and rolled her eyes. "Anyone in their right mind would just serve up a compromise version and be done with it."

"Uh-huh," I mumbled between bites.

"I do spoil you, I suppose. Some day, your wife'll have a bone to pick with me."

"Maybe *I'll* do the cooking." I prided myself on my egalitarianism. True: in my daydreams, I objectified women shamelessly. But I also believed they were the equal of men and should have

equal opportunities—including, ideally, the opportunity to objec-
tify me. In fact, my favorite fantasy about Cheryl Jantz entailed her
compelling *me* to. . . .

"So, Phil—how'd it go last night?"

I glanced over, startled. My mother's powers never ceased to
impress.

My father walked in, Sunday paper in hand, thereby delaying
the interrogation. "Morning."

"Good morning," I said, and seized the opening. "So, Dad . . .
what's new?"

Looking over, he sat down. "Not much, son; I just woke up."
My mom served him a plate's worth of smoky, arid, post-scrambled
husks. "Mmmm, perfect. Thank you, dear."

"Phil was just telling me about his date. What's the girl's name
again?"

"Uh, Kate."

"And her last name?"

"Y'know, I'm not sure," I said, and reached for my orange juice.
Granted, my parents didn't know Cheryl Jantz from Cheryl Tiegs;
then again, I'd long since become convinced that the gentle, loving
woman who'd given me birth was in fact part of a highly coordi-
nated, semi-secret network of moms stretched throughout our
community for the sole purpose of denying teens their freedom—
a kind of Underground Railroad-in-reverse. If the name "Jantz"
meant something to even *one* of these operatives, as it surely
did, then I—by virtue of their hyper-integrated hive mind—would
be toast.

My mom served bacon: floppy and pink for me, brittle and
black for my father. (In hindsight, it's a small miracle my Dad
never developed colon cancer—nor I trichinosis.) We mumbled our
thanks as she put the pan aside and joined us, yogurt cup in hand,
at the table. "So, did you and Kate have a good time?"

"OK," I said. And instructed myself: *Name, rank, and serial. . . .*

"What did you do?"

"Nothing much."

"Did you take her to dinner?"

"Yeah."

"Where'd you go?"

"Dos Banditos."

"Oh; nice. What'd you do after. . . ?"

"Joyce," my father said, refolding Section 1, "I think it's clear that the boy doesn't feel like talking about it." He seemed to be chiding both me (hence "the boy") and Mom—though given what followed, he may have been speaking in spousal code.

My mother eyed him, swirling her spoon in her cup, then stood up. "I'll get that bank statement," she said, and headed out of the kitchen. "It's in my glove compartment."

Her glove compartment. In *her car*. I stood, moving to follow: "I'll get it, Mom."

"Have a seat, son." This time, his tone was unambiguous.

I sat. And waited. And silently cursed my mother's olfactory prowess.

"Phil, is there anything you'd like to talk about?"

He seemed to believe that, in the preceding exchange, it was my mom's *gender* that had discomfited me, and that with her now out of the room, perhaps "us guys" could have a little heart-to-heart about the mysteries thereof. Despite his esteemed reputation in the field of cardiology, I remained unswayed. "Not really."

"Is there anything you'd like to ask me, son? Anything at all?"

I thought back to an April evening several years before when he had taken me to the Pig 'n' Whistle for a hot fudge sundae. . . .

On the drive home, gesticulating with his pipe, he'd filled me in on the facts of life. (Having read, by then, Todd's copies of *The Sensuous Man*, *The Sensuous Couple* and *The Mafia's Virgin Daughter*, I already knew a good deal more than my father realized.) "If you have any questions," he had said in summation, "I'll be happy to answer them."

"Well, yeah," I'd replied, gazing out the car window, "maybe one"—because there *was* something about which I'd wondered. "How often do you and Mom, um . . . do it?"

"Well, ah . . ." He paused. "Well." And paused again. "You see, it's . . . I'm not certain, uh, Phil, that it's. . . ." He puffed on his pipe.

"Sometimes, of course, we, ah . . . well, and then, naturally, there's a . . . a *range* of. . . ."

Taking pity, I leapt to his aid. "Like, a couple times a week?"

"Yes," he said quickly, and cleared his throat; he didn't actually *say* "harumph," but it was implied. "Yes, that's . . . that's about right." As I recall, we debated the Bucks' playoff chances the rest of the way home.

Locking eyes with him now across the breakfast table, I was disinclined to wade back into those waters. If I wanted to discuss the opposite sex, I'd phone a friend. Better to trade "bite me's" with Avery than more bumbling *bons mots* with my dad.

My mom returned, dropped an envelope beside my father's plate and looked at me. "Well, I don't know who this Kate girl is, but she does like her perfume, doesn't she?"

"Y-yeah," I said through a ragged smile.

"Smells like she spilled the whole bottle in there! Though whatever it is, it's not half-bad." She took her seat, picked up her spoon. "Next time you talk to her, ask her what she wears."

*   *   *

I frittered away my Sunday shooting hoops, biking by the lake, thumbing through magazines, watching summer reruns, neglecting my long-dormant electric guitar and, throughout, trying not to think of Cheryl Jantz. This last endeavor grew harder at bedtime . . . as did I. I'd deprived myself of "release" for nearly a week (a personal record), having set my sights higher than my own hand. But with my Jantzian prospects now dashed, I was in no shape to resist the clarion call from my crotch. I wouldn't think of Cheryl, though—not any more . . .

The stunning, slender blonde knelt naked on the floor, head bowed, wrists crossed behind her—the standard spoils-of-war pose from the covers of countless erotically-preoccupied sci-fi and fantasy paperbacks. I called my captive by name, and her chin tilted up, one stray, honey-hued lock tumbling over her widening eyes.

(This would be some of that shameless objectification to which I earlier referred.)

"That new movie of yours," I said sharply. "It blew."

"Oh, I *know*," she murmured in her hot Aussie accent. "I acted poorly. But it was hahd to feign int'rest in my leading man. For really, Phil, *you*'re the one that I want."

I wasn't ready to forgive her yet. "You ruined my date. Completely undermined it."

"I feel just *aw*ful about that." She rose to her feet and—conveniently morphing from slave-girl to seductress—climbed onto my bed. Poised panther-like on her hands and knees, she crept toward me. "Is there *any*thing I can do to . . . make it up to you?"

"What do you suggest?"

Then all at once she was on me, nose to nose and mouth to mouth, her nipples twin candy-corns pressed into my chest. I could feel her supple thighs parting, the dewy space between them yearning to take me in, then the heat of her breath on my lips as she spoke. "Phil," she trilled, "let's . . . get . . . physical."

And so, we did.

And it was good . . . while it lasted. But that's the problem with fantasy lovers: they so seldom snuggle up with you afterward—and they never stay the night.

* * *

My second week at Meigs-Childress proved arduous. Though the quality of my work remained steady, I was having trouble losing myself in, let alone enjoying, my duties as I had when there'd been an impending date to anticipate. Medical waste, now, was merely medical waste, and underexposed p.r. photos were . . . well, you get the idea. I came to think of the summer to that point as comprising two eras—B.C. (Before Cheryl) and A.D. (After Date)—and found myself waxing nostalgic even as I waxed the floors.

The waxing machine, a whirring, upright, pregnant-vacuum-cleaner-looking thing, was supposed to have an adjustable-height handle; I could never figure out how to lengthen it, though, so I simply hunched down over it and made do. At one point I glanced off toward one of the big front-lobby windows, caught a reflected glimpse of myself—shuffling, legs bent, from one foot to the other, my head tucked and shoulders jutting as I strong-armed the contraption from side to side—and realized that I looked for all the world like one of the urban gorilla slaves from *Conquest of the Planet of the Apes*: stooped and servile, mutely obeying my master, condemned to a life of menial labor in a dystopian high-rise hell.

I paused, staring at my remarkably anthropoidal reflection. Come to think of it, I *felt* like an ape from that film as well. I, too, was a creature constrained—not by an oppressive State, but by my own hormones and heart. Releasing the waxer, I pounded my fists against my chest and barked out a single, plaintive hoot that echoed bleakly off the marble floor. Naturally, my boss and his aide-de-camp—the chief housekeeper, Lorraine—chose that very moment to enter the lobby.

Mr. Puckett looked over at Lorraine, then at me. "Everything OK, Phil?"

"Yes, sir," I said, no doubt reddening. I could think of no reasonable explanation for my conduct and so offered none as the duo crossed the floor in front of me, Lorraine peering at me sideways. Hunching low, I resumed my work.

In only one respect did Week 2 trump Week 1: the paycheck. This time I had twice as much money to spend . . . on, regrettably, one fewer dates. But as I boarded the bus back to the 'burbs that Friday night, I resolved to stop sulking and get back in the game.

Taking my seat, I managed a smile. How had I turned the corner? Well, it didn't hurt that the weekend was at hand: two consecutive work-free nights. But in addition, the stitches I'd received right after asking Cheryl out had been removed earlier that same day, just before work. Perhaps this provided some closure. Perhaps those stitches constituted a frame of sorts around the whole Cheryl episode, and with the gash in my head now healed, the one in my heart would follow. I just needed a new direction—and in fact, as the bus trundled past a certain conspicuous downtown night spot, one such direction sprang to mind. . . .

The next morning, though, I awoke plagued with doubts. The scheme I'd hatched was unprecedented, impractical and, technically speaking, illegal. The Planet of the Dates was perilous enough; did I dare risk a foray into its Forbidden Zone?

Then again, given my state (or lack) of affairs, did I dare *not*?

An unintended answer arrived in Saturday's mail. Just before noon, while my folks were out, I answered the doorbell: it was our letter carrier, holding a large envelope marked "Certified and Registered" and addressed to me. I signed for it, ran it up to my room and tore it open. Inside was one of the 8×10s I'd sent to Craig Starling—the shot of the matronly dental patient leaning over the spit sink. With a thick red marker Craig had circled, for no apparent reason, the woman's right elbow. On the back of the photo, using letters cut out of magazine headlines, he had pasted this directive:

mESsaGe REcEIved. DO *not* dELaY. ProCeED to PLan B!

That clinched it. By responding in kind to my cryptic communiqué, my pen pal had provided the impetus I needed. I would do it. In fact, I'd go that very night.

Galvanized, I bounded into the den, grabbed the phone and dialed. His mother answered: "Hello?"

"Is Craig home?"

"Who's calling?"

"Hi, Mrs. Starling; it's Phil Corcoran."

"Hello, Phil! Just a sec'"—her voice all sweetness and light. If she'd only known. . . .

A click; then, "Phil?" His stereo was on: AC/DC, or possibly Nazareth.

"Hey, Craig."

"What's up?"

"I got your, uh, correspondence today."

"Correspondence?"

"The photo I sent you last week. The spit sink, the . . . Cuspimax 2000."

He said nothing for a moment. Then: "I can neither confirm nor deny any knowledge of what you're talking about."

"Drop it, man. It's me."

"How do I know that?"—ever the stickler.

Having initiated this folly with my initial mailing, I was in no position to complain. "You and I are, uh, fully authorized here; we have *carte blanche* from h.q. to discuss. . . ."

"Is this a secure line?"

I sighed mightily. "Listen, Craig. You can hear this or not"—I was speaking, by that point, less to him than to myself—"but the truth is, that message you stuck on the back, it . . . gave me a push in the right direction." I proceeded to tell him of my plans for the evening.

When I'd finished, Craig said coolly, "Again, I can neither confirm nor deny any knowledge of this, uh, dispatch you claim to have received. But as for where you're planning to go tonight, I *do* have clearance to inform you of the following." Then, an ear-shattering shout: "DISCO SU-U-UCKS!!!"

I grimaced—"Message concluded"—and hung up. Shaking my head, I returned to my room, where I opened the closet door and began pulling out an ensemble I'd worn but a handful of times before. The opinions of one hard-rockin' Hoosier notwithstanding, I was determined. In a matter of hours I would don silver shirt and white polyester pants, slip into midnight-blue platform shoes, blow-dry my hair, slap on some Brut, sling a faux-gold medallion around my neck and strut into the city with my fake ID to cruise for chicks at the area's preeminent discotheque-cum-pickup joint, Milwaukee's answer to Studio 54: the Park Avenue.

CHAPTER 4

Boogie Nights on the
Planet of the Dates

I suppose it's time I came clean about this: I was a teenage disco prince. But please don't judge me till you've walked a mile in my platforms.

You see, while the late-'70s disco craze was widely viewed as the last word in mindless conformity, for me it signified the opposite. In our lily-white, upper-middle-class suburb, and particularly at Hyper-Homogeneous High, disco—with its roots and popularity in both urban black and blue-collar white culture—was scorned for reasons more ethnic than aesthetic. Within our student body of 1,200, most of whom favored the arena-friendly cock-rock of REO Speedwagon, Journey and Styx, there were perhaps two dozen rebels who dared crank their Chic and do "Le Freak" for all to see and hear. This gutsy crew included most of the black kids bused in daily from the city, several members of the Modern Dance Club . . . and me.

Even among the misfits, though, *I* mis-fit a bit. Musical tastes on the Planet of the Dates were the chief means by which we teens bonded and, for that matter, self-segregated—a tribal dynamic, in essence—yet my own taste was wildly eclectic. I was as enthused about pop-rockers Boz Scaggs, Rita Coolidge and the Electric Light Orchestra as I was about disco; like Cheryl Jantz, I dug the harsh, guitar-driven sounds of Cheap Trick, Blondie and the Knack; and I found myself increasingly drawn to the offbeat lyrics and strange syncopations of New Wave pioneers Devo, the B-52s and Talking Heads. Call me broad-minded, but there wasn't much music I *didn't* like.

Except, that is, for the irredeemable pap churned out by REO, Journey and Styx.

By the summer of 1980, disco was on the wane—yet I, being underage, still had never "stepped out" at an honest-to-God discotheque. Now, as I drove downtown at 9:30 on that humid June night (under the auspices of meeting friends for mini-golf), my heart raced. Was I ready for this? I'd seen *Saturday Night Fever* three times: the R-rated original once, the PG reissue twice. I'd taken two disco dancing courses at the YMCA (yes, the Village People *were* on the play list) and practiced my moves religiously at home. Then there was that night the previous winter when my friend Danielle Payton and I had driven out to working-class West Allis to shake our respective groove thangs at an alcohol-free nightclub called DiscoTeen. . . .

As it turned out, we didn't linger long. For when Danielle and I walked in the door, a black girl with a white boy, you'd have thought we were aliens straight out of the *Star Wars* bar scene. Kids pointed and whispered and stared; dancing to black music was one thing, but having an actual black person amongst them—on the arm of a fellow Caucasian, no less—was quite another. Many a hostile glance was aimed our way; as we hit the floor (to the strains of Foxy's all-too-apt "Get Off"), I leaned in close. "Gee, Dee," I joked, "did we take a wrong turn and cross the Mason-Dixon?"

But Danielle didn't laugh—just looked up at me with anxious eyes and said, "Child, we crossed a line, all right. I'm thinkin' we'd better go."

. . . Even so, as I now pulled into a just-vacated street space a block past my destination, I wondered if I perhaps should have invited her along. I'd considered it—the downtown crowd was bound to be more open-minded—but she'd never seemed inclined toward anything but friendship. My best shot thus lay within the venue's indigenous population, and I certainly didn't want any potential Park Avenue paramours to see Danielle and me together and presume I was taken.

Of course, in striving to accommodate a hypothetical interest in me on the part of these as-yet-unmet older women, I myself was presuming up a storm.

I got out of the Pacer and, with the chicken-scratch guitar intro to "Stayin' Alive" playing in my head, strode up the street, jaw set, arms swinging—not quite Tony Manero, but a passable Tony-in-training. I paused in front of the Park Avenue's tinted front window to check my hair and admire my shirt: shimmering silver with a thick, red lightning bolt zigzagging across the front, from shoulder to hip. I adjusted my fashionably wide collar, took a deep breath and stepped inside.

"ID." I heard the man before I saw him; I couldn't have been carded sooner. With a practiced casualness—literally; I'd rehearsed at my bedroom mirror—I removed my wallet and produced the goods. The mustachioed door man inspected my card, then me, then the card again before handing it back. "Five-dollar cover."

That was a goodly chunk of change, though nothing a seasoned working man like myself couldn't manage. I handed him six singles—"Little somethin' extra for ya there"—and waited for a word of gratitude that never came. Rather, if his narrowing eyes were any indication, I seemed only to have aroused the man's suspicions. "Thanks"—the word was mine, not his, and after speaking it I hurried past him into the pulsating space beyond.

The Park Avenue was everything I'd hoped for: swanky and sumptuous, a grand, glimmering, bi-level disco palace. The translucent dance floor was laid out in a multi-colored grid and illumined from below by thousands of bulbs that flashed, rapid-fire, to the rhythm. Suspended above, a rotating mirror ball the size of a satellite sent a spectral web of light cascading across everything in sight. On the upper level couples stood, drinks in hand, elbows on the rail, gazing down at the dancers—who merited the attention: dodging and swirling, twisting and twirling, hard-eyed young men and haughty young women, black and brown and white together, united by the beat, by the heat, by their predilection for garish inorganic fabrics and, at this moment, by the powerhouse falsetto of Sylvester:

> You make me feel . . . mi-ighty real.
> Ooo! You make me feel . . . mi-ighty real.

Of course, the Park Avenue may have been many things, but "real" wasn't one of them. Then again, people didn't go there seeking reality; they went to escape it. As for me, standing open-mouthed and agog in the midst of it all, my own desire was to find, within and through this utmost *un*reality, one absolutely authentic woman . . . someone who, if I played my cards right, just might make me feel real. Mighty real.

Seated together at a table near the dance floor were three dazzling prospects: a blonde and two brunettes in their early 20s, stunningly attired in sparkling satin dresses. Nursing her drink, the highly animated short-haired brunette did nearly all of the talking while the others, flanking her, guzzled and grinned and hung on their friend's every word. The trio displayed true *esprit de corps*— Charlie's Angels, I thought, in between assignments. They seemed to be enjoying themselves, the one recounting some comically convoluted story and the others prodding her on. Still, every so often, one or another would glance toward the dancers as if yearning to join them.

Had no one yet asked these lovely ladies onto the floor? It seemed unlikely, given their looks. Or was that the problem: were the women prohibitively beautiful? Did no one here dare tender an invitation? Was there not a man in the house brave enough—or, as in my case, desperate enough—to risk rejection and shoot for the stars?

Apparently, there was not. But, I thought while in motion toward the trio, if the men were afraid to act, then maybe a brazen boy was what the job required. You see, I never lacked in confidence—only in competence to follow through. I was assertive to a fault, like a puppy bounding forth at full tilt, only to trip over my own outsized paws.

"Hi," I said, making eye contact with each woman in turn, then followed up my snappy opening line with the equally droll "How ya doin'?" I winced; at least my voice hadn't cracked.

The storyteller looked at her cohorts, then back at me. "We're doin' good," this apparent group leader said, sizing me up with lively green eyes. "How 'bout you?"

"Me too." I nodded, hands in my pockets. "Real good."

Straight-faced, she nodded back. "*Good* to hear."

The blonde stifled a laugh; the longer-haired brunette shushed her.

"I'm Cassie," the talkative one said. "This"—indicating the shusher—"is Tricia, and that's *Ahn*drea."

"Nice to meet you, Cassie . . . Tricia . . . *Ahn*drea. I'm Phil."

The brunettes, together: "Hi, Phil!"

*Ahn*drea, drinking, gave me a wave.

A new song began to play; I recognized the bouncy, Tinker-Toy synthesizer riff of "Funkytown," that inescapable disco confection by Lipps Inc. I was dying to dance, but Cassie indicated an empty stool. "Care to join us?"

"Thanks," I said, and sat.

"Don't think I've seen ya here before, Phil." Cassie turned to her friends. "Does Phil look familiar to you?"

Tricia shook her head. "'Fraid not."

*Ahn*drea tried to answer, but her words degenerated into another titter.

"It's my first time," I said.

"His first time!" Cassie placed an arm around each of her companions. "Did ya hear that, girls?"

Finally, the blonde spoke—"That's . . . hot"—then lapsed back into laughter.

"Now, *Ahn*drea," Cassie chided, "be gentle with our new friend. After all. . . ."

The three spoke in unison: "It's his first time!"

"My first time here, at this club," I blurted. "I've been to *others*"—though in truth, there had only been DiscoTeen. Tricia took out a compact, checked her make-up; I fumbled with my

medallion and studied my shoes. I was in over my head. I felt like
a double-agent who'd been exposed by three *femmes fatales*. No:
more like live prey being batted about by a pack of feral cats. I was
about ready to locate a mouse hole—or a mercifully quick trap.

Maybe Cassie picked up on my distress; maybe not. Either way,
she switched gears. "So tell us, Phil: what do you do? You in school,
or. . . ?"

"I work," I said evenly. "Building services and property
management."

This took the women aback; like Cheryl two weeks before, they
didn't know what to make of my title, though Cassie for one seemed
mildly impressed. "Management? So, is that in administration?"

I deliberated: that would be a *good* thing, right? "More or less."

*Ahn*drea, bored, played with her swizzle stick. "Well, how about
that."

Cassie raised her own drink, took a sip. "Where?"

"Meigs-Childress. It's this big professional building on—"

"I know," she said. "I'm a teller at First Wis. You're just down
the street."

"Yeah!" I heard my own ebullience, brought it down a notch.
"My savings account's at First Wis." Encouraged by even so distant
an affiliation—and by the apparent cessation of Phil-teasing—I
steeled myself and went for broke. "Uh . . . Cassie, was it?"

"Yeah?"

"Wouldja like to dance?"

Her friends, amused, exchanged another look, but this time
Cassie's eyes stayed on me. "Y'know what, Phil? I would." And with
that, she stood.

Out on the floor, a couple of feet apart, we slipped into the
rhythm with ease. Cassie's steps were flawless and her movements
fluid and oh, my God, what a *form*! Sleek and slender, she was
nearly my height with a tall, tapering neck, ivory skin and perfect
breasts that bobbed as she boogied. Long, sloping calves; thighs
till Thursday. As for her ass, I can only say that, my Methodist
upbringing notwithstanding, I now contemplated founding a new
religion. For each time she spun, her dress—a short spaghetti-strap

number the same gumdrop green as her eyes—whipped up and to one side, exposing the perimeter of a rounded realm that well may have been Nirvana.

My gaze, as you may have gathered, barely ever left her, but not until the second song—"You and I" by Rick James—did it hit me that Cassie's eyes had yet to fall on me. A shame: bolstered by the bass line and swept up by the sax, I was *on*, adeptly executing the steps I'd learned at the "Y" and tossing in some slick improvs for good measure. Still, what was the point of setting the dance floor aflame when the one you aimed to wow wasn't watching?

I reached out and took Cassie's hand and then, at last, she looked at me. Her face, framed by chestnut hair in a stylish pageboy, would have been striking even without its current cast: assured, collected, self-possessed. Swallowing, I eased an arm around her waist; she placed her free hand lightly on my shoulder. Just then a new song began: the celestial, synth-driven title track from *Xanadu*. "Hey," Cassie shouted over the intro, "you seen the movie?"

"Yeah," I answered, "last week."

She smiled at me. "I loved it!"

I smiled back. "Me too!"

Though we'd done well apart, we moved even better together. Gamboling with abandon, Cassie was more relaxed in my arms than expected as I guided her one way and spun her back the other; she responded so readily, it seemed neither of us was leading and neither following. A liquid energy coursed down her slender arms, into her palms and out her fingers; a rippling warmth enveloped me each time I pulled her close. And wafting around us all the while was the seraphim soprano of Olivia Newton-John:

> A million lights are dancing and there you are,
> A shooting star
> An everlasting world and you're here with me,
> Eternally. . . .

My heart seemed to be swelling within my ribs, pressing out toward my partner, aching for contact—but I caught myself, held my passion in check. I hadn't come this far to squander everything on an ill-timed kiss.

As "Xanadu" reached its big finish, I double-spun Cassie into a dramatic dip. We held the position, catching our breath, my dream-come-true date flung over my forearm with her head thrown back, lips slightly parted, eyes joined to mine. "Oh," Cassie sighed, "I hate this."

I nearly dropped her. "Uh. . . ."

She straightened. "This song. This *version*, I mean—I hate it. Don't you?"

The deejay had selected an old Beatles hit, re-mixed to a thumping disco beat. Cassie, being several years older than I, was probably a Fab Four fan back when they were still an active band; to her, this rendition no doubt qualified as sacrilege . . . though I kind of liked it. "I . . . uh, you're a great dancer, Cassie."

"Not so bad yourself." She raised a hand, flipped her bangs out of her eyes: an innocuous gesture rendered with heartbreaking grace. "Let's sit this one out."

"Deal. Can I buy you a drink?"

"Rum 'n' Tab. Thanks." She turned and headed back to her table—*our* table—thus presenting me with a most agreeable view. I'd developed quite a fondness for watching women walk away . . . appropriate, as my love life's rocky start had afforded several such opportunities. Heading for the bar, I recalled my last look at Cheryl Jantz: receding into her darkened home while verbally eviscerating the family pet. At the time, I'd been devastated. But one week later, with Cassie seated across that magical floor awaiting my return, last Saturday night had lost its bite.

Trying to catch the bartender's eye, I found myself wondering if perhaps I was *supposed* to have lost Cheryl in order to meet Cassie. Then I found myself imagining a proper date on some future night, with Tricia and *Ahn*drea nowhere in sight. Then I found myself wondering how Cassie's tongue would feel against mine. Then I found myself being grabbed by one arm and yanked away from the bar.

"Your driver's license," the massive, bald-headed bouncer said from his vantage point a foot overhead. "Please," he smirked—a little joke to himself.

I handed him my fake ID: a UWM student card with my own name and photo.

"This is not a driver's license." He didn't hand it back.

"I . . . I know," I said, voice shaky.

The bouncer folded his arms. "You have one?"

"I do." I cleared my throat, fixed my lips into a timid grin. "But y'see, the problem is, *on* my driver's license, if I *were* to show it to you . . . I'm only 16."

"Time to go"—he checked the card—"Phil."

"I'm not even *drinking*," I whined. "I'm just here to dance."

"Song's over."

I gazed off toward Cassie and company. Perhaps they'd witnessed my initial "capture," perhaps not—but they were watching now. "Can I say good-bye to my friends?"

He shook his head.

"It'll only take a. . . ."

"Do it from here." His tone invited neither bargaining nor begging.

I bit my lip. This time, apparently, it was the woman's turn to watch *me* walk away. *"Do it from here"*—that wasn't possible! Still, I couldn't just turn and go. Even Cheryl Jantz had managed an explanation of sorts. I had to tell Cassie something.

Catching her eye, I pointed at my watch, then mimed holding a telephone receiver to my ear, then shrugged, then waved good-bye.

Her face registered confusion—and who could blame her? I mean, what the fuck had I just said? Even *I* didn't know! As she raised her hand, fingers delicately opening and closing, a strobe light started to flash overhead, plunging Cassie's farewell gesture into somber slow-mo.

I headed back to the entrance, my unwelcome escort at my heels all the way.

* * *

Cursing under my breath, kicking at cigarette butts, I skulked and paced just outside the building on the off chance that Cassie might come looking for me. This stark stretch of street was the disco's depressing antithesis. There were no strobes or lasers, just a slowly flashing DON'T WALK on the corner; there was no crowd—just me and, half a block down, a bum dozing by a dumpster. And the music, from here, had been reduced to a muffled, bass-heavy blur.

After a minute the door swung open, and my head shot up; a black couple tumbled onto the sidewalk, arm in arm, laughing. They were fashion-model-attractive and dressed to the nines. "You think so, do you?" the woman purred.

Deep-voiced, her man replied, "You have somethin' better in mind?"

"Not tonight, I don't." She sighed, then snuggled up close. "Shit, Trey—not ever."

He rumbled out a low chuckle, his palm sliding briefly over her behind as they stepped past me and crossed the street.

I couldn't help it: I despised them.

I sat down on the curb and, staring at the pavement, put myself in Cassie's shoes. What did she think I was trying to say? "Oh, look at the time! I have a phone call to make. Places to go, things to do. Sorry, babe. Have a nice life." Would any woman in her right mind pursue a man—let alone an *almost*-man—who'd danced with her and held her close, then stiffed her on a drink and told her *that*? Head in my hands, I was near tears.

Again, the door swung open.

"Phil."

The bouncer. Standing alone. The neon "Park Avenue" logo reflected on his shiny bullet-head. My fake ID was clenched in his hand; he flicked it toward me, but as I reached out the card detached in mid-air: he'd cut it up. It landed in several pieces, two of them in the gutter.

"Get the fuck outta here."

I scrambled to my feet, glaring, and mumbled under my breath, "Starling was right. . . ."

He took a step toward me. "*What* was that?"

"DISCO SU-U-UCKS!!!" I screamed, voice fraying, then tore off my medallion, cast it into the storm drain and ran back down the block to my mother's car as fast as my blue platforms would take me.

CHAPTER 5

If at First You Don't Succeed on the Planet of the Dates

Let's skip the gloomy aftermath and cut to Monday afternoon—the last day of June—when I got off the bus one hour and one stop early, at the base of the First Wisconsin. I swiftly ascended the granite steps, lunch box in one hand, a lone red rose clutched in the other. Sweating profusely from the heat, the humidity and the attire (I'd put on a sport coat and tie, like the junior administrator Cassie thought me to be), I hurried toward the revolving door, eagerly anticipating the near-frigid conditions that surely awaited within.

But the building's overtaxed air conditioning system had blown out, and several maintenance workers—the First Wis version of *me*, I realized with a start—were erecting a series of ancient, wrought-iron electrical fans throughout the stale and stagnant lobby. As the crew activated each clamorous contraption in turn, the noise level quickly approached airport-runway dimensions. Wiping my brow, I got in line and scanned the long row of teller stations . . . and there she was, off to the right in a crisp white blouse. As I waited, I silently rehearsed the short speech I'd scrawled back home and committed to memory on the ride down.

Soon after I reached the head of the line, a teller beckoned; I stepped aside, ushering forward the customer behind me. A minute later, Cassie's station opened up and I, with jittery steps, made my way toward her. Stepping up in front of her, I noticed a triangular blotch of perspiration on her blouse, right at the collarbone, and smaller stains under each of her arms. If you for one moment imagine that any of this turned me off in the least, then you have never been a 16-year-old boy.

Cassie, straightening a stack of currency, had yet to look up. "Good afternoon. How may I help you?"

For lack of a check or a deposit slip, I placed my rose on the counter and slid *it* forward—only then noticing how much it had wilted during the commute.

She looked up, and as she recognized me her mouth dropped halfway open. Glancing about, she grabbed the flower and tucked it out of sight. "Well," she said softly. "This is a surprise." She fussed, again, with her stack of bills, eyes alternating between it and me.

"Cassie," I began . . . then paused, paralyzed by the smell of her: a perfume of some citrus scent—tangerine?—commingled with the faintest trace of the woman's own sweat. The bulky stationary fan behind her amplified the aroma, aiming it straight into my face. I nearly swooned, and though I vaguely recalled having readied a recitation of some kind, not a word of it came to mind. "Cassie. . . ."

"I'm working," she murmured, again looking about. "I can only talk for a minute; they watch me like a hawk."

"I don't want to get you into any trouble. . . ."

"It'd help if you had a transaction."

"Oh. Right." I removed my wallet, pulled out a twenty. "Tens, please."

Eyeing me, she took the bill.

My opening line came back to me. *Take two*, I thought, straightening the knot of my tie. *And . . . action!* "You're probably wondering what happened at Park Avenue the other night. . . ."

"I assume you got carded; I saw Floyd take ya out." She slid me two tens.

I slid one back to her. "Fives, please. So you knew I was underage?"

She took the bill. "Um, *yea-a-ah!* We all did, soon as we saw you." She slid me two fives. "Why'dja think we kept teasing you?"

I slid one back. "Singles. Then why did you dance with me?"

She took the bill. "Because you were kinda cute, and I wanted to dance, and, well, you asked. But, c'mon, Phil. What're you—16?" She counted off five singles in front of me.

I slid one back. "Quarters, please. Yeah, I'm 16, but only for the next month. Besides, I thought . . . I mean, the way we were dancing together and all. . . ."

"I'm eight years older than you. That's half your life! You must know girls your own age who like to dance and . . . and who like you." She slid me four quarters.

I slid one back, and as I did, an image of Danielle came to mind. "There's one, but . . . I don't think she'd want to be my girlfriend or anything."

"Ever ask her?" She slid me two dimes and a nickel.

I slid the nickel back. "Well. . . ." I cut myself short; we'd gotten off track. "Cassie, are you positive that nothing could, uh, develop between you and me?"

Wide-eyed, she looked right at me. "Sure—if I wanna get *arrested*!"

As if on cue, a short, pin-striped fellow wearing wire rims and a bad perm appeared by her side. I scanned his ID badge: Dale Seastrom, Accounts Manager. "How's it going, Cassandra?"—his tone accusatory.

"Fine, Mr. Seastrom." She flipped her bangs out of her eyes. "Just giving this gentleman his pennies." Which she did—along with a look: *Please leave before I get canned.*

The man folded his arms. "Quite the little tête-à-tête you're having, eh?"

Quite the little prick you're being, eh?—that's what I wanted to say. Instead, I somehow came up with this: "I was asking her about the . . . different kinds of accounts the bank offers. I'm saving up for college, and I, uh, wanted to know what my options are."

Mr. Seastrom appeared to buy my story. "In that case, you should speak with an accounts manager. *I'm* free, if you'd please come with me. . . ."

As I followed him away from the teller station, that glorious scent receding with each step, I turned my head and glanced back.

Smiling faintly, Cassie mouthed her thanks. Then, just as two nights before, she raised her hand and waved.

* * *

Half an hour later—armed with a brochure about money-market accounts, a First Wisconsin key chain and a receipt for my newly-purchased $1,000 certificate of deposit (I'd shifted it over from savings; Dale Seastrom may have been a little prick, but he was a persuasive one)—I made my way back through the loudly ventilated lobby toward the revolving door. I tried to sneak a peek at Cassie along the way, but some male teller stood at her station now. She must have finished her shift, or maybe she was on break.

I left the bank and headed for work, head bowed, dress shoes dragging across the steaming sidewalk. A dull clanging noise brought my head up, and I squinted out through the hundred-degree haze. Some big, brown dog—a thick-coated, overheated stray—had managed to capsize a garbage can and was dazedly sniffing at its contents.

Never had downtown been more depressing.

Returning my gaze earthward, I spotted something carved into the pavement below: two sets of initials, nestled inside a heart. I made a point of stepping on the accursed graffito—hard—as I passed it.

* * *

During my 7:30 break, I headed straight for the medical suite on 11. I was comfortable up there—though only to a point. For whenever I sat in the black leather chair at the oak desk with the brass **J. Theodore Corcoran, MD** name plate positioned in front of me, I felt compelled to maintain the same rigidly upright posture as my father.

Munching on carrot sticks and Cheetos, I stared at the phone. Sooner or later, I'd need to replace my fake ID—but I was hesitant to call my "supplier." I could make something up, but my big brother had an unerring ability to see through my chicanery and ferret out the truth. Even now, with his face smirking up at me from our Dad's desktop family photo, I could imagine Todd's reaction to what I'd done:

"What were you thinking? The fact that he demanded your driver's license should've tipped you off that the student ID wasn't gonna work. You shoulda just left; you ended up having to anyway! At least you'd still have the card—*douche bag*."

Not what my battered ego needed. No; the situation called for a *one*-way communiqué. I reached for my father's prescription pad, grabbed a pen and wrote:

> Hi, Todd, what's up? Bad news: looks like I've
> lost that awesome Christmas present you gave me.
> I've searched everywhere. Anyway, bro, I could
> really use another! THANKS. I owe you one!
> — Phil

I tore my note—along with the incriminatingly-indented sheet beneath—off the pad and shoved both into my lunch box; then, spirits sinking, I actually slouched in my father's chair. Earlier, I'd managed to occupy myself with four floors' worth of vacuuming, but now Cassie's words came back full-force. I was a kid: fun to tease, maybe to dance with, but not even a blip on her romantic radar. True, she *had* called me "cute" . . . but she may as well have been describing Strawberry Shortcake.

It was sweet, though, how she'd tried to steer me back toward "my own." And maybe she had a point: in all the time I'd known Danielle Payton, I had never suggested moving past friendship, simply assuming I'd be rebuffed. But what if she had been making the same assumption? Conceivably, Danielle and I could spend the rest of our lives bypassing a desire to which neither of us dared attest—not a bad movie premise, but unacceptable in life.

Or, at least, in mine: I picked up the receiver and dialed Danielle. As I did, it struck me that my friends nowadays seemed to exist largely on the phone. Yet another upside-down trait of the Planet of the Dates: the people I'd known the longest and best, like Avery and Danielle and Craig, had been reduced to disembodied voices, while my romantic prospects all appeared in the flesh. As her line rang, I decided that young Ms. Payton was up for a promotion.

"Hello?"—that familiar low-alto, welcoming as warm honey.

"Hey, Dee. It's Phil."

"Corky! Hey, what's up?"

I fiddled with my keyless First Wis key chain. "Not much. What's new with you?"

"Havin' a pretty good summer, at least so far."

Had she always sounded that sexy? "I guess we have some catching up to do."

"Yeah, I guess we do."

"You want to get together for lunch?"

"Love to."

I pitched the key chain toward my father's wastebasket; it hit the bottom with a *clang*. "How about tomorrow?"

At the end of my shift, I re-donned my sport coat and headed downstairs to check out for the night. Mr. Puckett looked up from his work and scrutinized my attire. "You makin' a play for *my* job?"

I laughed. "No, sir."

"Hot date, Phil?"

"Possibly," I said, turning to go. "I'll let you know."

* * *

The next morning, as I was adjusting the sprinkler on our front lawn, our anal-retentive retiree neighbor, Mr. Ruskin, beckoned to me from one lawn north. My impulse was to flee, but I pushed the urge aside; it had been years since I'd inadvertently punted a football through his kitchen window and into the fondue. So now I sauntered over to find out what he wanted, and when I reached him, he handed me a photocopied flyer covered with my own handwriting:

WORK WANTED !!
Lawn care, hedge trimming, gardening, gutter cleaning,
house painting (interior/exterior), furniture moving,
dog walking, pet feeding, babysitting, YOU NAME IT!
Motivated & broke h.s. senior-to-be, at your service.
Call Phil Corcoran at . . .

Mr. Ruskin folded his arms. "Does the offer still stand?"

"I landed a job right after I distributed these. But that's at night, so my days are free." I handed the flyer back to him. "What do you need?"

"Do you have a driver's license?"

"Yes."

"And access to a car?"

"Yeah; my mom's."

Mr. Ruskin folded the flyer neatly in two, then in four, then slipped it into the pocket of his ironed Bermuda shorts. "I have acquired some land," he began, his tone pedagogical, "up by Port Washington. Lakefront property, half an hour north. I plan to build a home there, eventually. At any rate, over the past month, I have had 50 saplings planted there. The landscaping service that performed the work would very much like to charge me through the nose to water those trees, but I suspect I can do better."

I nodded. "I suspect you can."

He stared at me for a moment, then turned, motioning me to follow.

Lined up against one interior wall of his impossibly fastidious garage were two rows of empty plastic one-gallon milk cartons, 25 per row. Mr. Ruskin dropped his voice to a near-whisper, as if disclosing the whereabouts of buried treasure: "There is no running water on the property as yet. You will fill the cartons here, by hose; transport them in your car; and then pour one into the ground at the base of each tree. I will need you to do this twice a week, unless we get a great deal of rain." He paused, weighing his next words with care. "While there, you may use the private beach, if you wish, and go swimming in the lake, provided you pick up after yourself *completely* when you are through. I am prepared to pay you $15 per trip."

I barely heard the amount; he had me by "private beach," the possibilities of which were endless. "I'm your man," I said, hand extended.

Mr. Ruskin inspected my hand, then took it, shook it. "Kindly start tomorrow."

* * *

Two hours later, newly showered and shaved, I got into the Pacer and headed down to the Coffee Trader for my date with Danielle. My thoughts en route, however, were directed toward a secluded beach half an hour north, where I envisioned two naked teens lying latched together at the water's edge, mouths joined, limbs entwined, white over brown over white like a great, sand-coated vanilla-chocolate Twistee Cone. . . .

"Shit!"—a red light; I hit the brakes. Crossing in front of my bumper, a businessman glared; I checked my rear view and backed out of the intersection. Clearly, I was getting ahead of myself. For my own peace of mind, as well as for the sake of the city's pedestrians, I would assume nothing about where things might go with Danielle. Perhaps we'd be friends; perhaps more. But it seemed only fair to let the girl herself have a say.

Not ten minutes later, her eyes went wide. "For real?"

"For real."

Danielle stared at me across the table, then looked down at her plate. "Oh, Corky. I . . . I don't think so." She picked at her chicken salad.

"Why not?" I had entirely forgotten my grilled cheese, riveted as I was on her exotic face: the wide-set brown eyes, the mahogany skin, the dear little chin, the ample lips that would not, it now appeared, be touching my own. "You *said* you didn't have a boyfriend. And we obviously like each other." Suddenly conscious of the other parties around us, I leaned in toward her and dropped my voice. "I find *you* attractive. . . ."

"You, too." She may have been tossing me a bone, but she seemed to mean it.

"Then what's the problem?"

She gazed out the restaurant window; a procession of East Siders strolled silently by. "Do you remember that other time we met for lunch? The day after Christmas. . . ."

"At the fish-fry place near your house—that really 'fly' joint down on Morgan."

Danielle smiled, amused as always by my efforts to sound "street" when talking with her. "Right. And do you remember I told you how, when you were in the men's room, one of the other customers came up to me. . . ."

". . . and he asked you, 'Why ain't you with a brother?'"

"Right."

"And you looked at him and said, 'That'd be incest!'"

We both laughed. "Right," she said once again . . . but then her smile faded. "Truth is, if you and I were to become, y'know, boyfriend and girlfriend, I'm pretty sure I'd end up asking myself the same thing."

"That's crazy, Dee."

"To you and me. But. . . ."

"It's bowing to racism."

"Not racism," she said. "Realism."

"So our skin's a different color. It doesn't matter."

"Mattered to the folks at DiscoTeen."

"It shouldn't have."

"But it did, child. It did, and it does. In ways that no white boy could understand." She reached out, placed her hand over mine. "Not even the sweetest white boy I know."

I had to smile at that, though it still spelled failure. "Gee, Dee. What a nice brush-off."

She shrugged. "I try."

Then, a thought: "Wait. I'm not *all* white. . . ."

"You told me," she nodded. "You've got a few drops of Cherokee—just like me. See? That's another reason not to: we could be related!"

"Yeah," I deadpanned, "that'd explain the resemblance. Hell, look at us; we could be twins." Then I tilted back my head and, with a sigh, stared at the wooden ceiling fan, watched its blades whirl round and round and round. . . .

"Phil."

Danielle never called me that. I lowered my gaze, met her eyes with mine.

A sly little smile flitted over her lips. Then she tilted her head down and, peering up conspiratorially, looked me dead in the eye. "Tell you what. If we're both still available, oh, 20 years from now, and *if* you still want to, not only will I go out with you—I'll *marry* you!"

"For real?"

"For real."

I gave her a crooked grin. "I'll still be white."

"By then, it may not matter."

"By the Year 2000 . . ." I mused for a moment, shook my head. "That's great. We'll have the wedding on Mars. I'll meet you in the chapel on Base Colony 4."

"Wherever you want," she said, and sipped her Fanta.

I reached for my own soda, flicked a finger at the straw. *We're so comfortable together! Always have been.* I pushed the drink away. *So, clearly, it'd never work.*

Danielle settled back in her chair. "Corky—tell me about your job. What is it you're doing again?"

"Building services and property management."

Her brow furrowed. "Oh . . . kay. And that means. . . ?"

I looked away—"It's just a job, Dee"—then reached halfheartedly for my sandwich. "Just a summer job."

* * *

Late the next morning, I drove 50 gallons of tap water up to Mr. Ruskin's property. The land was beautiful: three acres of grassy meadow, sprinkled with wildflowers of most every color, and bordered by pine forest on the west and a steep, wooded bluff down to

Lake Michigan on the east . . . but my heart wasn't in it. Emptying the first jug into the soil under the westernmost sapling, I wondered if my birth tree back in the 'burbs might be experiencing, at that moment, a twinge of betrayal. That was the closest I came to a snicker all day.

As I made my way eastward, the 50 newly planted trees were easy enough to spot, and I got a decent workout lugging all those jugs over hill and dale. I stashed the empties next to each trunk in turn, leaving them for *en masse* retrieval at the end; I'd brought along a pair of king-size Hefty bags for the occasion. This was not my idea, but Mr. Ruskin's; he'd prepared for me a full page of exhaustive instructions—and laminated it to protect it from the elements.

Reaching the bluff at last, I gazed down through cedar branches to the beach some 40 yards below. From what I could see, it was damned near idyllic: ten yards of tawny sand, then a few feet of wet stone leading out to the water's edge, all well-hidden by the C-shaped curve of a natural cove. "Private" indeed—not that it mattered: here it was, two days into July, and there were no writhing, rolling Twistee-Cones of *any* flavor in my future.

Under other circumstances, I'd have scrambled right down and gone for a dip; I'd gotten awfully hot trudging through that field under the midday rays, and the chilly lake would have felt great. But I couldn't bring myself to do it. *Salt in the wound*, I thought, and headed back to collect my empties.

Back home that afternoon, three five-dollar bills crammed into my pocket, I sat in the basement, in the dark, my Super-8 projector whirring along beside me, and tried to perk myself up with a trip down memory lane. Specifically, I'd chosen the P.C. Productions "Bloopers Reel," a compendium of outtakes from my two dozen movies to date. As amusing as some of these cinematic misfires were, I was finding it hard to get into the spirit of things:

The hypnotized title character of *The Mummy's Trance* emerged from his sarcophagus, which looked suspiciously like a refrigerator box fancied up with Magic Markered hieroglyphs. As the creature (played by Avery) limped off to wreak untold havoc, the camera—which had been shooting him from the waist up—tilted down just far enough to reveal the not-fully-bandaged boy's designer jeans . . . a blunder that had prompted us to rechristen our film *The Mummy's Pants*.

Why had each of the girls I'd approached focused so myopically on the differences between us rather than the similarities? Did they do that with everyone, or just with me?

From *Prehistoric Planet of the Apes*: Craig Starling, as gorilla-villain General Urko, high-tailed it across a barren stretch of the Forbidden Zone—i.e., the vacant lot behind Village Pharmacy—with a T-Rex model kit in hot pursuit. As Urko leapt over a storm drain, his black vinyl helmet came loose and tumbled to the ground. Though mere moments shy of becoming brunch, the General stopped, hurried back for his headpiece—then looked into the camera and spoke: "I shoulda just *left* it, huh?"

I was too young for Cassie, too square for Cheryl and too white for Danielle. Clearly, if I were to age eight years, develop a drug habit and somehow turn black, I'd have to beat the girls back with a stick.

The titular Vulcan from *Son of Spock*, played by me, strode purposefully across the bridge of the *New Enterprise*, heading for the "automatic" sliding door (which in actuality led to our downstairs bathroom). But Avery, who was struggling to operate the door from his crouching-place just below frame, only managed to execute the maneuver halfway, causing Son of Spock to step not through but *into* the door with a resounding THUD.

Which was a fair depiction of how I felt now. Sitting there watching the flickering screen, it struck me: the occasional blooper notwithstanding, as writer-producer-director of P.C. Productions, I'd been utterly in command, had wielded total control . . . yet now, in the world of romance, I was powerless. I was a walk-on, an extra, a mere face in the crowd. Wasn't there a girl somewhere who would "scout me out" as something more . . . who'd value and appreciate me for who I was, rather than rebuffing me for who I was not?

At that moment a vision appeared, its source a stretch of Super-8 chugging along beside me at 16 frames per second. The face on the screen belonged to a pretty young voodoo priestess striving to cure a certain long-suffering physician (Avery) of his dread affliction by exorcising the evil Mr. Hyde once and for all. (I'd been terribly proud of the title—*Cur[s]e of Dr. Jekyll*—and had used animation to erase the "s" in the opening sequence.)

In this outtake, the blue-eyed, black-robed priestess, arms uplifted, passionately invoked the aid of Damballah the Snake God to save "this poor unfortunate, this pitiable man who houses a fiend within his soul!" Then she struck a match and turned gravely toward the altar . . . only to find its lone candle already blazing. (I'd forgotten to extinguish it between takes.) After a moment's hesitation, the priestess exclaimed, "The candle has lit *itself*!" She shook out her match, re-raised her arms and intoned, "Thank you, Damballah, for this sign of your power"—an improv that might have worked were not Dr. Jekyll by then palpitating with laughter beside her.

As the actress, in response, finally broke character with a sheepish smile, I reached for the switch on the projector and froze the girl's larger-than-life image. I stood and walked right up to the screen, my own shadow falling abreast of the long, reddish-brown hair, the winsome grin, the unusually high-placed eyebrows that gave her that look of perpetual surprise.

"Stefanie," I said, savoring the name. "Stefanie Slocum. . . ."

CHAPTER 6

Independence Day on the
Planet of the Dates

When in the course of human events, it becomes necessary for one teenager to establish the romantic bonds which will connect him with another, so that the two of them might assume, among the powers of the earth, the united and equal station to which the Laws of Nature and of Nature's God entitle them . . . well, it's probably prudent for that teen to try his luck with someone who's hinted she might want to connect in the first place.

It hadn't really hit me till that mid-"Bloopers Reel" moment, but when I thought back to the days we'd spent together—shooting movies, be they in my basement "studio" or out on location; sharing pizza and pop afterward; a handful of jaunts to the Cineplex or the mall—I detected a subtext to Stefanie's words and actions. She'd been testing me, if tentatively—floating trial balloons and observing my reactions. I'd never needed to audition her for the three roles in which I'd cast her . . . yet all the while, she'd been trying *me* out for the role of first-ever boyfriend.

I was a decent actor, but that part had been beyond my range. Chalk it up to human development's practical joke, the Inter-Gender Time Lag: Stefanie, as a 13-year-old girl, naturally had been quite mature; I, as a 13-year-old boy, naturally had not. But now we were approaching 17. Presumably, I'd closed the gap . . . or narrowed it, anyway.

I could have called her on Wednesday afternoon, just flicked off the projector and picked up the phone. I could have asked her out for coffee—or to Summerfest; Atlanta Rhythm Section was scheduled to play. I could have . . . but I didn't. For the *possibility* of Stefanie was something to hold close, a treasure I could take out of my pocket for fervid contemplation. Part of me feared that she'd moved away, or that she had a boyfriend, or (worse yet) that she had neither a boyfriend nor any interest, now, in me. Having received Cassie's kiss-off on Monday and Danielle's on Tuesday, I had no desire to go for the hat trick. If more bad news was on its way, there was no need to obtain it today. As long as I refrained from contacting her, hope lived.

At work that night I pulled rest-room detail, but I didn't mind. I labored contentedly, as if under a wondrous spell. Spraying the inside of each john with alkaline-blue disinfectant, I thought of her eyes. Scrubbing, I saw her scribbling, as on the day we'd met, in her girlhood journal. Flushing, I heard the rush of female laughter, light, lilting and free. Bending, brush in hand, over the next bowl, I saw reflected on the water's surface not my own features, but those of the erstwhile voodoo priestess who, nearly four years before, had cast a time-release hex on my heart.

*   *   *

I waited till Thursday, a full day after my screening-room epiphany, then stepped into my father's study and closed the door. With no small amount of gravity, I pulled the City of Milwaukee phone book from its drawer, sat down at the desk and paged through to the listings starting with SLO. There she was—or, more accurately, there was Benjamin Slocum, her tax-attorney father—still on Shepard Avenue. And there was the phone number.

Staring at the seven digits, I sighed. Over the past 20-odd hours, the stakes had risen, for my longing had taken on a life of its own. Quite a nasty paradox: *because* I'd held out hope, the prospect of failure loomed larger. Shifting my gaze toward the slate-gray phone, I gave myself an internal pep talk: *You can do it; nothing ventured, nothing gained; there's only one way to find out.* Then I nodded firmly, picked up the receiver and dialed. I felt no pride in having done so, though, for the number I'd called was Avery's.

"Hello?"

"Hey, it's Phil."

"What's up?"

"Guess who I'm about to ask out."

He considered. "Cheryl Jantz's golden retriever."

"Bite me, Thompson; I wouldn't horn in on *your* turf. Try Stefanie Slocum."

"Don't mind if I do," he said. "I *saw* her last week, y'know."

This felt suspiciously like the set-up for a joke. "Let me guess: in your bed."

"Not a bad idea; the girl's grown up, and she's lookin' fine."

He sounded serious. He also sounded like competition. "Yeah? Where was this?"

"The Magic Pan on Jefferson. She's waitressing there."

I had eaten there a few times, though not lately. "Did you . . . talk to her at all?"

"Nah. Just watched her runnin' around, taking orders."

"You're telling me you didn't even say 'hi'?"

"I was with my folks! The place was packed; it was an hour wait, so we didn't."

Thank God. "Well, I'm goin' over there today to ask her out, so . . . hands off."

"Hey, I've known her as long as *you* have."

It was true; he'd been there at Atwater Beach the day Stefanie and I had met. "Yeah," I said slowly, and as I recalled that first meeting, an idea began to germinate. "But I . . . I knew her better. *I'm* the one who cast her; they were *my* movies. . . ."

"All right, all right. You've got dibs. But if you drop the ball, she's fair game."

"Deal."

"So," he said, sounding dubious, "you're headin' down there, huh?"

"You'd better believe it."

"What if she's not working today?"

"Then I'll find out when she is. Listen, there's something of yours I want to borrow. For when I see her."

"Sorry," he said, "it doesn't come off. You wouldn't know what to do with the extra inches, anyway."

Why did I put up with this guy? "Something else, jag-off. I'm coming over to get it. See ya in a few."

"And I should help you . . . why?"

I used a cutesy cartoon-animal voice: "'Cause we're best-est friends."

"Bite me, Corcoran."

"No thanks. I got a better taste in mind."

* * *

An hour later, charged with a wary excitement, I hopped off the bus at Jefferson and headed for the Magic Pan. No red rose this time; my offering, such as it was, resided in my lunch box. I'd supplemented my standard work attire of sneakers, T-shirt and jeans with a faded Levi's jacket inherited from Todd and a pair of mirrored shades. Nearing the restaurant door, I glimpsed my reflection in the adjacent glass: I looked hip yet apprehensive—Abbie Hoffman during a raid. Relaxing my shoulders, I grabbed the handle and stepped inside.

The decor was familiar: a shotgun marriage of '70s American eatery and wood-heavy Swiss chalet. Easy-listening music played: a Muzak version of the Bee Gees' "More Than a Woman" (*What the hell,* I'd always wondered, *a woman isn't enough?*). I stood in the lobby and scanned the three waitresses flitting from table to table in their knee-length blue calico dresses with white apron-vests and gathered maroon skirts. The servers were all fairly cute, but none, to my knowledge, had ever cured Dr. Jekyll or worn facial ape-pliances. Maybe Stefanie would come in for the dinner shift; I could zip back to check on my break.

Just then the kitchen door swung open, and into the smoking section she strode, pace swift, features set, auburn hair pulled back over her shoulders and a tray of crepes balanced on her raised right palm. She was a couple of inches taller than I remembered . . . and there'd been growth elsewhere, too. Stefanie filled out her bodice as pleasingly as the miniature Swiss Miss in those TV spots for instant cocoa, with the added virtues of being life-size and real. She stopped at a circular table, provided service-with-a-smile to a family of five, then turned and headed back to the kitchen . . . and, yes, she looked fine from *that* angle, too.

It was then that I noticed the hammering sound, a kind of muffled one-two punch, THUH-THUP, THUH-THUP, THUH-THUP, as of some construction project down in the building's basement. But the noise's source, I quickly realized, was much closer: it was the sound of my own blood pounding in my ears. What's more, my feet had gone clammy inside my Chuck Taylors, and I'd begun to break out in a sweat. For the stakes, now, had been raised higher still—*unbearably* high, should I fail—and so, to my shame, I found myself turning back and eyeing the exit. . . .

"Welcome to the Magic Pan. How many?"

The hostess, a middle-aged blonde in an ankle-length skirt, was smiling at me.

Well, that clinches it. I took a breath. "Just . . . just me. Smoking, please."

She eyed me over her bifocals, gauging my age.

"I won't be smoking, myself," I explained. "I just . . . prefer the smoking *section.*"

The hostess perused me a moment longer, then turned, menu in hand, and led the way. She seated me at the nearest booth. Keeping an eye on the kitchen door, I set my lunch box atop the table and unlatched but did not open it. Then I raised the menu in front of me, peeking over the top.

As Stefanie re-emerged, platter in hand, she executed a quick scan of her section and noted the new arrival. She hurried by—"Be with ya in a moment"—and proceeded to serve the couple behind me. I listened to her doing so, but didn't turn to watch. Seconds later, she was standing to my side. "Just yourself this afternoon?"

Menu still raised, I flipped open my lunch box, inside of which stood Avery's mammoth model kit. *Then* I lowered my menu. "Actually, we're two."

Stefanie's already-lofty eyebrows soared higher still, and a grin shot across her face. "H-how," she inquired, "would an elephant wind up in a Milwaukee creperie?"

I removed my sunglasses. "It's a woolly mammoth."

"Well, *that* explains it." She stepped closer. "Philip!"

I began to stand, arms opening in embrace . . . but my knee cap slammed into the table—*Agh!*—and an entire place-setting slid clattering to the floor. I staggered and wavered and undoubtedly blushed, for there it was again, my true identity: the over-eager pup.

As I made my second effort, she grabbed my arm and helped. "Philip Corcoran!"

"Hey, Stef!" To my great relief, I didn't sound as mortified as I felt . . . and *she* felt amazing when we hugged. The top of her head was just below my nose; her scent was familiar—thanks, no doubt, to the hours I'd spent leaning in close to chimpanzify her face.

She loosened her grip, drawing back to look me over. "This is such a surprise!"

"My job's just a few blocks south," I said, recovering, "and I'd heard you were working here, so I thought I'd stop by."

"I guess it'd be pretty weird if you'd run into me by accident. I mean"—she nodded toward the mammoth—"you probably don't lug that around on a regular basis."

"Actually, it's on loan."

She gave my elbows a shake. "I'm so glad you looked me up!"

"My pleasure." I nodded toward the booth. "Don't s'pose you could, uh, join me?"

"Well. . . ." She gazed off toward the hostess. "Maybe for a minute." As Stefanie sat, she stooped to scoop my utensils off the floor . . . and, bless her soul, made no reference to how they'd gotten there, just placed them on her tray. "You're looking good, Philip."

Was there any sound as beautiful as Stefanie speaking my name? "You too, Stef. That outfit . . . it's really flattering."

She rolled her eyes. "They must've come up with it back in '76. Red, white and blue—real Swiss, huh?" She raised her arms, examining her lacy sleeves. "The style's actually more German. Add in the Yankee-Doodle color scheme, and it's really kind of an Aryan-American mess." Bending toward me, she lowered her voice. "My first night here, I told Rick, the manager, that this is how we'd *all* be dressing if we'd lost World War II."

"What'd he say?"

"'Repeat that, and you're fired.' Apparently not the image they're after."

I patted the back of her hand. "Your secret's safe with me."

"Thanks. I need to get back to work, Philip. You staying to eat?"

"Absolutely."

"Great! Then we can keep talking in bits and pieces." Rising, she placed her hand in my palm and, ever the actress, tossed her head with a flourish. "In bits and pieces, dribs and drabs; in sweet, stolen moments along the way. . . ."

I grinned. "Guess I should say something really . . . suave here."

"Ideally, yeah."

I lifted her hand and kissed it. "An Alpine Cheese Sizzle and a Fresca, please."

Stefanie giggled, blue eyes a-glimmer. "Nice line . . . P.C."

And it was, indeed, in stolen moments that we conducted our on-again/off-again colloquy over the course of the next hour. We each learned a bit about what the other had been up to, but mainly we set about impressing each other with the wittiness of our semi-flirtatious banter. Drawing from a shared background in like scenes from the silver screen, we managed to improvise quite the run of romantic-comedy repartee. All in all, Stefanie Slocum proved remarkably easy to talk to. What's more, I made it through the entire meal without colliding into any inanimate objects. I was a tripped-up pup no more; perhaps all it took was the right girl.

When the check arrived, I was faced with a novel dilemma: how much to tip someone with whom you hope to become involved? Generosity was in order, yet *excessive* generosity could connote a kind of prostitution. I settled on $5 (about 45 percent), laying out a ten, a five, a single, a quarter, a dime, a nickel and a penny for my $11.41 bill plus gratuity—exact change courtesy of Cassie.

Returning to my booth, Stefanie took her seat across from me, folding her hands atop the table. "Lunch crowd's thinning out; I can spare a minute now."

Now . . . or never. "Y'know, Stef. . . ." I swallowed. "Maybe we should continue this conversation later, when you're, uh . . . off the clock?"

"You mean, like a date?"

I smiled, stuttered—"Y-yeah; exactly like a date"—and held my breath.

She smiled back. "Sounds like a plan, Cor-cor-an."

A curtain lifted as our interest in one another moved beyond the theoretical; we began speaking more quickly now, with unabashed enthusiasm. I shifted toward the front of my seat. "You doing anything for the Fourth?"

"That's tomorrow, right? Jeez, this summer's shootin' by! Well, I'm here till six. . . ."

"*We* get the day off. With pay."

She made a sulky face. "'Don't bring me down, Br-r-ruce.'"

I pointed at her. "E.L.O.—you like 'em too?"

"Love 'em! But anyway. . . ."

"Back to tomorrow."

"Right. I'm free at night."

"Great. Where would you like to go?"

She thought for a moment. "Want to watch the fireworks from Atwater Beach?"

More than anything. "Yeah. I do."

"Meet ya there at eight?"

"Great." I slid—*carefully*, knees pointed down—to the end of the bench. "And now, like a Stone Age working stiff, I guess I'll take my lunch box full of mammoth and be on my way."

Smirking, she stood. "How long'd it take you to come up with *that* one?"

"A while." I got to my feet. "You kept leaving; I . . . had to keep busy somehow."

Stefanie grabbed, at last, the bill and the cash. "Hey! Thanks, big spender."

I shrugged. "My job is—well, the pay's pretty OK."

She put a hand on her hip. "You haven't told me where you're working."

"Meigs-Childress, on Michigan. I'm in building services and property management."

"So, you're like a janitor—right?"

I must have beamed at her with the power of a klieg light.

And I thought as I hugged her: *You're the one.*

* * *

The next morning I sat alone at the kitchen table, nursing a glass of Tang and a bowl of the flying-saucer-shaped Quisp cereal: my "interstellar breakfast," as I'd called it years before. I'd since grown embarrassed of the designation—though not yet of the meal itself. Indeed, I adored Quisp, which had been taken off the market in 1978; at my insistence, my mom had stocked up. By the morning in question, I was down to my second-to-last box. Each spoonful— nay, each *saucer*—was a cherished gift.

Yawning, I slumped forward, elbows on the table. I'd had a long, tossy-turny night, and with ten hours to kill before my date, this promised to be a very long day. I reached over and grabbed that morning's Milwaukee *Sentinel*. This was years before the right-leaning *Sentinel* and the left-leaning *Journal*—the evening paper— merged into the middle-of-the-road Milwaukee *Journal-Sentinel*. Back in that two-paper era, our household maintained a subscription to each. Often, over breakfast, my father would cite *Sentinel* articles to validate his stances on the issues of the day; my mother and I dismissed his every contention, confident that the *real* version of whatever he was talking about would reach our doorstep by dinner.

A few pages into the July 4 *Sentinel*, following extensive, Carter-bashing coverage of the ongoing Iranian hostage crisis, the paper had printed the entire Declaration of Independence, signed and adopted 204 years ago on that day. I must've had it bad, for as I waded through the text, even Jefferson's lofty assertion of national self-determination brought to mind Stefanie Slocum. I pictured her at home after a long day's work: standing outside her shower, reaching back to unzip, declaring independence from that pseudo-Swiss dress. . . .

My father, entering the kitchen from behind me, stooped to see what item had so captured my attention. Then he placed a hand on my shoulder. "We are fortunate indeed," he declared, "to live in such a country."

I nodded, less grateful at that moment for my nationality than for the fact that only one of my parents was a mind reader.

He gave my back a pair of sturdy pats. "Happy Independence Day, son."

Yes, I thought as he headed for the fridge, *it just may be.* Independence from solitude; freedom from isolation; liberation from loneliness—and, in due course, from virginity. . . ?

"Uh, thanks, Dad," I said, and turned to Sports. "You too."

* * *

Nowadays, the beach hosts its own Fourth of July fireworks; the locals station their blankets and chairs along the spacious lawn of Atwater Park and watch from the bluff above. But back in 1980, it was a matter of heading down said bluff and watching *other* communities' fireworks from across the bay—the complication being that by the time the fireworks began, Atwater Beach had closed for the night.

The moon on that cool evening shone dimly on Stefanie's face. "There's a gap under the fence about halfway down," she said softly. "Follow me." Then she turned, a slender girl in a copper-colored sweatshirt and cinnamon shorts, and led the way through pines down the bluff, alongside the chain-link fence separating Atwater from the private property to the north.

It was fairly dark out, especially there in the near-woods; I'd have brought a flashlight if I'd known what was in store. Fortunately, Stefanie had made this trek before. She moved with an agility and grace that belied the steepness of our descent, and by following her lead, I too was able to negotiate the bluff with relative ease. We were, I realized, breaking the law twice: trespassing on some rich family's land in order to gain entry to a closed public beach. Still, Stefanie's conduct seemed far removed from, say, lifting a *mariachi*'s wristwatch. And anyway, I was too charmed by her to fret.

At the appointed spot, we crawled under the fence and resumed our descent. I stumbled once or twice, but the fence was there to steady me, and Stefanie just below to show the way. As the bank flattened out into grass and then sand, I drew up alongside her. My hand found Stefanie's, or hers mine, and we ran as one onto the self-same beach where we'd first met, giddy now with glee and with the allure of the forbidden, reveling in our success, our youth, the lap of the waves, the nip of the air, the vastness of the sky, the presence of each other.

"The jetty?" I asked, pointing toward the northernmost of three.

She nodded. "Let's do it."

I released her hand as we reached the line of cement blocks bumpily jutting out into the lake. This time, *I* led: clambering over the concrete, dropping to all fours as needed, getting back to my feet, then down again. I glanced over my shoulder, but in the dark, Stefanie blended into the bluff beyond; I saw her only when she stood, her top half-silhouetted against the violet sky. "You OK, Stef?"

"Dandy!"

"Almost there."

No sooner had we reached the jetty's end than the first of the fireworks, launched a few miles north from Klode Beach, streaked into the sky. As the yellow-white bloom of light exploded and the *BOOOM* rumbled over the lake, we exchanged a look of wide-eyed elation, then moved to sit down. "It's like a movie," she said.

"Well, that *is* how we met."

"Yeah, but—the *timing!*"

"I know! Even if I'd scripted this. . . ."

Another overhead explosion, this one red and green and
BOOOM.

She smiled—"Ya sure ya *didn't* script it"—and turned to me. ". . .
P.C.?"

I saw the reflected fireworks falling, falling, a cluster of comets
in each of her eyes.

I leaned down and kissed her.

She hooked her hands over my shoulders, her mouth opening
with mine, the taste of other-one, of not-me—of Stefanie. Stefanie
Slocum there in my arms, with the churning lake around us and
the incendiary sky above. I drew her up onto my lap, her thighs
scissoring apart, and she moaned a bit as our tongues coalesced,
the two of us now wholly swallowed up in the moment, in each
other, in the night.

BUH-BOOOM.

And I thought—don't laugh!—of Thomas Jefferson. Not the
man, but the message. For, having read his words in the *Sentinel* earlier, I heard them now in my heart. At that moment, even
though I knew I was jumping the gun, I silently prayed for that
glimmering day when Stefanie and I might "mutually pledge to
each other our Lives, our Fortunes and our sacred Honor," just like
the colonial signatories of yore.

Then I set the thought aside and, grabbing her sweet ass, kissed
the girl some more.

CHAPTER 7

Chills, Thrills and Spills on the
Planet of the Dates

"Whoa!" she exclaimed seconds later, yanking my hands off her tits. "*Easy*, slugger."

"Sorry," I said, duly chagrined.

Stefanie slid down off my lap; I retracted my culpable mitts and dropped them limply at my sides. She looked at me uncertainly. "There're a few places we're not going yet, and, well, that's two of 'em."

"Guess I got a little carried away."

"Yeah." She smiled. "But only a little." She reached out, took my hand in her own. "No need to do everything at once, is there?"

"'Course not. It's just. . . ."

"It's just what?"

"Forget it."

"What is it, Philip?"

I said nothing.

She shook my arm. "*What?*"

"Your butt. You let me grab your butt. Which seems at least as, uh, intimate as . . . and actually, in terms of, y'know, proximity, it's a lot *closer* to . . . uh. . . ."

Her eyebrows all but airborne, Stefanie grinned, clearly amused. And rightly so: I was being about as lucid and self-possessed as my dad was when I asked him how often he and Mom "did it."

84

I took another stab: "I mean, I wasn't gonna go *inside* your shirt. . . ."

"No," she assured me, "you weren't."

BOOOM: an explosion of crimson to the north—mirroring, no doubt, the one on my face. I was trapped in that timeless teen horror flick, *Return of the Inter-Gender Time Lag.* So much for closing the gap! Looking away, I gave it one last try. "It's just . . . hard. . . ."

"I imagine!"

". . . to know how far to go. What to do, and . . . when. And when not to."

"Would you like a little pointer?"

"Please," I sighed.

She took hold of my chin, turned my face toward her own. "Just ask me. It's as simple as that. OK?"

"OK; sure." Looking right at her, I mustered a smile. "That'll work."

She laughed, once—"'That'll work.' *God*, you're sweet"—and leaned in to find my lips: not a drawn-out, tongue-twisting kiss like before, but a kiss nonetheless, tender and searching and real. As if to say, *Don't sweat it, boy; I'm still around. And, no, you haven't lost ground.*

We sat out there on the jetty's end for a while more, necking and talking in alternation till the grand finale lit up the northern sky: *BOOOM, POP-pop, POP-POP-POP, buh-BOOOM.* "Stef," I said over the din, "I think we should climb back to shore. . . ."

". . . while we can still see what we're doing?"

"Precisely."

Stef led the way back across the water under blossoming eruptions of every hue; I followed just behind, thrilled by the view. (The *fireworks* were impressive, too.) Then we dashed across the beach, ascended the bluff and made our way back through the park to our bicycles, which were locked to a rack near the flag pole. Thumbs hooked into the pockets of her shorts, Stefanie glanced up at the moon. "I had a great time, Philip."

I unlocked the chain—"Me, too"—pulled it out through the spokes and, regretfully, moved our bikes apart. As was my habit, I slung my bike chain over my head and shoulder like a sash.

"Now *there's* a look," Stefanie said. "'Suburban punk,' huh?"

I laughed. "Right." Then, the inevitable moment of truth: "Stef, you, uh . . . want to do something next week?"

"Next week?" she asked, mounting her bike.

Lucky bike. "Yeah." I slid onto my Schwinn. "I thought we could. . . ."

"How 'bout tomorrow night?"

"Tomorr—yeah! I mean. . . ." I laughed out of sheer joy. "Yeah!"

"Dinner and a movie?"

"Sure," I said, and we spoke in unison: "That'll work!" Then we leaned our bikes toward one another, one foot each on the ground, and kissed once more before pedaling off, I to the north and she to the south, both of us heading home.

* * *

The next day—Saturday—I drove up to Mr. Ruskin's acreage, watered his 50 saplings, retrieved the empties and stashed them in the car, all just as I'd done before. But that's where the similarity ended, for this time, once my work was complete, I scampered straight down the bluff and through the cedars to the promised "private beach."

The hour I spent there was part scouting expedition, part celebration. As I walked the quarter-mile expanse, I gazed less at Lake Michigan than back to the west where bluff and beach met. There I noted numerous nooks and crannies where, hypothetically, a couple of teens could lie hidden on the sand, doing pretty much anything they desired. "When she's ready," I murmured to myself, "when Stef says, 'Yes'"—and shivered in anticipation.

Then, for lack of a cold shower, I stripped down to my Jockeys and raced into the surf. We Milwaukeeans are a hardy stock, accustomed since toddlerhood to swimming not in the oceanic bath water of our Floridian friends and Californian cousins, but in a

Great Lake roughly the temperature of the glacier that carved it. Once you've waded in knee-deep, it's best just to "suck it up" and dive. Sure, it's cold, but the worst of it's over; you can only warm up from that point on.

Eyes open underwater, I breast-stroked out as far as I could in a single breath. (It occurred to me that, for now, this was the only "breast stroking" I'd been permitted.) When my lungs insisted, I broke the surface, hungrily sucking in air, then dropped to my feet and stood there, chin-deep. I turned and gazed back toward shore, pleased with how far I'd come . . . and with how far I'd come lately in another way as well.

Predictably, I found myself wishing Stefanie were there beside me—though not for the reasons you think. Maybe the lake's frigidity had done its job, or maybe swimming into deeper water had somehow given *me* depth. But at that instant, what I longed for wasn't so much to get my hands on her as for the two of us to, say, toss a Frisbee or a Nerf football, each of us diving to make the catch; to coax and cajole one another closer, then splash each other with neither malice nor mercy; to give chase, laughing and shrieking, through the surf, from beach to lake and back again; to lie side by side on the sand atop a single, shared blanket and talk till dusk. For, as much as I wanted a lover, what I craved even more was a girlfriend.

Don't look now, I thought while diving back under, *but I think you've got one.*

* * *

Stefanie opened the front door and gave me a peck on the lips. "Hey, handsome."

This, I could get used to. "Hey, gorgeous," I said, eyeing her above-the-knees black skirt and short-sleeved denim shirt. Then I peered past her into the house. "Should I say 'hi' to your folks, or. . . ?"

"They're out of town; it's just me this weekend."

I liked the sound of that. "Where'd they go?"

She leaned against the doorway. "You know they're both law-
yers, right?"

I'd forgotten this. "Yeah."

"So they have all these conventions and annual meetings
and stuff; they usually wind up going together. This time, they've
enrolled in a continuing-education seminar."

"Maybe someone'll teach 'em how to spell 'Stephanie.'"

"Oh!" she said, and poked me in the ribs. "Harsh! I told you,
Philip, it's an. . . ."

". . . acceptable alternate spelling. I know."

"Well, as long as that's settled. . . ." She reached for the door
knob. "Shall we?"

Moments later, we got into the car and pulled away from the
curb. "How was work?" I asked, quickly adding ". . . honey?" for
satiric effect.

She played along: "God, Carol, it's a jungle, lemme tell ya."
Then she rolled down her window and described her day: the noon-
hour throngs, the prissy "*ass*-istant manager," the aching feet, the
dropped tray. "Sometimes I wonder if it's worth it," she concluded,
"but then I think of all the people who've never had a seafood crepe.
If *I* don't serve it to them, who will?"

I dabbed at my eye—"That's beautiful"—and turned right.
"Well, I worked today *too*, y'know." Heading south on Lake Drive, I
described my stint on Mr. Ruskin's land.

When I was done, she turned toward me. "Let me get this
straight. While I was on my hands and knees, picking up pieces of
broken glass and peeling unraveled crepes off the floor, you were
swimming in the lake . . . and getting *paid* for it?"

"Dinner's on me."

"You'd better believe it!" She placed a hand on my thigh . . .
which made it tingle. "Sounds nice up there, though—your neighbor's beach. Take me some time?"

I placed a hand over hers. "You bet!"

Through no effort on my part, our itinerary recalled my dates
with Stef's three most recent predecessors. Though the outcome

was much improved, the evening's events played out like "Phil's Greatest Hits"—or, more accurately, misses—sequenced in reverse:

We began with dinner at the restaurant of her choice, which turned out to be Coffee Trader. While Stefanie and I exchanged quips, sips and forkfuls by candlelight, I marveled to myself that just four days before and three tables away I'd sat opposite Danielle Payton, staring up at the ceiling fan in near-despair, a hapless victim of romantic apartheid.

Later, as we exited through the front waiting area, a song we both liked came over the sound system: "Strange Magic" by E.L.O. "Hey," Stefanie kidded, "wasn't this the love theme from *Cure of Dr. Jekyll?*" Without a word, I took hold of her; then and there, before hostess and diners-to-be, we started swaying to the music. It was the slow-dance my early exit from the Park Avenue had prevented Cassie and me from sharing—and with a far more fitting partner.

And where did we head after dinner? To the same Cineplex where Cheryl Jantz and I had survived *Xanadu*—survived it individually, that is; *not* as a couple. As Stef and I pulled into the lot, she commented, "I haven't been here in ages."

"I was here two weeks ago," I said, hunting for a space. "For *Xanadu*." Glancing off toward the marquis, I was unsurprised to find that title already missing in action.

"Who'd ya see it with?"

"Cheryl Jantz."

"Who's Cheryl Jantz?"

"No one," I said, steering left. "Just this stoner chick I used to go out with."

"Really."

I pulled the Pacer into an empty spot. "We only saw each other a couple of times."

"Should I worry?"

I shifted into PARK—"You have absolutely no reason to"—and cut the engine. "Though I . . . wouldn't mind if you did."

"Oh," she teased, "so that's *flattering* for young Philip, is it? Well, now, let me reach back in time and give *you* a name or two. . . ."

I took out my wallet. "Stef, I'd actually *pay* you not to."

She laughed, pushed it back. "Get the tickets, and we'll call it even."

"Deal."

We saw the movie that Cheryl and I had intended to see, but which had been sold out on that June night: Stanley Kubrick's much-hyped "masterpiece of modern horror," *The Shining*. The premise is simple: a struggling writer (Jack Nicholson) is hired as off-season caretaker of the mountain-top Overlook Hotel; from November till May, Jack, his wife Wendy (Shelley Duvall) and their young son are to be the snowbound resort's sole occupants. But in fact, they're far from alone: the Overlook is swarming with the ghosts of previous lodgers—malevolent spirits who prey on Jack's weakness, drive him to madness and bid him to "correct" his wife and child . . . with an ax.

I adored *The Shining* from first frame to last: its accumulating sense of doom; its flashes of dark humor; the pioneering Steadicam shots, barreling down the hotel hallways and, climactically, through the snow-covered hedge maze; the soundtrack's deft use of unsettling themes from Bartok and Penderecki (whoever the hell *they* were); and Nicholson's bravura performance as a man whose mind gradually disintegrates before his family's eyes, and ours.

Stefanie had a different reaction. Having read and enjoyed the Stephen King novel from which the film was derived, she couldn't help but fixate on the many liberties Kubrick had taken. "That's not in the book," she repeatedly whispered, determined to set the record straight.

The last straw for her came when Jack leapt out from behind a pillar and buried his blade into the abdomen of his son's would-be rescuer, played by Scatman Crothers. As jarring as this moment was for those of us who hadn't read the book, it was downright traumatic for those who had: apparently, the literary version of Crothers' character sustained no such blow, *saved* the boy and his mother . . . and survived. Thus, as Jack's ax met its mark and Crothers collapsed, Stefanie jerked back in her seat, dropping her pop; the cardboard glass burst open between her left foot and my right, making a generous contribution to the ever-stickier Cinema 6 floor. She pointed at the screen: "That doesn't happen!"

I, too, gestured toward Crothers' blood-gushing corpse: "Apparently, it does."

Happily, her qualms with the script did not dissuade her from snuggling with me for most of the movie's 143 minutes, nor did she decline my unspoken invitation to neck during the closing credits. When the lights came up we disengaged, stood—I, of necessity, with a hand in my pocket—and headed up the aisle with the rest of the audience. "Your, uh, purist objections aside," I asked, "what did you think?"

She tipped her head one way and then the other, considering. "It was good. It creeped me out; I guess that's the real test, right?"

"Plus, it *did* make you drop your Coke."

"True. They could put that in the ads: 'Soda-spillingly scary.' I just wish it had stayed a little closer to the book."

Having slogged my way through the novel *Carrie*, I considered Stephen King something of a hack: strong on set-up but weak on characters and language—a far cry from the genius of a Kubrick. But I took Stefanie's hand and kept my opinion to myself.

We talked, on the drive home, about other horror movies we'd seen, discovering in the process much common ground. Neither of us had cared for *The Exorcist*, but we both admired *Psycho*, she for Tony Perkins' "risky" performance and I for the plot twists and frenetic editing. This led to a discussion of Hitchcock's work in general, during which we each learned a great deal: I about acting, she about production. I also developed a new understanding of the word "complementary"—and inwardly forgave her for liking King.

Then, outside her house . . . the unexpected: we stepped onto the front stoop and found the door slightly ajar. Stefanie stood there, eyes wide, and stared. "H-how . . . how'd this happen?"

"You closed it on the way out, right?"

"I *thought* I did." She looked up at me. "Didn't I?"

I racked my brain. "I . . . remember you reaching back for the knob. But by then, I think I was turning toward the car."

She looked, again, at the door. "Do you remember hearing it close?"

"No. But I . . . don't remember *not* hearing it, either."

She glanced inside the house. "Lights are off, like they were when we left."

"Does anyone else have a key?"

"Not that I know of."

I inspected the lock, then the knob. Stefanie watched in expectant silence, as if I actually knew what I was doing. Gingerly, I opened the door and checked the other side. "Well," I ventured, channeling Jim Rockford, "it wasn't broken into; there'd be marks. You probably just didn't close it all the way."

"But what if . . . what if they broke in somewhere else, and *left* through here? Or. . . ."

Or didn't leave at all. "Let's walk around the outside and have a look."

Hand in hand, we circumnavigated the Slocums' two-story brownstone, checking the windows by the light of street lamps, the locked back door by the gleam of the moon. Halfway around, we heard the *Hooo, hooo* of a nearby owl. Stef and I exchanged a look, and I was tempted to throw in a line of standard-issue haunted-house-movie dialogue: "This place gives me the creeps," or "Sure is quiet—*too* quiet." But her eyes were so filled with dread, I just squeezed her palm instead.

Returning to the front, we stood again on the stoop. "Well," I said with an authoritative tone, "no signs of forced entry. I think it's safe. Though we *could* call the police."

"I'd . . . rather my parents didn't find out about any of this. They just started leaving me on my own; I don't want 'em thinking they made a mistake."

Amen to that. "Why don't we go in and check it out ourselves, room by room?"

She sighed, threw up her hands. "What else *can* we do?"

We made our way through the front entry hall and, blindly, into the kitchen. "Shouldn't we turn some lights on?" I whispered.

"And let 'em know we're here? Hell, no!" Stefanie groped for and found the flashlight atop the fridge. She flicked it on and opened the drawer to the right of the stove. She handed me something, then removed something like it for herself. By the flashlight's dim glow, I saw that I was holding a butcher knife.

I swallowed, hard.

Then we both noticed what Stefanie was holding—a turkey baster—and as she quickly exchanged it for a knife of her own, I squelched back a nervous laugh.

Without a word, we cased the entire first floor: kitchen, pantry, washroom; living room, dining room, den. We looked behind the curtains, pushing them apart with our knives; we checked the closets, holding our breath with the opening of each door. As we reached the bottom of the stairway, I placed my lips to her ear and whispered: "I'll go check out the second floor. You'd better stay here, in case anyone comes runnin' down."

"So I can do what? *Fight* them?"

"No, babe." I pointed to the back door. "So you can get the fuck *out*."

"Oh." Smiling thinly, she handed me the flashlight. "That'll work."

I padded up the stairs and stepped into her parents' room, my beam illumining in turn the king-sized bed, the twin dressers, the eerie, wall-mounted faces of various stern Slocum ancestors. I checked inside the closet, then proceeded to the bathroom.

The floral-print shower curtain was closed. With the *Psycho* theme music playing in my head, I reached up, grabbed the mottled plastic and yanked it aside: nothing—other, that is, than a bad case of ring-around-the-drain.

Then it was over to my girlfriend's room, which I'd been hoping to visit under different circumstances. I stepped through the door, and *Shit!*—my beam lit up a young man's face, life-sized, startled and staring right at me. And for good reason: it *was* me, reflected in Stefanie's full-length mirror.

Once my aorta kicked back in, I lowered my knife and advanced to the closet: uninhabited. Then I checked under her bed: post cards; a scrapbook; a small, stuffed panda; a torn-open, half-empty box of tampons. I lingered over this last item, vaguely aroused by so graphic a reminder of her femininity, then shook it off and got to my feet.

She saw my beam descending the steps. "Well?" she asked in a stage whisper.

I waited till I'd reached her. "Your parents need to scrub their tub."

She gave me a look. "I'll pass that along."

"Otherwise, all clear. That just leaves the basement."

"This time, I'm comin' with."

We'd saved the worst for last: the Slocums' cellar was a dismal area that seemed, by flashlight, distinctly macabre. Cobwebs connected the furnace to the rear wall; the billiard table brought to mind a massive casket; flesh-colored stockings dangling from the laundry-room clothesline resembled severed legs. Eager to ascend, I guided my beam onto the one closed door, which was covered with peeling gray paint. "Where's this lead?"

"We call it the game room."

I had a bad feeling about the game room. "What's it for?"

"Storing things."

"What kind of things?"

"Board games, puzzles . . . Christmas ornaments . . . uh, some canned food. . . ."

I opened the door, and in we went. I pulled the chain beside the overhead bulb, bathing the room in light. It all looked strangely familiar: the pale yellow walls, the shelves laden with dried foods and canned goods, the lone metal pipe protruding from the ceiling, the cardboard boxes stacked by the door. "Wa-a-ait a minute," I said. "I've been here before."

"I . . . don't think so."

Then it hit me. "Oh, Christ."

"What is it?"

"Remember that scene in *The Shining*, right after she knocks Jack out with the bat, and she drags him into the storage room and locks him up, and he's trapped in there till the ghost-butler comes and lets him out?" I swept my arm—and, thus, the knife—from wall to wall. "Look at it. It's *this room*!"

She shook her head, began to dissent—but then her eyes wandered, taking it all in. . . .

We charged out of the game room and up the steps, two at a time, to the ground floor, where we slammed and locked the basement door and turned on every light in sight. We revved up the stereo, cranking WKTI as loud as the speakers could bear, and ran back to the kitchen to put our weapons away. Then, standing by the stove, we fell into each other's arms: shaking with laughter, hanging on for dear life.

"A-a-a-agh!" she screamed. "Damn your eye for art direction!"

Which *really* cracked me up. "Y'know, Stef," I finally managed, "if ever there were a night when a guy might, uh, justifiably talk his way into *staying*. . . ."

"This would be it," she nodded. "But . . . it isn't." She pulled back a bit, though still in my arms. "The neighbors might see you leave in the morning. What would my parents think?"

Hell—what would mine think if I didn't come home till tomorrow? "Gotcha."

She raised a hand to my hair. "Besides, Philip . . . it's still pretty soon."

"'No need to do everything at once,' right?"

"Right. But feel free to grab. . . ." Stefanie averted her eyes; smiling, she pointed behind her. "*You* know."

I hastened to comply. "I don't suppose your folks are leaving town again in . . . oh, a month or so?"

"No—but *I* am. For all of August."

Stunned, I released her cheeks. "What? What the heck for?"

"Youth Acting Camp in NYC. I've been looking forward to it all year!"

"Boy, that's . . . terrific."

"Philip, Philip, Philip." She clasped her hands around my neck. "That's three whole weeks from now. And I'll be back by Labor Day; we have our whole senior year ahead of us!"

"Yeah," I sulked, "at different schools."

"So? I'll still be living right here, a grand total of, what—a dozen blocks away?"

"Sixteen."

"Is that right?"

I nodded, my sullenness starting to falter. "I . . . I counted. Back when we met."

"Well, believe me: you 'count' now, too." She gave me a kiss. "Don't you forget it."

"I won't." Yet already, a part of me had begun to wonder whether Stefanie would meet someone in New York—some studly-yet-sensitive young thespian who would make her count me out. . . .

Then I set the thought aside and, grabbing her sweet ass, kissed the girl some more.

CHAPTER 8

Ticklish Business on the
Planet of the Dates

The following week, our jobs conspired to keep us apart: Stef was on the day shift while I, of course, worked nights. But we waged a counter-conspiracy through daily phone calls that fairly simmered with adolescent sexual tension. We even managed to plan and pay one visit apiece to each other's workplace.

Tuesday night, at the outset of my break, I took the elevator down to the lobby; spotting her through the glass, I bent down to the floor to unlock the revolving door. Stefanie stepped right in, then raised a hand between us. "Are there cameras?"

I glanced over my shoulder, saw one mounted high on the wall. "Right there."

"So . . . at this very moment, somebody's watching us on a screen?"

"Yeah. But it's OK; I told 'em I had someone coming."

"Oh." She eyed the security-cam. "Then I guess the question is, do you *want* them to see us kissing?"

I pictured old Casey, the building's avuncular night watchman, seated at his station around the corner and down the hall. I stuck my hands in my pockets. "What if the answer's 'yes'?"

She stepped closer, stood on tiptoes and, wrapping her arms around me, planted a long, drawn-out wet one squarely on my lips. I could just make out the distant sound of Casey sending forth an appreciative "Whooo-*hoo!*"

Stefanie came up for air but didn't release her hold, staring right into my eyes from inches away. Her actions took me aback; never had I seen her so forward, so bold. Then it struck me: this wasn't Stef—not really. This was an eager young actress who, spotting a camera, had decided to put on a show.

But, oh, what a show!

A lock of my hair had fallen over my eye; she pursed her lips and *blew* it away. "Tell me, big boy"—her voice a husky purr—"you want some more?"

"Stef, I'm . . . not sure I do!" I squirmed a bit. "Not here and now, I mean."

Her posture relaxed as she slipped out of character; her tone turned playful. "Well, then, if that's *it*, we should take a curtain call. Let's just face you toward the audience. . . ."

I broke free—"Duty calls"—and knelt down to re-lock the door. Once the bolt had been extended (and my own "bolt" retracted), I stood up straight and turned toward both Stef and the camera, arms out to my sides. "Is this what you wanted 'em to see?"

She shook her head. "*Hard*-ly."

I'd gotten an OK for her visit from Mr. Puckett the night before, so I led her straight up to my father's office; Stef plunked herself down in the black leather chair and fawned over the freckle-faced, nine-year-old Philip in the desktop family photo. Then I led her down the hall to the examination room. Closing the door behind us, I offered her a complimentary physical. Sadly, no dice—so instead I donned gloves, pulled the medical-waste bag out of its receptacle and demonstrated my *Andromeda Strain*-inspired biohazard-disposal protocol, complete with dramatic countdown. My task completed just shy of "zero," I turned to face her. "Well?"

She flashed a thumbs-up: "Soda-spillingly scary!"

From there it was down to the photo lab, where I explained my "intelligence work" in hushed tones, then nabbed from the trash three 8x10 glossies—a corporate head shot, a low-angle view of a man undergoing dialysis, and a young Asian couple's saccharine-sweet engagement photo—and tucked them under the leg of my jeans. Stefanie's chuckle was ambiguous; I folded my arms. "Are you laughing with me, or at me?"

"Yup."

In the hair salon, she all but pushed me into one of the chairs and insisted on trimming my sideburns. "They don't need it!" I protested.

She wrapped a bib around my neck. "Just a little touch-up."

"Miss, do you have a license to do this?"

"Sure. It's hanging right next to your photo-stealing permit."

As the razor's electric *bzzzz* closed in on my head, I clamped my eyes shut. "Please be careful."

"Hey, I'm the one who has to *kiss* this face." She switched sides. "So I'm quite motivated not to screw up."

Not the highest-minded of motives, but it would do.

"Ta-da!" She handed me a mirror.

I inspected one side, then the other. "Not bad. Edges are nice and straight. But . . ."

"The left one's shorter, isn't it? I can fix that." *Bzzzz. . . .*

Moments later, I re-checked my reflection, only to find that she'd overcompensated: the *right* sideburn was now shorter. I didn't like where this was heading. "Perfect!" I said, and flew from the chair.

Our last stop was the vacant dance studio. We faced each other in a seeming infinity, standing as we were between four mirrored walls in the center of the glossy, wood-paneled floor. That glossiness, incidentally, was my handiwork; I'd mopped the night before. I was about to mention this when Stef asked, "Did you see *Saturday Night Fever*?"

"Three times," I replied, suppressing my recent disillusionment with disco.

"Remember that scene. . . ?"

That was all I had to hear. I grabbed her hands and began to side-step in a clockwise arc; Stefanie, facing me, did the same, and soon the two of us were twirling, twirling, hands enmeshed and arms outstretched, round and round and round.

As our speed increased, the railings and reflections behind her streaked sideways, wiping into a horizontal blur. Her face, now the sole object in focus, shone with glee. She released a shriek, high-pitched and clipped. "Philip! How do we stop?"

"Stefanie! We don't!"

"We just keep goin' till. . . ?"

". . . we turn into butter!" *And melt into each other.*

Instead we decelerated, fell into one another's arms—and fell down.

The background was in focus now but was sliding counter-clockwise at an alarming rate. "Oooof," she groaned. "I'm nauseous. . . ."

"Close your eyes till it passes." I struggled to my knees and reached for Stef . . . but her image was in motion, and I missed. "Funny how they left this part out."

"I was just thinking that! The scene ended with Tony and what's-her-name still grinning 'n' spinning. . . ."

Shakily, I stood. "Instead of sprawled on the floor, ralphin' all over each other."

Eyeing me woozily, she took my offered hand. "And on that charming note, it's time for me to go."

My Thursday visit to her workplace was far less eventful. I arrived mid-afternoon and was shown to a table; no sooner had I sat than Stefanie burst out of the kitchen, a tray balanced on each palm, her white frills flapping and blue dirndl skirt a-whirl. She was a vision, a bustling, breathtaking Bavarian beauty, and when she reached my table, I told her so.

"*Danka, mein herr.*" She curtsied. "Dining alone?"

I nodded. "Yeah, it's over between the mammoth and me. She's back with Avery, and I'm . . . seeing someone else."

She lowered her voice. "I'd kiss ya, but . . . *you* know."

"You're kissing me now," I said. "With your eyes." And thought: *if Avery heard that, I'd* never *live it down.*

I ordered my usual Alpine Cheese Sizzle but saved room for an ice cream crepe as well. By the time the latter arrived—festooned with a *double*-dollop of dark-chocolate shavings (truly, it's who you know)—business had slowed enough for Stef to take the seat across from me. "I've got maybe two minutes."

"I'll take 'em." Under the table, our hands met. "So, the folks here treatin' ya right?"

She shrugged. "No complaints."

"And they're cool with you taking August off?"

"Oh, they don't know."

"You're kidding."

"I don't think they'd have hired me if they had."

"Yeah, but Stef. . . ."

"I wasn't gonna stay on for the school year, anyway."

I leaned toward her. "Do your parents know?"

Stefanie laughed. "My dad's the one who *suggested* it!" She deepened her voice: "'Each for himself, Steffie. You give 'em a week's notice; that's all they deserve'—this, mind you, from someone who once founded a *commune!*"

I pictured big Ben Slocum, attorney-at-law, seated in the lotus position in torn jeans and tie-dye, strumming a sitar. "Do you ever remind him about that—about those days?"

"'Ancient history,' he says. 'Summer of Love's over, kiddo. Screw them before they screw you.'"

"God." I shook my head. "Has it really come to that?"

"I don't know; he's pretty sharp. When Carter let the Shah in for medical treatment, my Dad said, 'Big mistake.' Next thing you know. . . ."

"Right."

She glanced behind her. "I've gotta get back before they miss me. See you Saturday?"

"And talk to ya tonight."

"Right." She gave my hand a squeeze—"Now kiss me, you fool"—and winked. ". . . if only with your *eyes*."

* * *

I spent a chunk of Saturday morning dealing with two pieces of correspondence: one sent by me, the other *to* me. First, clipping letters from the previous week's issue of *Time*, I composed the message "MisSION AccomPLISHE*D*" and Elmer's-Glued it to the back of my photo of the Asian couple staring into each other's eyes. I slipped the shot into an envelope, addressed it to Craig Starling and galloped downstairs to greet the day.

"Breakfast, Phil," my mother called from the kitchen. "Cream of Wheat."

In the middle of summer? I thought, but said only, "Just leave it out; I'm going to the post office." I reached for the front door. . . .

"Oh; that reminds me."

Cautiously, I turned back.

She stepped into the hallway, a missive of her own in hand. "We got this yesterday from Todd; he's coming home to visit next weekend."

"Great," I said, taking the proffered post card. *Greetings from Florida* it read, in garish yellow script. The obviously doctored photo showed a busty, bikini-clad beach babe stooping to pick up a seashell as an open-mawed alligator prepared to sample her ample ass. I shook my head: my brother, the aesthete.

"There's a message on there for you."

I turned the card over, skimmed down to the terse P.S.:

> Tell Phil I found that comic book he wantid.
> I'll bring it when I come. But it'll cost him.

Want-id? *Oh: my fake ID!* Great news—though that *last* bit. . . .

My mother retrieved the card. "What comic book's he talking about?"

Here we go, I thought, and slowed down my breathing like a perp hooked up to a polygraph. "'The Incredible Hulk.'"

"What does he mean, it'll cost you?"

"It's a, y'know, misprinted issue. Where the Hulk is purple instead of green. A real rarity. So, I'm guessing it wasn't cheap."

"Oh." She nodded, turned, walked away.

It worked; it *worked!* She didn't have a clue! Was her power dwindling . . . or mine increasing?

Either one'll do.

* * *

Just before noon, I filled Mr. Ruskin's watering jugs while he provided superfluous supervision from the side ("The cap on that one seems a bit askew . . . Careful not to dent the handle!"). Annoyed, I packed up the Pacer in record time, then headed south to Stef's. She must have been watching for me, because the front door swung open just as I pulled up in front. Out she came, all but skipping down the walk in lemon-yellow shorts over a purple one-piece swimsuit. She opened the door and hopped in. "Hey, handsome."

"Hey, gorgeous." I gave her a kiss, and off we drove.

We flirted and chatted, teased and joked all the way up to Port. At one point, she tugged at my raggedy tan shorts and asked, "What's with these?"

"I know they're kinda shot," I said, "but they're *real* comfy; they're my favorite pair."

"Mine too, Tarzan: they're barely there!"

Arriving at Ruskin Ranch (as I'd taken to calling it), we parked on the private dirt road, got out of the car and set about the task at hand. I'd given Stef the option of hitting the beach while I made the rounds, but she insisted on pitching in: "I don't want to get tired of it before you even get there. Besides, the work'll go faster this way."

"Well, thanks." I hefted four jugs from the trunk and bent low to set them down.

"Did anyone ever tell ya," she asked, "you have a dandy li'l butt?"

I grinned—objectified at last!—and took a step toward her.

Stefanie, smiling, took a step back.

"Oh-h-h," I said admiringly, "you know just how to play me, don't ya? You're a pro."

"There's no script, P.C. Just makin' it up as I go."

We went our separate ways for the watering; I probably hit about 30 saplings and Stef the rest. Then we hooked up for jug retrieval, one jumbo lawn bag clutched in her hands and the other in mine. Once the empties had been collected and stashed in the car, I scooped my *Planet of the Apes* beach blanket off the back seat, and we set out together for the beach.

"Just the one blanket, huh?" she asked, wading through knee-high prairie grass beside me. "If you'd mentioned it, I'd have brought one, too."

"Yeah, but *then* where would we be?"

She looked puzzled. "I give up: where?"

"On separate blankets."

She laughed. "Now who's the pro?"

"Makin' it up as I go."

When we reached the beach, Stefanie raised a hand above her eyes and gazed out across the lake. "They say you can see Michigan on a clear day, but I don't know."

I looked south toward Milwaukee, where a single white building was visible. "Hey, is that the First Wis?"

"It's so tiny," she marveled. "It looks like a Chiclet!"

"Yeah, we are pretty far from home. Y'know, way out here"—I moved closer—"anything could happen."

"Yeah"—she sidestepped—"like . . . going barefoot!"

I sighed. *Well, it's a start.*

We slid out of our sneakers and deployed them over the outstretched blanket's four corners. "Y'know," I said, pulling off my Pat Benatar concert T, "this is a private beach. We could take it *all* off if we wanted."

Stefanie shimmied out of her shorts—"Don't waste any time, do ya?"—to reveal the bottom half of her purple one-piece, a French-cut model that exposed generous amounts of hip, including the most exquisite pair of iliac crests since my Visible Woman model kit.

Scratch that: they were *better* than Vizzie's.

Aware, now, that I was gawking, she raised her arms and turned, once, all the way around, the fabric of her snug little suit clinging tightly to her caboose.

"*Yow*za! I mean—very nice." I undid my "Tarzan shorts," worked them down my hips and let them fall to the sand; in one meant-to-be-sexy motion, I scooped them up with my foot and kicked them several yards away.

She lifted a hand to cover her mouth, but I could tell from her eyes she was giggling.

Undeterred, I stepped toward her wearing only the kelly-green Speedo I'd bought at Boston Store the day before. I leaned in for a kiss. . . .

. . . but Stef bolted for the lake. "C'mon!" she shouted, bare feet bursting through the surf, flinging up twinkling rings of water. "Let's get—*Shit!* Oh, jeez, *br-r-r-r!* Let's get you cooled down."

I bounded out after her. In no time at all we were hip-deep, splashing each other determinedly from a remove of 15 feet. I was living a dream; hadn't I envisioned this scene? *My kingdom for a Nerf football*, I thought, but settled on lunging toward her—"A-a-a-agh!"—impervious to her splashes, titillated by her screams, grabbing her waist and hoisting her up, legs kicking, arms flailing, throwing us off balance as her shrieks lapsed into laughter and we toppled into the lake. "*Br-r-r-r!* Get off!" I hollered from below, straining for the surface. "I'm not your lifeboat!"

"You sure? 'Cause I . . . think I felt a rudder."

I revisited this remark later as we lay on our backs, side by side on my *Apes* blanket, I atop the image of Cornelius and Stefanie, appropriately, over Zira. "You seem awfully fascinated," I began, "with a . . . certain part of me."

She stretched out her arms, slid her palms under her head. "Which part would that be?"

"My, uh . . . 'rudder.'"

She smiled, her cheeks beginning to redden; she closed her eyes. "Do I, now?"

"Uh-huh. You keep bringing it up."

"Yeah . . . and *talking* about it, too."

"Seriously." Turning onto my side, I couldn't help but admire her smooth right bicep, the subtle scoop of the pit beneath. "What gives?"

"Well, what do you expect? It's, y'know, completely foreign to me; I . . . don't have anything like it." She lowered her voice. "I mean, there's this . . . *thing* you guys have, this kind of . . . fleshy, floppy, dangly thing, and somehow, just by the power of suggestion it turns into this . . . this big, honkin' *bone*. What's up with that?"

She had a point. "When you put it that way. . . ."

"Don't you feel the same way about me—about what *I've* got . . . there? I mean, that's pretty foreign to you, isn't it?"

"Sh-sure," I said, a big, honkin' bone forming at that moment. I reached down, made a discreet adjustment. "Sometimes I think of it as this damp, cramped cavern with kind of a . . . a steamy stream coursing through it. Secret and submerged, and surrounded by darkness."

Stefanie shifted beside me, eyes still closed. "Go on."

"Last year in school, we studied Greek mythology, and. . . ."

"The River Styx?"

"Exactly."

"Huh." She smiled. "I like that." A mosquito alighted in her arm pit; with the flick of a finger I banished the bug from that hallowed hollow, thus inflicting upon Stef an inadvertent tickle. "*Eeeep!*" she squealed, arms slapping to her sides, then craned her head toward me. "What was that for?"

"You were about to get bit. And not by me."

"A 'skeeter?"

I nodded. "Sorry if it. . . ."

"Don't be." She raised her arms, slowly, into the previous, prone position. Then she lowered her head back onto her hands and re-closed her eyes. "I . . . think there's more of 'em."

"More. . . ?"

"Mosquitoes"—and bit her lip in anticipation.

So I rose to my knees and proceeded to guide a fingertip up, down, over and around the tender depression under one arm, then the other, then both at once. Stefanie shook and shuddered and, eventually, squeaked; what's more, I couldn't help but notice two bantam "bones" of her own pressing up through the violet nylon, one at the tip of each breast. Just like the new Chapman's window mannequins, or my Farrah poster back home—only *so* much better. In response I lightened my touch, now barely grazing her goosebumpy flesh. . . .

"Ohmygod*stop*!"

I stopped. "Too much?" I asked, surprised by the breathiness of my own voice.

"No. No"—her eyes shut tight. "Please keep going."

"Even if you tell me . . . ?"

"Cantaloupe."

I opened my mouth to speak—"Uh"—closed it; opened it again. "*What*?"

"Don't stop unless I say 'cantaloupe.'"

I eyed her suspiciously. "Stef, have you done this before?"

"No! No, I swear. I've only . . . read about it."

It somehow hadn't occurred to me that *girls* might peruse those publications, too.

Her eyes opened just a bit, two sun-splashed blue slits. She spoke, then, with an endearing timidity: "It could be our . . . c-code word, y'know? For 'Stop?'"

I swallowed—"Gotcha"—and recalled, just then, her boldness at my workplace four days ago. Sure, the smoldering temptress she'd assayed for the front-lobby security-cam had been hot . . . but this was infinitely hotter, for she wasn't acting now. This was no role; this was Stefanie Slocum.

Again, she began to blush. "And . . . if you want to, Philip. . . ."

"Uh-huh?"

". . . *while* you're doing it?"

"Yes?"

"You . . . could kiss me."

I nodded. "That'll work."

Stefanie nodded back. Then, with a sigh, she closed her eyes.

CHAPTER 9

Brotherly Love on the

Planet of the Dates

On Thursday afternoon I sat hunched over my desk with a purple marker, transforming a Marvel back issue into an alibi. My exertions were probably unnecessary: what were the odds that my mom would want to view the comic book in question? Still, in accordance with the Boy Scouts credo, I labored on, leaving in my wake panel after panel of floral-hued Hulks. Just as I reached the final page, the bedroom door swung open; I dropped the pen and feigned reading. "Mom," I shouted over the stereo, "could ya please knock?"

"Knock ya *out* if you call me 'Mom' again."

I turned: my brother stood in the doorway, looking tanner than usual but otherwise unchanged. "Hey, Todd! Didn't hear you pull in."

He glared at my palpitating speakers. "How could ya, with this New Wave crap playing?"

Rather than engage him in debate about the music's merits, I stood and crossed toward the amp. As I bent down to lower the volume, Todd bent down to stop me.

"Leave it," he instructed, his hand encasing my wrist.

"Grows on ya, huh?" My words faded as I caught a glimpse of the doorway, for stationed just behind my brother's denim-clad legs was the most astounding pair of gams I'd ever seen: sumptuous, smooth and gloriously disclosed by blue jeans cut off just below the crotch. The high-placed hips angled in sharply toward a flat, bared belly; the capacious breasts, at once pointy and plump, strained against the confines of a hot-pink halter top. My eyes followed a slim neck up to pouty red lips, a kewpie-doll nose and a waterfall of strawberry-blonde tresses worthy of a Clairol commercial.

Standing up straight, I shook my way out of Todd's grasp. "Hi."

"Hi." She slid a finger into my brother's beltless belt loop and smiled at me, all teeth, curves and curls. "You must be Phil."

"Yeah, I. . . ." Stepping forward, I shook her hand. "Hi."

"I dig the Costello. *Armed Forces*, right?"

"Right!"

"It rocks."

I'm not sure which pleased me more: her comment, or the grimace it elicited from Todd. "Listen, babe, I gotta talk to the kid."

She released his loop and, with a dainty wave, backed away from the door. "Don't be long. . . ." she said, eyes flitting to my brother. ". . . Bronc."

He closed the door behind her. "Now, listen. . . ."

"'Bronc'?"

"None of your business." He shook his head. "It's . . . an inside joke."

"She's gorgeous, bro'. Way to go."

Todd permitted himself a meager smile. "You don't know the half of it."

I reached again for the volume knob—

"I said *leave* it." He pushed me toward my desk; I half-fell, half-sat in my chair with a *thwump*. "We're gonna have a private conversation, and I suppose that whiny guitar-nerd of yours is as good cover as any."

"Your girlfriend seems to like him."

Ignoring the comment, he reached into his pocket and pulled something out, then thrust it in front of my face.

My eyes re-focused, and there before me was the fake ID of my dreams: a laminated card from the Florida DMV with a birthdate exactly two years older than my own . . . and a photo of me. Not the most flattering shot—he'd clipped it from the infamous 1979 Corcoran family Christmas card—but recognizable. "All right!" I enthused. "This'll get me in *any*where!" I reached to take it . . .

. . . but he snatched it back. "Not so fast, little man. Let's talk turkey." Todd looked suddenly perplexed; he pointed past me. "What the . . . ?"

I scooped up and handed him my copy of Hyacinth Hulk. "*This* is what you brought me, as far as Mom knows. A misprinted issue; very rare."

He shook his head, tossed the comic book back. "You want the card?"

"Do I!"

"Then, let me tell ya somethin'. For the next three and a half days . . ."

"Whatever you want, man."

". . . till her and I leave. . . ."

"Anything!"

He nodded, slowly, and folded his arms. "Your ass is mine."

* * *

". . . and thus began my current state of indentured servitude."

Reminded, no doubt, of her own salaried subjugation, Stefanie glanced briefly toward the hostess station, then turned back to me. "Jeez. Is it worth it, Philip?"

"Do *you* have a fake ID?"

"'Course I do."

"Well, if we want to go out together, then I'll need one, too." I reached for her hand under the table. "Really, it's . . . not that bad."

She stroked my thumb. "You bra-a-ave, brave man."

"He had me wash his car. Big deal; I like washing cars! But the main thing he wants is a lookout—y'know, for his girlfriend and him. My folks stuck 'em in separate rooms."

"What's her name?"

"I don't know! I keep trying to catch it, but he always calls her 'babe.' I just think of them as Todd and the Bod. I mean, Stef—you should see her."

Her eyes narrowed. "Really."

"Oh, but that's . . . I didn't; I—don't. . . ."

She grinned. "Keep squirmin', Sherman. I'll tell ya when to stop."

"You've got nothing to worry about, Stef. I'm crazy. . . ."

"I know." She gave my hand a squeeze. "I'm crazy, too." A new easy-listening song began to play; Stef tilted her head, trying to identify it. "That's . . . 'Copacabana,' right?"

I nodded. "A Muzak version of Manilow. Seems kind of redundant."

She looked back at me. "Listen, I'm telling the manager today. I decided to take your advice and give 'em two weeks' notice after all."

"*Das ist gut, fraulein.* May as well leave on decent terms."

"I suppose." She stared at the table. "I'd better get back to work," she said—but didn't move. Neither of us spoke for some time. Stefanie's dirndl-skirted colleagues periodically fluttered by as the Muzak continued to play. "Y'know," she finally said, "I'll miss this place."

"Me, too. And the lunches here with you."

Releasing my hand, she slid out of the booth. "Well, you can always come here next month and *think* about me." She straightened her hem. "I wouldn't mind that. Picturing you here. . . ."

". . . all alone in a corner booth, pining away. *Alpine*-ing away. . . ."

She groaned.

"Sorry."

"You'd have no one to flirt with but a mammoth in a box."

"That does it," I griped. "I'm now officially depressed. Back to the kitchen with you!"

She kissed the air. "Talk tonight."

And so we did. Sprawled in the den, I dialed her up after work, and as we spoke I tore open the latest mailing from Craig Starling. He'd returned to me the photo of the saccharine-sweet couple—glued inside the bottom of a Pan Am vomit bag. Craig had successfully decoded my latest message, for over the image, in haphazard script, he had scrawled a single word: "Congratulations."

"So," I asked, "how'd it go, giving notice?"

"Oh, fine. They weren't upset. They even said they'd hire me back . . ."

"Great!"

". . . if the restaurant weren't closing."

"You're kidding. When?"

"September. Apparently the whole chain's in trouble."

"Man." I turned the vomit bag over, bent and re-bent the clasps. *What's happening here? First, Fotomat; now. . . .*

"Hey, Philip. What's your tomorrow look like?"

I flung the bag aside. "Not good. My brother cornered me when I got in tonight and gave me my marching orders. Which are more like stay-at-home-and-do-nothing orders."

"Why's he want that?"

"Our parents are going to a wedding in the city, so I have to hang out downstairs while Todd and the Bod are up in his room. I'm to 'stay the fuck away' from his door unless the folks come home early, in which case there's a special warning knock he's directed me to use."

"Jesus. Are you allowed to have company?"

"'Fraid not."

"Well, how about tomorrow night?"

"Family dinner. The five of us are going out; I have no choice." A sudden inspiration: "Hey—wanna make it six?"

"Hmmm. Well, I *am* kind of curious to meet this. . . .'Bod.'"

"Stef, you're a lifesaver."

"And you," she said, "are Good 'n' Plenty"—then groaned at her own joke. "Darn it, P.C.; you're rubbin' off on me!"

* * *

If there's one thing tougher than being a teenage boy whose girl-friend feels there's "no need to do everything at once," it's being that same boy trying to watch TV while his brother emphatically nails his own centerfold-worthy squeeze one floor above.

I'm pretty sure Todd didn't out-and-out *intend* for me to hear them. Initially I couldn't, thanks to the quadraphonic speakers blaring side 1 of Supertramp's *Breakfast in America* behind his locked bedroom door. But then the record ended.

"Gahhhd," moaned the Bod.

"Oh, *God!*" concurred Todd.

—this theological exegesis delivered to the disco-drum accompaniment of a bedpost pummeling a wall at 110 beats per minute. Understandably, neither party saw fit to break away at that moment and flip the album over. For my part, I wasn't sure whether I wanted them to or not. Feeling feverish, I cranked the TV volume and tried to focus on an old "Twilight Zone." But Serling's story line—some miserable sap gradually realizes he has died and gone to hell—brought me right back home . . . as did the following scream from above:

"Yeah, gimme that *cock,* ya stallion!"

"Bronc," I thought, horny and queasy now in equal measure. I headed for the bathroom, where I hesitated, torn between the Jergen's and the Tums.

And then—I swear to God—my brother *whinnied.*

I grabbed the Tums.

They kept at it for close to an hour, then quieted down . . . only to resume after a 20-minute intermission. Act II was even longer, Todd's endurance presumably enhanced by the, uh, climax of Act I. Through it all, his stereo remained silent, clearing the way for more audio porn from on high. Nowadays, you can pick up the phone and pay $1.95 a minute to hear what I was getting for free—yet I'd have paid that to shut them up.

"Zuck! Ooo, Zuck!" Todd bellowed at one point, leaving me to wonder whether *this* was her name, or part of it. There were two Zuckers and a Zuckerman at my school—though the Bod was nothing like them. The matter was clarified by his next utterance: "Zuck, zuck, *zuck* it, zweed-heart!" I stared at the ceiling in disbelief: somehow, the throes of passion had conferred upon my suburban-born brother the diction of a north-woods fishing guide.

Gazing out the window, I longed to go out and mow the back lawn—or, better yet, to hop on my Schwinn, hightail it to Stef's and tickle her silly—but such thoughts were pointless. I'd been ordered to remain at my post while Todd indulged his.

Eventually, I heard the two of them stumble into the upstairs bathroom, and it was during the subsequent very long, very loud shower that the phone rang. "Hello?"

"Hi, honey."

"Hey, Mom."

"We're just leaving the reception. Listen, dinner's at 6:30."

"OK. I'll tell Stef."

"It'll be good to see her again."

"Yeah. Uh, how was the wedding?" I asked, the muted *thunk-splash-thunk* of boisterous shower-sex wafting down around me.

She sighed. "It was beautiful. Terribly romantic."

Thunkita-thunkita-THUD!

"Great," I muttered. And thought: *Love is in the air.*

* * *

That evening, the six of us sat around a seafood-laden table at the Red Lobster on N. 76th St., glancing about in strained silence. Conversation was sporadic, tending toward the selective and/or secretive—as when Todd, seated to my left, whispered something to the bra-less Bod who, giggling, kicked him under the table. I followed my brother's lead, leaning toward Stef and advising her to "save room for cantaloupe."

She nearly gagged on her scampi.

It was the good Doctor—characteristically overdressed in a light blue sport coat and navy tie—who eventually broke the ice with one of his Paternal Proclamations: "Well. What a pleasure it is to have you two young ladies with us tonight."

Stefanie smiled. "Nice to be here, Dr. C. Pass the hush puppies, please?"

The Bod reached them first, snagged one for herself and then leaned forward with the basket—her rather imposing breasts nearly snuffing out our table's lone candle in the process.

Stefanie stared at the retreating cleavage, then caught herself and covered with "I, uh, like your pendant."

"Oh, thanks!" The Bod fingered the small oval stone. "It was a present from my friend, Sidney. He's a photographer."

"How nice," my mom said tersely.

My father poured himself some water. "A commercial photographer?"

The Bod giggled; Todd slung an arm around her and, mouth half-full, answered for her: "He's really more of a . . . nature photographer."

She kicked him again.

My father then launched into a lengthy discourse on the genius of Ansel Adams, during which oration Stefanie and I, between sideways snickers, concentrated mainly on our meals. Ultimately, my mother cut in with, "Are you still acting, Stefanie?"

"Yes, I am—whenever I can."

"In fact," I said, "she's going to acting camp in New York next month."

Stefanie nodded—"*All* month"—and shot me an apologetic smile.

My folks exchanged a look that I, for once, couldn't begin to read.

Todd gestured toward me with a forkful of crab. "He made her play a monkey."

"First of all," I began, "it was an ape, not a 'monkey'. . . ."

". . . and second of all," my girlfriend cut it, "Philip didn't *make* me do anything. It was my privilege to portray Dr. Zira." She looked right at Todd, addressing him directly. "Your brother happens to be a very talented filmmaker."

I gazed over at her, tingling with pride. *My hero!*

My parents looked rather impressed, too.

"Whatever," Todd grumbled, and resumed feeding his face.

"I was in a movie once," the Bod offered.

"Cool," Stefanie said. "What did you play?"

"A stewardess."

I reached for my Fresca. "Did you shoot on a set, or in an actual plane?"

"Well, mostly at Motel 6."

My father opened his mouth, then closed it.

Adjusting her napkin, my mother looked off to the side.

I set down my drink. "Hey, bro'. If you're comin' home for Christmas, we should try to get Packers tickets; they're hosting Denver. You know: the . . . *Broncs?*"

The Bod looked quickly at Todd, who leaned up against me and grabbed my upper arm—tight. He hissed two words into my ear—"Watch it"—then let me go. "Just may need to *keep* that comic book."

Stef appeared concerned—I'd have to explain it to her later— and my mom was downright baffled. Peering over her half-glasses, she looked from Todd to me and back again, then shook her head. "It's like you kids speak a whole 'nother language."

* * *

On Sunday morning I knocked off more chores for my brother, but the afternoon brought a reprieve when T and the B headed for Bay-shore Mall. I rang up Stef and then sped over to her place, watering jugs in tow. Pulling up in front of her house, I congratulated myself on my foresight: I'd filled the jugs and packed the trunk the night before, knowing full well that if my window of opportunity opened, I'd need to dive right through.

A smiling Stefanie slipped out the door, candy-cane scrumptious in a cherry tank top and white shorts. She raced down the walk and hopped right in.

"Hey, gor—" That was all I managed before she grabbed my head and mashed her mouth into mine—this, mind you, with nary a security-cam in sight. "Wow!" I said when at last she let me. "What's all that about?"

She shrugged. "It's prob'ly 'cause we're alone together, but I know it's not for long. Like when they give a prisoner one night with his wife. . . ."

"A conjugal visit."

"Right!" She buckled up. "How much time *do* we have?"

I pulled away from the curb. "Two hours, tops. I don't want to push it; I'm already on the warden's shit list."

"Yeah," she said, taking my right hand. "What was all that about?"

I filled her in on "Bronc."

Stefanie laughed. "Gives new meaning to 'horsin' around.'"

"If they'd been a couple of strangers, I guess it could've been sexy. But when it's your own brother, no matter *who* he's with, it sorta . . . negates the hotness. Y'know?"

"Not really; I'm an only child."

"Oh; right. Well, then picture your parents. . . ."

"Gotcha." She shuddered. "Next topic!"

I pulled onto the expressway, heading north. "Hey, did you see the look *my* parents gave each other when I mentioned your acting camp?"

"Yeah. What's the story?"

"I have no idea."

"Maybe you should ask 'em."

"Maybe I should." We both fell silent; I suspected that she, too, was contemplating our imminent separation. "I'll . . . miss you, Stef."

"Philip. I'll miss you, too. But it's only for a month." She gave my fingers a squeeze. "Stay outta trouble, huh?"

I laughed. "That should be easy."

"How will you keep busy?"

"Well, I'll still have my job, five nights a week—and these trips to Port. Plus, I've been thinking I might dust off the ol' Super-8 and shoot another movie. Not a cheesy one, like before. No talking apes! Something . . . decent, original, new."

"Cool." She moved her hand lower, resting it on my knee. "Save a part for me!"

At Mr. Ruskin's acreage, I got out and opened the trunk. As Stef stepped up alongside me, I noticed how the sun brought out the red in her reddish-brown hair. Before I could mention it, she gave me a poke, then spoke: "I have a surprise for you."

I tried to decipher her grin. "Hmmm. Does it involve your swimsuit? Or, better yet . . . the lack of one?"

She shook her head—"Nah, I've got it on underneath"—then tapped one of the water jugs. "It involves *them*. Go ahead and start watering; I'll meet up with you at the end."

Curiosity piqued, I set about the task at hand, lugging the first half-dozen jugs out toward the trees. At first my girlfriend hung back, pacing beside the Pacer and watching me. But once I reached the second sapling, Stefanie darted, fox-like, into the field and raced to the base of the first. There, she crouched low and vanished into the underbrush . . . only to pop up seconds later, eyes trained my way, waiting for me to reach tree number three.

And so we progressed, moving from one end of Ruskin Ranch to the other, I blazing the trail and Stefanie ever lagging one tree behind. We must have looked like two big kids playing either follow-the-leader or else the strangest game of "tag" in history. At each stop, my undeniably vulpine girlfriend squatted on the ground (not, I presumed, to mark her territory) and busied herself doing something-or-other that the high grass hid from view.

At long last, I reached sapling #50. Kneeling, I emptied the final container into the arid soil surrounding the tree's wrist-thick trunk. Then I stood, turned and—there she was! Startled, I bobbled the empty jug . . .

. . . which Stef reached out to nab. "Thanks!"

"What now?"

"Turn your back, please."

I complied, gazing far down the bluff. The wind had picked up, and there was a slight chop on the lake; the water looked great. "Want to hit the beach?"

She turned me back to face her—"First, let's put these away"— and gave me back the jug I'd dropped. There was writing on it now: a pair of Magic-Markered inscriptions in Stef's girlish cursive. On one side of the white container, in red, she'd etched "Wyoming"; on the other, in blue, "Equal Rights."

I stared at her handiwork. "Uh. . . ."

"C'mon," she said, tugging at my elbow. "Let's visit the Dairy State."

Which made no sense, as that was where we were. Still, we backtracked across the meadow to sapling #49, where I found a jug labeled "Wisconsin" / "Forward," and it was then—recognizing our state motto—that I understood. "My God," I said, gazing out across the vast field. "Did you have these memorized?"

"Nah. Though *you* ought to by the time I get back! I'll quiz ya." She produced a folded crib sheet from her pocket. "I copied them from an almanac. I got the idea when we were out here last week: 50 trees; 50 jugs . . . 50 states!"

It seemed I'd found someone whose thought processes were as peculiar as my own, a girl with a similar . . . well, less a sensibility than a nonsense-ibility. "So, you figured you'd make my job a little more interesting, for when you're gone?"

She nodded.

"Ingenious," I said, tapping the "Wisconsin" jug with my foot. "You've certainly, uh, 'shed your grace on these.'"

"Well," she said, "our first date *was* on July Fourth . . . right?"

I took her in my arms—how could I not?—and kissed her. I kissed her long and I kissed her hard, taking hold of her behind and pressing her hips to mine. Never had I felt so patriotic.

In due course, we moved on to West Virginia ("Mountaineers Are Always Free") and Washington ("By and By") and so forth, reciting each motto aloud—often with wry asides—while pitching the empties into our two jumbo lawn bags. Working together, we quickly wended our way back to Alabama ("We Dare Defend Our Rights"). Then we ran to the car, stashed our Heftys, grabbed my beach towel and barreled down the bluff.

"How long?" Stefanie asked, her voice as bumpy as the trail underfoot.

I checked my watch. "Shit. Twenty minutes, tops."

"Damned conjugal visits! That's barely time to. . . ."

"Conjugate."

Reaching the beach, we stripped down to our suits and charged straight into the bracing lake. We made our swim a quick one, essentially a condensed version of the previous week's epic splash-fest—an abridgment the bemused Stefanie went out of her way to highlight. "So I splash you," she stated as if skimming a script. "There; then you splash me . . . right. Now what?"

"Uh, fifteen seconds of improvised merriment. And, *action!*"

Moments later, we ran back out to the blanket and threw ourselves down. Stef stretched out on her back, arms over her head. "Is it just me, or is this place *crawling* with mosquitoes?"

Never let it be said that Philip Corcoran can't take a hint. Kneeling over her, I placed a fingertip to her right pit—but she shrieked at my touch. I tried the other side and got the same response. "You OK?"

"It's weird. I guess I'm more ticklish some days than others."

"I wonder how come?"

"Prob'ly has to do with my . . . cycle."

That, I found hot. "You want me to stop?"

"I . . . didn't say that." She closed her eyes. "H-hold me down."

I nodded. Then, clamping her wrists together with one hand, I tickled her with the other, at first tentatively—I didn't want to *hurt* her—but then rather mercilessly because I loved how it made her squeal and strain. Besides, it seemed to be what she wanted; we had our code word, and though she came close, she never spoke it. Instead, heels drum-rolling the beach, she quivered and writhed and tossed her head, ruby hair a-whirl, bursting out with cries of "Canta, canta, can't afford a new car!" and "Canta, canta, can't a girl get a drink in this town?"

We were both shaking with laughter. Of course, I was as aroused as I was amused, so I slipped in a nice, wet kiss. As I pulled back, our eyes locked; Stefanie's giggling abated. I placed my palm on her rib cage, then began sliding it up the slick fabric of her suit; she closed her eyes as I reached her left breast. I gave the nylon-covered mound a single, exploratory squeeze, then started to massage it. I'd never felt a breast before (though not for lack of trying) and so had nothing with which to compare it. But it was heavenly.

Call me crass, but it had turned out to be quite a day for jugs.

As her nipple pressed up into the center of my palm, I thought of *Logan's Run* and the tiny glass "life clock" each citizen, by law, had implanted in that same spot. The moment you turned 30, your palm crystal started blinking, and you had to turn yourself in and die. On the plus side, though, you'd spent the bulk of your brief life romping between the sheets with willing young lovelies like this one . . . so maybe it was worth it.

As I circled the nub with my thumb, Stefanie's eyelashes fluttered, but her lids stayed closed. Breathing rather quickly now, she seemed to be enjoying what I was doing . . . and if it felt this good *through* the fabric, just imagine. . . .

Her eyes shot open. "Cantaloupe."

I stopped unzipping her suit. And thought: *It's more of a navel orange.*

She was still sort of panting. "It—it's good, Philip. Really. But it . . . it's enough."

"OK." Releasing her wrists, I took a deep breath.

"For now, I mean. No need to do . . ."

". . . everything at once."

She nodded. Her face was flushed . . . and not from the sun.

I couldn't help but ask her: "How's tricks in the River Styx?"

She shook her head, exhaling—"*Hooo*, boy"—then looked down at my Speedo. "Hey, you really *can* see Michigan from here!"

"Huh?"

Sitting up, Stefanie reached between my legs and delivered a slow, deft stroke from base to tip. Just one, as gentle as it was excruciating. Then, eyes dancing, she scampered to her feet. "'If you seek a pleasant peninsula, look about you.'"

* * *

That evening, my parents strolled over to our neighbors' for a drink, so I spent another agonizing hour-plus on sentry detail. This time, I actually had occasion to use that "special knock" Todd had taught me, thanks to which he and his girlfriend managed to get dressed—barely—by the time my folks walked in the door. Until their return, though, I dwelt in damnation. In fact, owing to what had—and hadn't—transpired earlier on the beach, putting up with the hullabaloo from above was even harder than it had been the day before. As was I.

Todd and the Bod rose early the next morning and hit the road; the time had come for my big brother to take his own special brand of sunshine back to the Sunshine State. But before he departed, he must have crept into my room and, like the Tooth Fairy's evil twin, slipped a little something under my pillow.

It was, of course, my fake ID. Taped to a box of Trojan Ultra-Slims. Along with a heartfelt note:

Don't fuck up.

I sat on the edge of my bed, turning the gift over in my hands— and in my head. It was often a challenge not to despise the guy. But at that moment, for perhaps the first time since toddlerhood, my capacity for brotherly love knew no bounds.

CHAPTER 10

Such Sweet Sorrow on the

Planet of the Dates

If I wracked my brain, I probably could call to mind one or two *other* incidents from that next week. All would pale, however, in comparison to the afternoon of Sunday, July 27 and what turned out to be our last get-together before Stef left for camp.

What momentous event transpired then? Did I lose my virginity? In a word . . . no. But even so, I saw, heard and touched the twinkling edge of a miracle.

* * *

Our initial plan for Sunday had been another trip north to water the trees, but Mother Nature beat us to the punch. "Albert the Alley Cat," TV-6's Bronx-accented weather-puppet, had forecast "sunny skies an' low humidery"—but Albert was not a credentialed meteorologist. Staring out at the morning downpour, I phoned Stef, and together we hatched a somewhat unorthodox Plan B: we'd still hit the highway, but this time we'd head south and discover where a half-hour's drive in *that* direction took us. She suggested, though, that we return to her house at 3, when her folks would be attending a fundraiser downtown. My girlfriend thought the two of us could "use a little privacy."

I concurred. Actually, I shivered in anticipation, *then* concurred . . . then leapt into the Pacer and hydroplaned to Shepard Avenue.

Minutes later, as we drove past General Billy Mitchell Airfield with its old WW II bomber plane displayed out front, Stef dropped a bomb of her own. "I've got some kind-of-bad news, Philip. Y'know how I was supposed to take off for New York on Wednesday?"

Did camp get canceled? I wondered hopefully. "Uh, yeah?"

"Well, my parents have decided to make a 'family trip' of it. So, we're driving out together . . . and we're leaving tomorrow."

"Tomorrow?" I looked at her. "When'd this happen?"

"They've been talking about it for a while. My dad never takes off from work, though, so I assumed it'd fall through. But last night, he said it's a go."

"So . . . this is it?"

"Only till Labor Day." She gazed out the windshield into the rain. Her profile at that moment was lovely—though the sky beyond had never looked so gray.

"I wish I'd known. I was gonna get you something, a going-away present."

"We can find something for each other," she said, and pointed ahead. "Down there."

"Or . . . back at your place?"

She smiled, looked away.

As our car approached an overhead pedestrian bridge, I spotted a young black couple standing up there in the rain. Snuggled together under a shared umbrella, they were facing our way and talking. Not a bad day for a romantic walk—but wait: wasn't that Danielle?

By then, we were passing underneath. I'd only gotten a glimpse, but I was certain; I'd seen her before in that olive-green slicker, and she did live mere blocks from the spot. It was Danielle, all right . . . but who was the guy? I supposed it didn't much matter—*as long as he isn't white. Gee, Dee, you don't waste any time.*

Yet as I eyed the retreating bridge in the rearview, my ire subsided. Sure, Danielle and I had differed on whether we two should date, but what did that matter now? Shouldn't she have someone to love, too? Dee was a great girl; she deserved the best. Inwardly, I wished her luck . . . then wished the same for Cassie.

And, what the hell, for Jantz as well . . .

"How's the new movie coming along, P.C.? Any ideas?"

The question brought me back. "Um, actually . . ." I turned toward her. "I have two. I'm not sure which one to do."

Lightning flashed to our left, then distant thunder rumbled; Stefanie rested her hand on my leg. "Maybe I can help. What are they?"

"Well, I've always wanted to do a film about time travel: about how going back into the past could change the course of the future."

"Sounds cool."

"But I also want to do something about the Loch Ness Monster."

She laughed. "What—attacking Milwaukee?"

"No!" I said, a bit incensed. After all, I'd essentially made that movie; had she forgotten *Lost Island*? "No, it would take place in Scotland. I was there for a week, two summers ago. . . ."

"You were?"

I nodded. "With my folks; my Mom has cousins in Edinburgh. One of *our* 'family trips.' Anyway, since we were that near Loch Ness, I pretty much insisted we make an excursion up there, which we did. I had my movie camera along, and I got some killer location footage—you know, stuff I can intercut with whatever I end up filming here."

"Get any shots of Nessie?"

"No—but not for lack of trying!" I proceeded to tell her the whole story of how my parents—who, strangely enough, have never shared my fascination with sea serpents—checked me into a bed-and-breakfast and then departed, driving down to Inverness for the night. My small third-story room looked out on the Loch, so I pushed the desk right up to the window and set up a fairly impressive amateur observation station. There I sat with my movie camera, still camera, tape recorder, binoculars, sketch book and note pad laid out in a handy array before me. At sunset—a sunset that, due to the northern latitude, stretched on for hours—I sat at my post, coolly surveying the choppy waters and scribbling notes at 15-minute intervals: "7:45: Still no sign. . . . 8:00: Wind has changed direction. . . . 8:15: Slight disturbance on the surface! Could it be. . . ?"

"It wasn't," I said in conclusion. "At least, not that I could tell. But if some plesiosaurus or some huge, mutant eel *had* shown itself while I was there, well . . . the debate would be over, 'cause we'd have incontrovertible proof of the creature's existence today."

I looked over: Stef was grinning from ear to ear. "What we have instead," she said, "is the cutest story I have ever heard."

"Well," I mumbled, "I was only 14."

"I know. But, c'mon, Philip—let's be honest: if you made that trip today . . ."

I nodded. "I'd do it again. The exact same way."

She leaned over, kissed my cheek. "Too bad you *can't* go back now. While I'm away, I mean; it'd help kill time. Are you guys traveling at all next month?"

I changed lanes to pass a truck. "They are. Oh, which reminds me: *that's* what that look of theirs was about—the one at Red Lobster."

"You mean, when you mentioned my acting camp?"

"Right. Their 25th anniversary's next month. They weren't planning to go anywhere, but now, all of a sudden, they have plane tickets to New Orleans! It's like, now that I have a girlfriend, they're afraid to leave me alone . . ."

"But when they found out I'd be away . . ."

"Precisely."

"That's the thing about parents," she mused. "You think you have 'em right where you want 'em, but then they pull something out of their sleeve."

"Yeah—something that reminds you they've been doing this a lot longer than us."

She nodded sagely. "That's what nature gives 'em. So they'll have a fighting chance."

Coming into view on our right was the sign for Exit 340 and the Bong Recreation Area. I had never visited the Bong Recreation

Area . . . nor passed its signage without making a crack: "What kind of 'recreation' do you think goes on there?"

Stefanie laughed. "That stoner friend of yours might know. Cheryl . . . Janz?"

"Jantz," I corrected. "Yeah; she might. Hey, look!" I pointed toward a roadside edifice looming up in the distance, its roof edged in battlements, with three turrets on top. From each turret waved a rather damp flag: the Stars and Stripes; the state seal of Wisconsin; and one banner depicting, quite simply, a whopping hunk of cheddar. "The Cheese Castle! Ever been?"

"Nev-uh"—this with an English accent.

"Well then, milady," I grandly proclaimed, "exit three-four-zero it is."

As we strolled the linoleum aisles, a Wings song playing overhead, Stef didn't bother masking her disappointment: "There's this place I've been to in South Dakota called the Corn Palace, and it's a palace that's actually, y'know, made out of corn. Tens of thousands of ears. So when they called this the Cheese Castle . . ."

"False advertising," I concurred. "Have your dad file suit."

"Nah, my mom's the litigator." Stef stepped over to the meat cooler. Maybe it was the sight of her standing there in short shorts and a semi-wet T, comparison shopping—grabbing different lengths of salami and giving each one a squeeze—but I was getting pretty hot and bothered. (Of course, for a not-quite-17-year-old boy, that's basically the status quo.) As she picked up a toothpick and daintily popped a sausage-slice into her mouth, I beat back the urge to bend her over the counter and give her a free sample of my own.

We ended up purchasing one salami (an ego-crushing 12-incher), a bag of cheese curds and two wax-encased novelty cheddars: one shaped like a Guernsey cow, the other like our home state. I held the latter cheese aloft—"Forward!"—and out the door we strode. And it was then, standing just in front of the Cheese Castle, listening to the *pop-pop-pop* of the rain on the awning, that things got interesting. For immediately north of the Castle stood a small roadside motel. And on the afternoon of Sunday, July 27,

1980, at the very moment Stefanie and I glanced toward the neon sign in front of that motel, one word lit up:

VACANCY

I looked at her. "You see that?"

She nodded, eyes on the sign. "Weird."

"Seems like a . . . suggestion."

A flash of lightning to the east, then a gravelly rumble of thunder.

She looked at me. "Well, we . . . *did* want some privacy."

A chill of expectancy shot up the height of me. The length of me, too. "That'll work."

Again, she turned toward the sign; her brow furrowed.

"Of course, we wouldn't have to do anything that . . . that you weren't ready to do."

"Of course!" She smiled lopsidedly—"I mean, thanks"—then looked, again, at the motel. "Wonder how much it would cost?"

Boy, did *that* not matter. "It's on me."

"No," she said firmly. "We'll split it. I think . . . before I go off to camp, maybe *this* is what we're supposed to give each other."

Hallelujah! "They'll probably card us both."

She lifted her purse. "I'm covered; how 'bout you?"

"You bet," I said, patting my pocket. And thought: *God bless you, Todd Corcoran.*

She took my arm—"Shall we?"—and we dashed into the rain.

"They" carded us, all right, but our fake IDs did the trick. "We're used to it," I told the Paleolithic proprietor as he shakily handed over the room key. "People always think we're younger than we are. Personally, ha-ha, I don't mind! Y-y'know?"

The man squinted out through thick-lensed glasses. "*What'*sat?"

Stef stepped on my foot. "Thank you," she told him, then steered me toward the door.

Outside, we fought back laughter all the way to the room. "Jeez!" she teased. "Mr. Smooth Operator! 'Why, yes, my good man: people *often* mistake me for 16.'"

"Shut up!" I muttered, reaching out—but Stef eluded my grasp. I chased her around the corner and past the ice machine and then, all at once . . . we were there.

Room 7.

I unlocked the door, and we stepped inside.

I can see it today as clearly as if I were standing again in the doorway. Two full-size beds. A chair, a desk, a dresser; an ancient-looking TV. A mini-fridge; a tan-colored telephone; an Amana air conditioner, sealed in with duct tape. Off-white walls and a stucco ceiling. Blue-gray indoor/outdoor carpet. A small, wall-mounted mirror. A cheap, framed print of some calla lilies. Behind beige drapes, a single front window affording the room's lucky lodgers quite the scenic view of I-94.

"Nice," we said in unison—and meant it. Because, drab and dreary as our motel room was, it was ours.

Closing the door, I noticed the "Do Not Disturb" tag hanging from the inner knob; I made a move for the tag, but Stef grabbed it from my hand, saying, "We prob'ly don't need to be any more conspicuous than we already are."

"Guess not."

She held the tag up in front of me, flipped it back and forth— "You want it? As a souvenir?"—and slid it down the front of her top. . . .

"Oh, man."

. . . then rolled her eyes and blushed. "Jeez. I can't believe I did that!"

I reached for the tag. . . .

. . . but she pulled it out herself. "Patience," she said, turning away to set down door tag and cheese bag alike. "Let's not get ahead of ourselves."

I stepped up close, placed my hands on her hips: "I . . . don't mind getting behind."

More lightning; more thunder.

Stefanie moved away. She looked at one bed, then at the other. "So," she said brightly, "which one do *you* want?"

Enough was enough: I lunged. She, with a shriek, dropped onto the left-hand bed as I flung myself down beside her. And then . . .

then we just sat there, side by side, hands locked around each other's forearms, shooting silly grins at each other and fighting back the giggles for a solid minute. Finally, she relaxed her grip. "About your movie . . . I have an idea."

I had some ideas, too . . . but those would have to wait. "Shoot."

"Combine the two subjects—Nessie and time travel."

"How?"

"Beats me! That's your job, P.C."

"All right. Any other suggestions?"

"Let's take off our shoes."

There is, to my knowledge, no *Guinness Book* listing for fastest sneaker removal. But if there were, then a picture of me in that motel room would serve as the graphic. With time to spare, I let my socks follow suit, then glanced over at Stef.

Head bowed, she was holding her own tennis shoes, one in each hand, staring at them. She set one down on the floor and fiddled with the other. Her demeanor had changed—owing, I presumed, to our being alone together in a motel room, and to our now having taken that first concrete step toward . . .

Lightning. Thunder.

"Stef?"

"They were uneven," she said softly, then looked up. "The laces . . . were uneven."

I'd never wanted her more.

And she must have seen it in my eyes, heard it in my sigh, felt it in the pull between us—a force that rivaled anything in the sky outside. She reached for me: afraid, yet swayed by all we'd found in each other. Off came our shirts and our shorts and her bra—the kind that, helpfully, unhooked in the front, and *God* they were pretty and plump—a frantic, almost hostile kiss punctuating the removal of each garment. As her B-cups hit the carpet she all but threw her face at mine, her front teeth breaking the skin of my lip.

I did not stop to visit the ice machine.

And of course, the storm itself was a tremendous turn-on: the crackling lightning, the booming thunder, the heavens opening as we opened to each other.

And of course, Stef—being less nervous once we were underway—did pause briefly to make a quip about my erection: cupping the crotch of my underpants, she smiled and said, "A disturbance on the surface! Could it be. . . .?"

And of course, as she lay back with her wrists above her head, I pinned them to the bed and meted out the tactile torment she both dreaded and craved.

And that's when it happened.

She didn't say "cantaloupe"; she didn't say a word. Just closed her eyes, then parted her thighs and clamped them around my knee. Then she began to rock. Her hips moved up and down, up and down, rhythmically riding, riding. She'd found a way to harness her ticklishness and funnel the feeling elsewhere: between her legs, into her core . . . into the River Styx. It was happening gradually, a drawn-out, deliberate build, but it was happening—little thanks, really, to me. I was there, I was helping . . . but Stef was making it happen.

Though her jostling breasts were a wonder below, what held my gaze was her face—and the discovery within its dear features of whole new expressions. I sensed dampness against my knee as she ground into me, her breaths coming ever more quickly now, ever more shallow and short. "Keep going," I murmured, myself short-breathed—though I doubt she heard: she was slipping into another dimension, traveling through time, cracking the code, unfolding, progressing, evolving and evanescing before my very eyes.

I heard her cry out, but by then she wasn't Stefanie; she was fireworks and waterfall and sorcery and song. She was, in short, Oregon: "She Flies with Her Own Wings."

She cried out again, but for my part, I was dumbstruck. Humbled by her transformation; awed by the mystery, the glory of it all. And stricken by a realization:

By this time tomorrow, she'll be gone.

When she had finished and hurled herself down—eyes averted, now less a force of nature than a near-naked, self-conscious girl— I took her into my arms, pressed her pounding heart to mine and held her, just held her. Didn't stroke; just held her. Didn't kiss; just held her. Didn't ask for a turn of my own, though God knows. . . !—just shut up and held her for a long, long time. Till finally, she spoke:

"Philip."

"Yes, Stef."

She snuggled close. "Miss you."

* * *

If this were some Hollywood teen sex comedy, you know what would happen next. As soon as Stefanie left for New York, all the girls who'd rejected me would have a simultaneous change of heart. Cheryl Jantz would decide to take a walk on the mild side; Cassie, weary of guys her own age, would access my bank account, look up my phone number and give me a ring; Danielle Payton would see, at last, past my white skin to the indisputable soul mate within.

Hell, for good measure, Olivia Newton-John's tour bus would break down in front of my house; dropping the mower, I'd rush to her aid. And she would be . . . appreciative.

But this is not some Hollywood teen sex comedy. The various women who'd spurned or ignored me did *not*, in fact, return en masse, asking me for one more chance.

Only Cheryl Jantz.

CHAPTER 11

The Plot Thickens on the

Planet of the Dates

To you, my situation may not seem to have posed a major dilemma. But it did. I mean, stop and consider: a movie about both time travel *and* the Loch Ness Monster?

It was July 31st. Stef had been gone just three days, yet already I longed for her as I'd never longed before: with a sweet, slow, sinuous ache that crept into each waking moment. Also, I was horny as a triceratops in heat. So I seized upon this movie project as a welcome distraction . . . the problem being that my blue-eyed Muse had given me an assignment I hadn't a clue how to tackle.

I've often found a good run to be the best cure for a quandary; jogging invariably jogs my brain, shaking loose an idea or two. So it was on the last day of July. For as my feet pounded the pavement three miles out, it came to me. I would make a movie about a pair of scientists in the not-too-distant future—a husband-and-wife team, like the Curies—who secretly develop a means of traveling through time. Oddly, their method only works on life forms; they can't send back a rock or a rifle, but they *can* go themselves. For the answer lies in "the submolecular makeup of that most basic yet most magical elixir, the source and key component of Life itself: water."

God, that's good. I picked up my pace. *Should've brought a notebook!*

And, let's see, this water-based method only works *within* water: the journey must start and end in an ocean or lake. The lake, for instance, right outside their lab.

Oh, and did I mention that these scientists were Scottish? Well, they were now.

Anyway, they activate their apparatus and head back to the Cretaceous Period, and there, in the sea covering what will become Great Britain, they encounter a plesiosaur. After a harrowing struggle, they trap the great ocean-beast in a containment field, intending to bring the creature back alive as rather graphic evidence of their method's success.

Hence the movie's title: *Proof Positive.*

But in their ambitious zeal (movies like this always end up as cautionary tales), they forget to factor in the additional mass—about 25 tons' worth—an omission that throws their computations out the window. Consequently, they only make it as far forward as the 6th Century A.D. As they land back in the same lake where they started, the overtaxed machine shorts out, the containment field deteriorates, and the plesiosaur breaks free and . . . and devours its captors. Yeah, just gobbles up the both of 'em, then and there. Which is fortuitous for all plesiosaur-kind, because (cue dramatic music) the *eggs* she's carrying need the nutrients!

In the final sequence, the plesiosaur dives down to the lake bottom to lay her eggs, then charges to the top. Her toothy head and serpentine neck break the surface, and she lets out a mighty roar as if to announce her arrival—and to foretell the generations of her progeny now destined to populate that lake for all time. Cut away to the shore and a lone, kilt-clad fisherman (if I could con Craig or Avery into wearing a skirt). He drops his rod in disbelief, points to the rolling waves and exclaims, "Ach! Ther-r-re be a *Monster-r-r* in *Loch Ness!*"

"Yes!" I exclaimed, kicking into a sprint. Ingenious! It would be an "origin story," like in Marvel Comics . . . only the audience doesn't know that till the end! This stuff was golden; I had to get home and write it d—

Whoa! Braking, I nearly flew head over heels: right in front of me was an expanse of just-laid sidewalk—a 40-foot length of wet cement.

Panting, I looked down, the toes of my sneakers poised at the brink. I crouched and extended an index finger, preparing to spell out some random obscenity. But thanks to the influence of the absent Stef, I wound up operating on a less profane plane, drawing a heart and, inside it, "SS + PC."

Stefanie, my Stefanie . . . a thought I'd revisit in the shower.

"Hey!" A rather rotund man was emerging from the front door of his house—the house with the new stretch of sidewalk.

I stood up and gave him a half-hearted wave.

"What the hell ya think you're doin'?"

"Oh, c'mon," I said. "It's wet cement. It's . . . Americana. A suburban tradition."

"Not at *my* house, it's not." The guy seemed pretty steamed, so I backed away as he approached. He knelt (no small effort) to examine my sentimental hieroglyph. "S.S.," he said, then swiped his hand across the heart, wiping it out. "You a Nazi or somethin'?"

"Takes one to know one" was the best I could come up with.

But I guess it was enough: the guy looked pretty pissed off. He hefted himself back up to his thick, sandaled feet. "I see you out here again, I'm calling the police."

"Don't you mean the Gestapo?"

(All right—in truth, I didn't think of *that* line till I'd turned and begun jogging home.)

As I ran, I hoped the fate that had befallen my handiwork wasn't some kind of sign.

* * *

Nearing our house, I noticed someone seated on the front stoop. A moment later I saw that this figure—small; female?—seemed to be smoking. My Mom had a short friend who smoked, but why would Mrs. Samet be sitting outside? Then I noticed the figure's very un-Mrs.-Samet-ish attire, and I slowed to a walk as it dawned on me: Cheryl Jantz.

She flicked some ashes to the ground and looked up. "Hey. How goes it."

By now I was nearly in front of her. "Hey . . . Cheryl." *What the hell?*

"Your ma said you were out for a run. Figured I'd chill. Chill for Phil."

She's met Mom? I glanced toward the front picture window, and sure enough: there beyond the glass, peeking out from behind the living room curtain, was Joyce Corcoran, P.I. (a longer-running series, by the way, than "Mannix" and "Cannon" combined). My mother looked me in the eye, brow knitted in consternation, then slid out of sight.

I returned my attention to Cheryl. "I was . . . just out running."

She took a drag. "Kinda got that from the outfit. Plus, like I said, your ma. . . ."

"Right." I felt completely out of sorts. It's not that I was displeased to see her—just shocked to the core. True, Cheryl *had* said she might look me up some time. But I didn't actually expect that to happen, and certainly not via a house call. This wasn't in the script . . .

"Have a good run."

"Yeah, I did."

She held out her Marlboros. "Want one."

"I don't smoke." She was still holding the pack aloft, so I went on: "My dad used to, but he quit. It's weird: he kept his pipe—it's just sitting there on his desk! He's a doctor, and he kind of scared me off tobacco; see, he's got all these really graphic photos of cancerous lungs."

Cheryl nodded, took another drag. "Wicked."

She was missing the point, so I dropped it. "What's up, Cheryl?"

"Plenty." She stood. "Kinda hot out."

Yeah, I thought, *when you wear an army jacket in July.*

She dropped her cigarette, stamped it out. "Can we go inside."

My shower, it seemed, would have to wait. "Uh, sure. Why not?"

I took her down to the basement, which was, in summertime, the coolest part of the house. It also had the advantage of being nearly soundproof, as long as you kept your voice down and/or the music up. On top of that, the stairs squeaked so loudly and with such minimal provocation so as to serve as a surefire parent alarm.

There was a nasty gray couch down there that used to reside in our living room but got demoted back when I was in diapers; Cheryl threw herself on top of it, slouching low. She gazed blankly at my guitar case and Peavey amp gathering dust across the room. I turned on our little no-frills basement stereo and, knowing her taste in music, stuck some Cheap Trick on the turntable. "You want a soda . . . lemonade. . . ?"

"Nothin'." The music began to play: the bombastic opening bars of "Surrender." Cheryl nodded to the beat. "Right on."

I sat down beside her, establishing a two-foot neutral zone.

She looked at the zone, then up at me. "I got busted, Phil."

"Whoa—that sucks. For what, possession?"

"I *wish*." She looked away. "Nah, I was sellin'."

"Shit."

She reached into her shirt pocket for her Marlboros.

Joyce's son sprang into action: "Not . . . not in the house, OK? Sorry, but. . . ."

"Whatever." Cheryl put away her smokes and proceeded to invert herself on the sofa, resting her ankles on top; her head drooped toward the cellar floor, raven hair a-dangle. "They nearly put me in Juvie; they were gonna send me away 'cause I had priors. But then this kick-ass social worker steps in 'n' gives Your Honor this *killer* sob story. It was all 'abusive father' this and 'broken home' that; she's goin' a mile a minute, just pullin' stuff out of her *ass*."

> Mommy's all right, Daddy's all right
> They just seem a little we-e-eird
> Surrender. . . .

I looked at the stereo, then back at Cheryl. "Uh-huh."

"Long story short, I got one more chance."

"Cool," I said—and meant it. I hated the thought of her behind bars. Well, maybe I'd *fantasized* about it a time or two, in a fly-on-the-wall way. But not as an actual occurrence.

"I'm cleanin' up my act. No more coke, no more speed, no more 'ludes, no more . . ." Clearly, this next one was tough to say—and not just because most of her blood had by now made its way past her neck. "No more pot." She shook her crimson head. "Kills me, man, but it just ain't worth it. Can't get busted again. Gonna have to get my kicks else-how."

"Like, by hanging from your ankles?" I'd meant it as a joke.

"That, and booze." I must have given her a look, because she added, "I ain't goin' for sainthood, OK." Cheryl smiled a crooked smile. "You look kinda cute upside-down."

Her color was beginning to concern me; I placed a hand on her shoulder and gave her a tug. "Can you just, uh. . . ?"

"Fine." She righted herself, then closed her eyes and breathed in deep.

"Good rush?"

She shrugged. "I've had better."

"This is all really interesting, Cheryl. But what I'm wondering is, why tell *me*?"

She opened her eyes but looked away. "I thought maybe. . . ." She trailed off and, with heavy lids, blinked twice.

"Maybe what?"

"Maybe you could help."

*　*　*

"What she wants," I told Avery that night on the phone, "is a non-fucked-up friend."

"Yeah? For what, exactly?"

"Just to hang out with. She's lookin' for someone who won't get her into trouble. And who can maybe show her how to have fun *without* altering her neurochemistry . . ."

"Or committing a felony."

"Bingo. She said she wants to 'chill in Philsville.'"

"But there's plenty of other boring goody-two-shoes out there," noted my ever-helpful bud—who, unlike me, did smoke the occasional "bud" himself. "Did she say . . . why you?"

"Actually, yeah." I adopted a tone of Jantzian dispassion: "'Of all the squares I know, man, you come the closest to bein' cool.'"

He laughed. "Sounds like a greeting card."

"Right, from the new Hallmark Burn-Out line."

"You gonna do it?"

"I told her, 'Sure.' But, to tell you the truth . . . I'm not sure at all."

"'Cause of Stefanie?"

"Well, yeah! Not that anything would happen with Cheryl; it wouldn't. But it feels kind of wrong. I'm in a real bind."

"Not at all," Avery said, all soothing reassurance. "We can solve this in two easy steps: Jantz moves to Philsville, and Crepe Girl relocates to. . . ." Then, with swagger: "*Ave*-ry-town!"

Why did I put up with this guy? "You wish! No dice, jag-off."

"Don't worry, I'll take real good care of Slocum's . . . magic pan."

Cussing him out, I hung up. It was, after all, my turn.

The next morning I sat under my birth tree with a pen in my hand, the half-finished *Proof Positive* shooting script on my lap . . . and Cheryl's request still on my mind. A breeze drifted in from the east; I closed my eyes, leaned back against the trunk. *Let's figure this out.*

Granted, the timing couldn't have been better. Stef would be gone for a month, and other than the movie, nothing had come along to claim my free time. So I really had no excuse not to help her. Besides, in the great card game of life, there was no question that Cheryl had been dealt a lousy hand. I didn't say anything when she mentioned her social worker's "killer sob story" about neglect and abuse, but in my heart I knew every word of it was true.

I guess I've always had a savior complex. I was the kid who brought home wounded animals—a broken-winged robin from beneath this very tree; a lame squirrel; a semi-squashed *caterpillar*, for God's sake!—and did my damnedest to nurse them back to health. In a way, Cheryl Jantz was just an extension of these previous "projects."

The difference being that Chirpy had a red-feathered breast, not a pair of cute little human ones; Earl had a long, fuzzy tail, not a round one wrapped in tight denim; and Kate R. Pillar had, to my knowledge, no interest whatsoever in getting into my pants.

* * *

August 1. First day of my birth month; second day of Operation Jantz. Per my suggestion, Cheryl showed up at noon, when I knew my mom would be away. I was intent on minimizing contact between these two females, who couldn't have been less alike if they'd tried, and the older of whom had voiced "grave doubts" about the younger.

When I answered the bell, I found that Cheryl was not alone: stacked up beside her were the various component drums of a full rock kit. They were not in cases, yet appeared brand-new. "Hey," she said, drumming her fingers on the snare.

"Hey yourself. What's with these?"

"Just picked 'em up. Nice, huh."

"Yeah. They must've cost a fortune!"

She snickered. "Likely. Anyway, I was hopin' I could keep 'em here. Looked like you had room in your basement."

"I guess. But. . . ."

"And you play guitar, don'tcha."

"Yeah."

"So I figured we could jam. *That*'d be safe 'n' legal, right."

She had a point.

It took us two trips to get everything downstairs, and midway through the second, a question sprang to my mind: "How the hell did you get them over here?"

"Friend dropped me off." She hefted a tom-tom higher on her chest, guiding it clear of the banister. "He picked me up at the store where I . . . got 'em."

We reached the basement, and I set down the big bass drum. As she began assembling, I took out my Fender and started tuning by ear. I rarely made time for playing music—yet always had a blast when I did. *Hmmm,* I thought, *could Cheryl turn out to be a good influence on* me?

She held up the snare and inspected it. "Got a little scratched. Must've scraped it on the wall comin' down." She shrugged, then resumed her assembly.

"No cases, huh?"

"Nah, they . . . came right off the floor."

And then it hit me: somehow, this willowy wisp of a recovering stoner-girl had just executed the most ambitious heist in local shoplifting history. Wait—did housing the goods make me an after-the-fact accomplice? *Oops. Not such a good influence after all.*

"Your ma doesn't like me, does she."

I looked up from my D-string. "Cheryl, she doesn't even know you."

"She doesn't like me." Her eyes locked with mine.

I appreciated her candor; she deserved to be treated in kind. "No, she doesn't. But I do." I turned back to my guitar.

Cheryl worked on her cymbals. "We were, like, lab partners or somethin', right."

I nodded—"Sophomore year, in Bio"—then laughed. "Remember that experiment they had us do? Where everyone had to put a sample of their urine in a test tube and spin it around in that machine to measure the enzyme level?"

She paused, concentrating. "Yeah . . . yeah, I remember."

"The machine held two tubes at a time. So there was your tube, and there next to it was mine, and they were spinning around, side by side. And I. . . ." I looked away, embarrassed, but went ahead. "I remember picturing what *parts* of us those samples had come from. And thinking, 'Jeez, that's . . . kinda hot.'"

"I was just glad it wasn't a drug test.'" Her assembly complete, Cheryl stood looking at the kit for a moment, then bent down for her sticks.

I glanced at her decidedly non-squirrel-like "tail," then forced my gaze back to the drums. "That's quite a step up from the dashboard."

"Fuck, yeah. Ya ready."

"Don't you have one of those drumming stools—a 'throne'?"

"Wasn't time to grab it. I set 'em high; I'll play standing. Oh, here"—she pulled a cassette from her pocket, handed it to me— "Let's tape it."

"Really?"

She shrugged. (Cheryl shrugged a lot; it was one of her favorite expressions.) "Could come in useful," she added.

I stepped over to the stereo, stuck the tape in and got it rolling. "It's just a little condenser mike; it'll sound like shit."

"Likely."

I picked up the Fender and slid out my pick. I hit a chord— loud—and Cheryl hit a drum roll—*way* loud—and we were off, chasing and racing each other into a high-volume, high-velocity, no-holds-barred jam.

How to categorize the ensuing "music?" This was punk rock, only sloppier; grunge, a decade early, only uglier. This was garage rock's drooling back-woods cousin: basement rock. I broke my high-E string three minutes in . . . but who needed two Es, anyway? Or a bassist or a singer or a "song structure?" Not us—not for what we were doing. Because we weren't so much playing as venting: she, the prickly pangs of multi-drug withdrawal, and I, a bottom-less pit of sexual frustration that my motel-room liaison with Stef had only served to redouble. Despite all the differences between us, Cheryl and I made noise as one. For we met in a place we both could claim—a place of craving and pain.

She bobbed like a boxer: bending for the snare hits, straight-ening for the cymbal crashes, pounding the bass drum with one foot while the other struggled to keep her aloft. Her hair whipped the air, all but covering her face—yet through the stringy black strands I saw her eyes coasting over in my direction. She shot me a euphoric smile, threw back her head and mouthed two words:

"Right on."

* * *

Up in my room at evening's end, I lay down and thought of my darling Stef. No, not *those* thoughts; not exactly. I was picturing us in bed—but not during sex. Rather, I saw us lying together under the covers, side by side, grinning at each other in rapturous, post-coital bliss. I imagined my hand resting lightly on her hip as we spoke in the low, cozy tones I could only assume devoted couples used for pillow talk. And it dawned on me then that, as much as I wanted the sex, maybe, just maybe I wanted this more.

I slipped out of bed and stepped over to my desk. I sat down and composed a long, tender, semi-suggestive letter to Stefanie Slocum. Then took out my colored pencils and drew, from memory, a loving portrait of Stefanie Slocum. Then turned out the lights and fell asleep thinking of Stefanie Slocum.

Then dreamt of Cheryl Jantz.

CHAPTER 12

Spicy Developments on the

Planet of the Dates

I spent the weekend mowing lawns, watering trees, shooting hoops and steering clear of Cheryl. She phoned on that sweltering Saturday to see if I wanted to go cool off in the lake. The prospect of watching her strip down to a swimsuit (or, more likely, to panties and a T) held a great deal of appeal. The honest answer to her question was "yes," I did. But the answer I gave was: "I'm pretty busy. Let's shoot for next week."

Wait till Wednesday, I thought while hanging up. *Maybe even Thursday; play it safe.*

Biking over to Cheryl's on Monday morning, I couldn't help but think back to the last time I'd been there: the tail end of our disastrous first date six weeks before. I remembered the crickets chirping and "What the fuck, it was worth a shot" and that cursory kiss and, finally, Cheryl swearing a blue streak at her long-suffering dog as she slammed the front door shut.

But another door had stayed open that night: "Maybe I'll look ya up some time."

No point denying it: I was glad she had.

I veered up the walk to Cheryl's mother's semi-crummy townhouse, then hopped off and locked my bike. The door was wide open, so I walked right in, closing it behind me. "Cheryl?" I shouted. "It's Phil."

"Kitchen," came the reply.

Following the voice, I stepped past a groggy golden retriever lying in the front hall, gnawing at a leather sandal. I smiled down at him. "Hey there, Scout."

The dog glanced up and gave a half-hearted growl, then returned to the task at hand.

I found Cheryl seated on the kitchen counter, flanked by an assemblage of small glass bottles. She was slouched to one side, swinging her feet—one sandaled, one bare—and smoking. And it wasn't a Marlboro dangling from her hand; it was a joint.

"Cheryl!"

"How goes it."

I didn't try to mask my disappointment. "You said you'd given that up!"

She looked at the doobie, then back at me. "Chill, Phil. It's only dill." Then she broke into a goofy grin: "Hee-hee-hee!"

I surveyed the bottles standing to either side of her—cinnamon, tarragon, basil, paprika—then stepped forward, snatched away her spliff and gave it a sniff. The odor called to mind chips 'n' dip from some stale, smoky cocktail party of yesteryear. "Jesus, Cheryl. How many of these spices have you tried?"

She grabbed it back. "Eleven-teen, give or take—and every one of 'em licit 'n' legal."

Was "licit" even a word? Either way, I had to admire her ingenuity. "Hanging upside-down lose its thrill?"

She shrugged.

"Are they . . . having any effect?"

"This one—maybe." She took a drag. "The label said 'dill *weed*,' so I was hopin'."

"You do seem kind of . . . happy."

"Could be the dill, or could jus' be hearin' myself say, 'Chill, Phil, it's only dill.'" Then she laughed so hard that she snorted and, dropping the joint, tumbled off the counter.

I caught her. And noticed how compact and girlish she felt in my arms. And how nice her hair smelled, especially compared to the spliff. "Your front door was wide open. Better watch it; your dog could run away."

"Yeah," she mumbled, "he sure could."

I set her down on her own two feet, then picked up the doobie and tossed it in the sink. "Let's get you focused on something else."

"You name, I'm game."

"You want to go to Radio Doctors?"

She nodded—"Right on"—then looked down at her feet. Brow furrowed, she began to search the floor. "Now where the *fuck* is my sandal."

* * *

We biked side by side to Farwell, then headed south into the city, I on my Schwinn and Cheryl on a European racer: a men's model (and, as such, a bit big for her), onyx-black and gorgeous. The vehicle's every part screamed "state of the art"; watching the smooth revolutions of her feet, I felt a twinge of envy. "Nice bike."

"Thanks."

"Is it new?"

"Well, yeah"—she looked over—"for me."

I shook my head. "You've got to cut back on the larceny."

"Unlikely."

"Cheryl . . ."

"Fine," she sighed, "I'll . . . phase it out. Can't quit everything at once, y'know."

Reaching Milwaukee's best-stocked record store, we parked at the rack outside. I slid my chain lock through her wheel as well as my own, but she went me one better, dipping into her army jacket for a hefty iron bracket lock: "Can't be too careful." Then she shot me a sly smile.

Which made me wanna. . . .

I looked away. *That's not why I'm with her; that isn't why we're here.* Glancing up at the storefront signage, I hoped Radio Doctors would prove therapeutic for me as well as Cheryl, the distraction of its vast vinyl offerings curing us both of our particular temptations.

The slender young woman manning the counter—clad all in black, with short, spiky hair to match—looked up from the latest issue of *Record Mirror* ("Exclusive Elvis Costello Interview!") as we approached. "Hey."

"Hey," I answered, eyeing the Buzzcocks button pinned just above her lovely left breast.

"Lookin' fuh anything in pah*ti*culah?" An English accent, sexy as sin.

Jesus. I took a breath, then told myself to *give it a* rest*!* I mean, seriously: did I need to further complicate my personal "Dating Game" Home Version by trying to add a third contestant? What was with me? "Nah, we're just. . . ."

"Just lookin'," Cheryl cut in, then grabbed my arm and dragged me off to ROCK. Which suggested she'd noticed me noticing Ms. Buzzcocks and was . . . jealous?

I dug the idea. More than I should have.

To the accompaniment of unfamiliar punk rock blasting overhead, we worked our way through the section alphabetically, pausing to compare notes on the bands we liked: B-52s, Cheap Trick, the Cure, Devo. . . .

I tapped a finger at that one. "Their version of 'Satisfaction' blows me away."

"Right on." Cheryl pulled out an album: "Fresh Fruit for Rotting Vegetables" by the Dead Kennedys. "I don't know which name's cooler: the record's, or the band's."

The band's name bugged me. "There've been too many dead Kennedys already."

"Yeah, we could use a dead Reagan or two."

"Y'know," I said, "his campaign's in town next week; he's coming to give a speech."

"Oh, we should *go.*"

I looked at her. "What for?"

"See what kinda freak show turns out for that clown."

When we reached S, Cheryl grabbed the latest Styx LP and, with a chortle, showed it to me; I obliged her with a fairly realistic retching sound. She discreetly pulled out her black Magic Marker, added an N between the last two letters of the band's logo and placed the album back on the rack. "Score," she murmured, and moved on.

I felt a bit queasy—this time for real. For while the *band* Styx deserved such ill-treatment, the river of that name held other associations. I dropped my head, looked down at the floor. Stefanie could not have seemed farther away.

At the end of the aisle (Warren Zevon), we turned and started back. But this time we skipped the obvious selections and pulled out LPs whose covers intrigued us, as well as those we'd heard were good. Occasionally Ms. Buzzcocks would take note of our selection and contribute a pithy remark: "Side one kicks arse . . . Sucks . . . Overrated . . . Bloody brilliant." Thus did we receive our initial education about Siouxsie & the Banshees, the Psychedelic Furs, Gang of Four and the Cramps—or about one woman's opinion of them, anyway.

Cheryl and I were bopping to the overhead music, which was accelerating song by song. "Man," she said. "Fuckin' *rocks*."

I turned to our tour guide. "Who is this?"

"Ecks, from L.A."

"The Ecks?" I looked off toward E. "Who're they?"

"Naught *the*. Just . . . X." She held her forearms in front of her, crossed in the middle.

I walked back to the end, and there it was: an album called "Los Angeles" whose grainy, black-and-white cover showed a large wooden X, set aflame like a KKK cross and blazing away in the night. The image matched the music, for over a buzz-saw guitar, knife-in-the-gut bass and machine-gun drums, a man and woman sang together, keening and off-kilter:

> Sugarlight, sugarlight, I can't believe
> Swallowing one bulb after another in the
> City of electric light. . . .

I didn't have a clue what it meant—yet I felt the song to my core.

"Naught too shabby," Ms. Buzzcocks said, "f'r a pack o' Yanks."

I turned toward Cheryl, primed to defend our national honor, but she'd slipped off to Cassettes. I joined her there, where she'd pulled out the Cramps' "Songs the Lord Taught Us" and "London Calling" by the Clash. Standing to her right, poring through Grateful Dead tapes, was an aging hippie couple. The man was tall and haggard, with a tie-dyed bandanna on his balding pate; his moon-faced mate wore a lacy yellow dress, and her waist-length gray hair was festooned with daisies and baby's breath. Once, their kind had predominated in places like this, but by 1980 they just seemed quaint.

The man addressed the woman with emotion: "No, no, it didn't bum me out at all."

She lifted her wide eyes toward him. "Really?"

"Nothin' bums me out, Starflower. I don't *let* it bum me out." He held up a Dead cassette. "It's all in how you look at it."

Cheryl took a swipe at the tape; it sailed from the man's hand and clattered to the floor.

"Hey!" he shouted. "What the fuck?"

Starflower gasped.

Cheryl shrugged—"Bummer, huh?"—and stepped away.

I followed her, watching over my shoulder as the stunned hippies retrieved their goods. What had gotten into her? Was it the music? I glanced toward the counter: Ms. Buzzcocks stood watching, amused. It was clear where *her* sympathies lay.

"I'm leanin' toward cassettes," Cheryl said blithely, still nodding along to X. "They're more . . . portable."

I could see where this was heading. "Don't even think about it. I'd say you've blown our low profile; 'Mary Punkins' over there has her eye on you."

"She may've met her match." Cheryl pushed me sideways. "Stand ri-i-ight about. . . ."

I grabbed her tapes—"My treat"—and walked them up to the counter, along with two LPs for myself: "Los Angeles" and the Pretenders' self-titled debut. Cheryl followed, stopping just behind me. As I forked over $30, I could feel her leaning lightly against me, her tiny breasts touching my back, as if we were in a storm and I was her wind break. I wasn't sure what this display meant amongst her people but took it to be positive.

"Y'know," the clerk said, "if ya'd loik to check out some *local* acts . . ."

I turned back to Cheryl, mere inches away. Her breath was still dilly: "Fuck, yeah."

". . . then you ought to get 'ope."

—at least, that's what it sounded like. "Hope?" I asked warily. Was this presumed punker some kind of evangelist—a born-again shepherdess in wolf's clothing?

The clerk held up a cheap-looking photocopied magazine, stapled together along the left-hand margin, whose cover showed a severed head impaled on a stake. "*HOAP*," she repeated. "*Head On A Post.* Just a dollar an ish, an' it's chock-a-block with info on the 'ole local scene."

"We'll take a couple." I gave the clerk two more bucks, then grabbed the mags and handed one to Cheryl. As we left the store she held *HOAP* out in front of her, staring down at that grisly cover, gray eyes shining like a kid's on Christmas morn. It frankly warmed my heart to see her so enthused about something she couldn't smoke.

But this wasn't just about Cheryl. Punk rock, you see, was growing on me. I found it edgy, gutsy, exhilarating. Not the way the Park Avenue had exhilarated me; that was all about suave sophistication, glamour and glitz. Punk was disco's polar opposite: a lack of style, a lack of decorum, a lack of elegance, civility and grace—a lack, it seemed, of even the vaguest pretense toward those things.

And in their place? Volume. Velocity. Candor. Rage.

And far more affordable clothes.

* * *

Sitting in my room with the stereo playing low, I tore open a pastel-blue envelope, pulled out the matching stationery, gave it a sniff and smiled: *There's my girl.* The scent was faint, to be certain. But it was Stef.

Her letter, written in eager, looping cursive, began with a bang:

Hey, handsome! Just 3 days in & already it's been
the week of my <u>life</u>! This place is AMAZING.
It's like everyone here speaks the same language.

I smirked. "English?"

Yeah, I know: English. Ha, ha.

She knew me well.

Seriously, Philip: imagine yourself at a camp where all
you talked about was movies, all you did was make
movies, you had weekly visits from professional
movie directors, & then, at night . . . you watched
movies! What that would be for you, this is for me.

I was genuinely, unreservedly happy for Stef. And no, I wasn't
envious.

The ratio here is about 3 girls per guy. . . .

Well, maybe a little.

. . . & of the guys who <u>are</u> here, about half of
them seem pretty darn interested in each other!

That certainly beat having them interested in her.

Then there's this crazy kid, Pike, who wears a cowboy
hat & boots ALL the time, no matter how hot it is—
& it's been <u>sweltering</u>. He's from a cattle ranch in
Wyoming (or <u>says</u> he is) & speaks with a drawl; he
wants to be in movies, but "only Westerns." (Which
by the way have been dead in Hollywood for YEARS.)
I'm starting to wonder if his whole life story is an act!

Why was she going on about this possible faux-cowpoke?

I miss you terribly, Philip—every day & every night.

Better. . . .

When I think of your touch, the River Styx gets slick.

Now we're talkin'!

> I'm so sorry I won't be there for your birthday, but I
> WILL make it up to you when I return. I can hardly
> wait to see (etc.!) you again. In the meantime, water
> those trees for me. And when you do, remember:
> KENTUCKY!   ♥, Stef

I had yet to memorize the state mottoes, so I'd have to check the jug. On the back of the letter, some time later, she'd added a P.S.:

> Just found out who the final week's Visiting Artist
> is going to be. Would you believe: KIM HUNTER!
> She's in town to do some play on Broadway . . . or
> off? I'll be sure to compare notes with her, one Zira
> to another. (AND getcha her autograph!)   XOXO

Wow! Dr. Zira herself, in the flesh! Probably not in the *fur*, though; an appearance in chimp make-up would be too much to ask. After all, it was summer. But still. . . .

A knock at my door, then my mother's voice: "Honey?"

"Yeah."

She looked in—"Just saying good night"—and glanced at the letter. "From Stefanie?"

The question was rhetorical; *she*'d brought in the mail. "Yeah, from camp."

"How's she doing?"

"She's having a blast."

My mother said evenly, "She's a lovely girl." Her statement seemed as much a slap at Cheryl as an endorsement of Stef.

I nodded. "Yes, she is. 'Night, Mom."

Eyes fixed on my own, she returned the nod. "Good night."

As the door closed, I refolded the letter and returned it to its envelope. No reason to feel guilty; I'd done nothing wrong. Stef and I were rock-solid. I hadn't put a single move on Cheryl Jantz. I was getting her on track—not into the sack.

But if that were so, then why hadn't I told her about Stef?

I stripped down to my shorts, grabbed *Head On A Post*, put on my headphones and cranked "Los Angeles" as high as I could bear. *It just . . . hasn't come up.*

* * *

On Friday, it came up.

I awoke that morning in a profound state of Stef withdrawal, missing her even more than before, and so stumbled down to the basement in my boxers, slouched into a metal folding chair and projected her onto a six-foot screen.

I bypassed *Prehistoric Planet of the Apes,* in which—like the famous actress she soon would meet!—Stef sports ape makeup throughout. I also skipped *House of Usher*; though an effective little chiller (you haven't truly experienced the darker works of Poe till you've seen them enacted by 13-year-olds), Stefanie appears in the film as Madeline, a largely inert quasi-corpse—*not* what I was currently looking for. Instead, I selected her P.C. Productions swan song, *Cur(s)e of Dr. Jekyll.* For here, playing High Priestess Idemas Norab (the name of Voodoo's wily trickster figure, spelled backward), was Stef in all her charismatic glory: casting hexes, invoking the Snake God, swooping about in her long, black robe, subduing Mr. Hyde, outfoxing London bobbies—well, *a* London bobby (we only had the one costume)—and playing to the camera like a pro.

After the end credits, I rewound and watched it again. This time, I focused solely on Stef—not just her actions, but her *re*actions—and found subtle grace notes I'd not noticed before. Like the way in which, as Jekyll chronicled his whole wretched history, she gradually bowed her head, ever-more-burdened with empathetic grief. And the shudder with which she greeted his mention of that first murder. And, finally, the way she leaned toward him before proclaiming, "By Damballah's scales, good sir, I swear: your torment ends *today*."

Wish mine would, I thought . . . yet three long weeks remained.

Halfway through my third viewing, I heard what had to be my mother coming downstairs. (It was laundry day.) But then the interloper spoke: "How goes it."

I sat up straight in my chair—"Hey"—feeling slightly exposed in my boxer shorts though protected, for now, by the dark.

She stepped in front of the screen, gazing toward me, and for one surreal moment, Stefanie's image appeared over Cheryl. "Your ma said you were down here," this Stef-yl creature said. (Clearly, my mother hadn't realized my state of undress.) Cheryl moved to stand behind the drum kit. "Whatcha watchin'."

"Just this little . . . horror movie I made."

She picked up her sticks. "Cool."

I hit freeze-frame (on an intense image of Avery in mid-transformation) and filled her in on the plot to that point, then flipped the toggle forward and let it roll. Occasionally, Cheryl augmented the action with a drum fill or dramatic cymbal crash, but she didn't speak again till the closing credits:

"Stefanie Slocum," she read aloud. "Slo-cum."

It was odd hearing that name coming from those lips—almost as odd as seeing the one girl projected onto the other. "What about her?"

"Well, *does* she."

"Does she what?"

"Come slow." Cheryl hit a rim shot, then put down the sticks; she made her way to the light switch on the wall.

"Well, I don't think . . ." Then all at once I was sitting there in my boxers, bathed in light. Cheryl gave me the once-over twice, and though it made me blush, I didn't exactly mind.

"What, is she your girlfriend or somethin'."

"Yeah," I said. "She is."

"Unlikely. As of when."

"Fourth of July or so."

She reached into her jacket pocket, pulled out a pair of black horn-rimmed glasses and slipped them on. "How come I never seen her."

"She's at camp this month, in New York." I crossed one leg over the other, trying to act casual. "Acting Camp."

Cheryl smiled with one side of her mouth. "She needs it."

I let that go. "I didn't know you wore glasses."

"I don't."

I pointed at her face. "So, that's an optical illusion?"

"They're not mine," she said, walking toward me; she stopped just in front of my chair. Apparently she wanted me to stand, but at that moment it would have been . . . revelatory.

"Whose *are* they?" I asked, keeping the focus on her.

"My ma's new boyfriend."

"Doesn't he need them?"

"He's an asshole," she said, as if that explained everything.

"Do they . . . help your vision?"

"Nah; everything's all smeary and smudged." Then, I got it: this was of a piece with the body-inversion and the dill-ijuana, just another creative attempt by Cheryl to alter her consciousness and mess with her senses—while staying within the law. She folded her arms. "Your 'girlfriend' doesn't go to our school, does she."

I shook my head. "Riverside."

"City girl, huh. Looks kinda young."

"She's our age. That movie's three years old."

"How's she look now."

"Really good."

Cheryl regarded me for a moment. "Ya fuck her yet."

"Not. . . ." I grimaced, then pointed at Cheryl's face. "That's *got* to be bad for your eyes."

She shrugged. "Likely. But I kinda dig it." She reached down, uncrossed my legs and plopped herself onto my lap, facing me.

Straddling me. Then she whipped the glasses off her face and slipped them onto mine. "See."

What I saw was a corroded, close-up likeness of a crafty little she-elf—a watercolor portrait left out in the rain. "Trippy."

"Yeah," she said, and scooted forward.

I was feeling dizzy. I wasn't sure how much of that was from her mom's boyfriend's optometric prescription and how much was from the proximity of Cheryl's crotch to mine.

She placed her forearms on my shoulders. "Ya look like Costello."

I began to reach for the glasses but then hesitated, unsure of what she might do if my hands were thus occupied—and unsure, too, of whether I wanted her to or not. What *did* I want? I wanted her to back up, and I wanted her to slide closer. I wanted her to step away, and I wanted her to strip. I wanted her to leave, and I . . . and I. . . .

. . . placed my palms on the hips of the blurry watercolor girl and gently lifted her off.

Cheryl stood, re-claimed "her" glasses and stuck them high on her head like a barrette. "Goin' to Madison this weekend to see my friends. Wanna come with."

I had no real plans for the next two days, and a road trip sounded like fun. What's more, I knew there were influences in our capital city from which she could use safeguarding . . . but who would safeguard *me*? Could I trust myself to spend a night with Cheryl Jantz—and out of town, to boot? The answer was obvious: "I can't."

"How come."

"I have . . . a commitment. Why don't you stay, and we'll hang out here?"

"Nah." She pulled two tapes from her jacket pocket—the ones I'd bought her four days before. "These rock; been listenin' to 'em non-stop. Figured we could trade."

"Cool. My records are upstairs," I said, and stood, for it was now safe to do so. "Y'know, I've been reading about this Starship Club in *Head On A Post* . . ."

"Me too."

"If you stayed in town, we could go check it out."

"Rain check." She handed me the tapes and took a step back. "I'm outta here."

"Cheryl, this is probably gonna sound real square, but your 'friends' in Madison. . . ."

"No worries," she said, heading for the stairs. "I'm not dealin'; I'm not buyin'; I'm not even using. Ain't worth the risk; I know that. But they're still my buds."

I began to follow. "Right, but when you're *with* them. . . ."

"I'm over it, Phil. You helped me get there. Don't need that kick any more."

"You sure?"

"Positive. And, besides. . . ." She looked over her shoulder and gave me a cryptic smile. "Got my eye on a new kick now."

CHAPTER 13

Poodles, Punks and Politics on the

Planet of the Dates

I wound up wishing like hell I'd gone to Madison. Could I have kept my hands off Cheryl, and hers off me? Who knows? But by staying home, I stumbled into the most embarrassing moment of my life.

It started out innocently, with a Friday phone call from Stefanie's mom. "Ben and I are having a cook-out tomorrow night," she said. "It's going to be our neighbors, plus a few friends and their kids. It occurred to us that if Steffie were in town, you'd be there, so . . ."

I'd always had a crush on Bonnie Barr-Slocum. She was trim and fit for 40-plus, with the taut, tan summertime skin of a tennis addict. I appreciated that she never talked down to me—that she'd referred to her husband as Ben, not "Mr. Slocum" or "Steffie's father." Too, there was her hot hyphenate surname and the fact that she wore skirted business suits and worked outside the home—in a courtroom, no less. She reminded me of the "I can bring home the bacon, fry it up in the pan, and never-ever-ever let you forget you're a man" gal from that perfume commercial. And on top of all that, she'd given birth to Stefanie Slocum.

". . . can we count on you?"

I wanted my girlfriend's parents to know that they could, in fact, count on me—for this and more. "I'd love to come." So, the die was cast.

There are a few things you'll need to know before we go any further. To begin with, I'm lousy at recognizing faces; always have been. Often, I wind up "introducing" myself to someone who replies, "Uh, we've met." I'd fit in well on the Planet of the Apes, for to me, most humans look pretty much alike.

Secondly, in 1977 I had visited the home of Stefanie's Uncle Russ, a thirtyish bachelor who lived across town. At Stef's suggestion, we had filmed portions of *House of Usher* in his basement, which looked rather like a Victorian prison cell. (What was it with the Slocums and their cellars?) The shoot went well, except for the sporadic interference of Russ' toy poodle, Laddy. A natural-born ham, the dog kept darting into frame, capsizing candles, pulling at Stef's increasingly tattered shroud and generally wreaking shin-level havoc.

Russ, incidentally, was a short, stout man with bushy brown hair and a woolly beard.

The vice principal of my high school, Mr. Varland, was likewise a short, stout, thirtyish bachelor with bushy brown hair and a woolly beard. Perhaps you see where this is heading.

One final datum: after arriving at the cook-out, saying my "hellos" to Stefanie's folks and nabbing some hors-d'ouevres (which included, I kid you not, proscuitto-wrapped *cantaloupe*), I nabbed some punch from the "adult" punch bowl, and so was feeling foot-loose by nightfall.

So I'm standing there, drink in hand, next to Mr. Varland—who, for his part, recognized me at once and called me by name—but I'm *thinking* he's Stef's Uncle Russ. After all, it was a Slocum party, not a school event; how was I to know Mr. V. was a family friend? Unfortunately, over the course of our five-minute chat about the Brewers, the bratwursts and the balmy weather, not a word was spoken that tipped me off as to who this man next to me actually was.

We reached a lull . . . but I had the perfect topic. Rocking back on my heels, I swished the punch around in my glass and turned to the man beside me. I leaned down, placed a genial hand on his shoulder and said with a smile, "So. How's my favorite little toy poodle doing?"

Mr. Varland stiffened; his fluffy head swung toward me, eyes wide, mouth open and aghast. "I am *not* your little toy poodle!"

* * *

Pedaling beside me, Cheryl laughed so hard that the cigarette fell from her lips. "No shit!"

"That's what he told me." We took a left, heading south on 6th.

"Jesus. What the fuck did ya say to *that*."

"It was a miracle. Somehow, I sobered up in two seconds flat, and I realized it was Varland. So I say, 'Uh . . . no, but you *own* one, right?'—knowing that he doesn't. And he says, "No!" And I say, 'Well, one of the school administrators does. I thought it was you.' Then I just walk away."

"Man. Nice cover."

"But it was so humiliating! What'd Varland think: that I was *coming on* to him?"

"Likely," she said. "And in a fuckin' freaky way."

"I am so screwed, Cheryl. When school starts, he'll be on my case somethin' fierce."

"Chill, Phil. He won't dare."

We stopped at a busy intersection; I looked over. "How do you mean?"

She lit a new cigarette. "So you made a mistake. An honest mistake. As stupid as you felt, imagine how it was for him. I mean, what's the . . . normal response to 'How's my favorite little toy poodle doin'?'"

"Oh, something like, 'What the hell are you talking about?'"

"Exactly. But Varland assumed you were talkin' about him. Which means that, on some level, he must see himself as . . ."

"A toy poodle."

"Right. Now you know that. And he *knows* you know it. And he knows you know there's plenty of people at school who'd love to know it, too. Follow?"

Somehow, I did. "He can't touch me, can he?"

The light turned green, and we moved on.

"That story's your trump card. Long as you don't go spreadin' it around, you're . . ."

"Invulnerable." I felt greatly relieved. And grateful. And impressed: I'd never seen Cheryl so cogent. Spending two weeks drug-free seemed to have transformed her; maybe she *was* like Kate R. Pillar after all. For, as with the injured insect I'd returned to health and then to the woods, Cheryl had a new lease on life. She was a clear-headed, sharp-witted butterfly, newly sprung from a murky marijuana-leaf cocoon. Or something like that. "Hey," I asked, "how was Madison?"

"Sucky. Everyone was toasted—everyone but me. And no, I didn't slip, if that's what you're wondering."

"I didn't think so."

"Didn't get laid, either."

It surprised me that Cheryl would have any trouble attracting a lover. I told her so.

"Nah," she said, "that's not it. There's one guy, a bud o' mine, who wanted to. A month ago I would've, 'cause he seemed kinda hot—when I was stoned. But now. . . ." She trailed off, and we took our right turn in silence.

"*You're* not getting high," I offered, "but maybe your standards are."

"Yeah." She eyed me. "Maybe."

We turned left on 8th and soon reached our destination: one of the oldest edifices on Milwaukee's South Side. We veered onto the curb, passing an assortment of flags, campaign signs and star-spangled streamers on our way to the building's expansive parking lot. So much for separation of Church and State: the Reagan/Bush '80 rally was being held right in the shadow of Our Lady of Perpetual Something-or-Other Roman Catholic Church.

We got off our bikes and walked them into the lot, the better to negotiate our way through a large and growing crowd. Cheryl spotted a rack, so we made our way over. "Y'know," she said, "I never really biked much before."

"No?"

"Never had a decent bike." She secured her lock. "I like it."

"You're good at it. And it's good *for* ya, too—very healthy."

She pulled out another Marlboro and lit up. "Likely."

We'd been curious to see just who would take off from work on a Tuesday afternoon to hear a speech by the arch-conservative former Governor of California and newly anointed nominee for president. The answer, in a word, was locals—and lots of 'em: blue-collar Polish-Americans with swarms of kids scampering around them, young sons and daughters they'd brought along to witness this historic event.

The realization spooked me, for I did follow politics a bit— partly out of genuine interest, and partly because, well, it made me feel like a grown-up—and I knew that these should have been Carter supporters. Our president's labor record was stellar; why would these working-class white ethnics with mouths to feed give the time of day to the G.O.P.? The term didn't exist yet, but in hindsight it's clear: I was witnessing the birth of the Reagan Democrat.

We made our way through the crowd to a phalanx of counter-demonstrators whose picket signs indicated their affiliations: National Organization for Women, Sierra Club, Urban League, NAACP. Their number was small, but the sight of them was heartening. As we slid in amongst these few kindred spirits, I felt a chill, a kind of counter-cultural thrill. We were rebels, just like those protesters back in the '60s! It was a little dangerous, just a bit scary. Cool, I thought, and turned to Cheryl. "You think he's getting turn-outs like this all over the country?"

"Prob'ly." She shrugged. "People are idiots."

"It said in *Time* that the race is a dead heat. Wish we were old enough to vote. . . ."

A voice to my side: "Corky!"

There, coming toward me, was a green and white "Re-Elect Carter/Mondale" sign—and, hoisting it up from below, Danielle Payton.

I moved toward her. "Dee!"

Her sign lowered, tilting sideways as we embraced. "How you been?"

"Great!" I said, squeezing her tight. "Look at you! You're, what . . . working for the President?"

"Child," she laughed, "I'm *workin'* for the Colonel; I'm doin' register at KFC. Been volunteering for Carter, though—just a few hours a week. Mostly in the office: stuffing envelopes, makin' calls. But they wanted us to 'have a presence' here today, so. . . ."

I felt a twinge of inadequacy: I may have *read* the news, but Danielle was helping to make it! Talk about "grown-up". . . . "It's so cool that you're doing this!"

"Hey, it's fun. We've got a really good group, and we're all pulling together. It's kind of like being on a sports team, only playin' for something that matters."

In Packerland, such statements were sacrilegious, but I let it pass. "Y'know, I've been meaning to call you."

"Been a little . . . busy, Corky?" She tilted her head down and, peering up, looked me dead in the eye, that conspiratorial smile of hers playing once again on her lips. "Heard you found yourself a lady."

I smiled back. "You heard right."

"Is it serious?"

"It is."

She gave me a high five. "Yeah, I'm seeing someone, too."

I nodded—*Her rainy-day boy on the bridge*—and said, "I'm really glad for you."

"Guess it's lookin' iffy for that wedding of ours on Mars."

It took me a moment, but then I remembered. "Gee, Dee, don't be so sure! That's *years* away . . ."

Cheryl stepped up to join us. "Hey, Payton."

Danielle nodded. She looked at me, then back at the cigarette-puffing burnout before her. "Uh . . . hey. You were in Miss Martin's class, right?"

"Right."

"Sorry, but I'm blanking on your name."

On stage, some pin-striped party shill had stepped up to the podium to deliver an effusive introduction; I stayed focused on the girls. "Dee, this is Cheryl Jantz. We're, uh, not . . ."

"Christ," Cheryl cut in, "can you believe the turnout for this lunatic."

"I know." Danielle glanced around. "It's scary. I mean, if you look at his record on education, race, women's rights . . . well, it's all in here." She handed us each a pamphlet.

I scanned it, then read aloud: "'A longtime opponent of the Equal Rights Amendment' . . . 'Claimed 80 percent of air pollution is caused by trees'. . . ."

Cheryl flicked her ashes, then cozied up beside me. "Plus, under his drug policies, I'd be in *prison*."

Danielle looked at her for a moment, then back at me. "That right?"

I tried, again, to clarify the nature of our relationship but was drowned out by the sound of some 2,000 people cheering as one. For there, ambling up the steps to the accompaniment of a Sousa march, was a broad-shouldered man in a crisp, navy-blue suit, whose mahogany hair—shellacked into a kind of proto-pompadour—belied the many crimps and creases on his road atlas of a face. As the ovation persisted he stood tall on the platform and soaked it all in, smiling and waving, waving and smiling.

His head bobbed, quavered, pivoted to scan the crowd. On cue, a blonde-haired girl of five or six, clad in a traditional Polish dress, stepped up in front of him with a bouquet. He took the flowers, tilting his chin to one side in an "Aw, shucks" gesture I didn't buy for a second, and placed them on the rostrum—then bent way, way down to grace the top of the Polish Princess' head with a kiss.

"Looks like my sister," Cheryl muttered.

"Gabby?" I asked.

She nodded. "Little bitch."

Yikes! I looked at Cheryl. Was the epithet meant for Gabby, or for the Princess? I made a mental note to follow up later and returned my gaze to the stage.

As I watched the Governor, a single word kept coming to mind: "prehistoric." He looked like a well-preserved yet antiquated life form, a being not of our day but of an epoch long past, resur-rected through some ill-advised genetic experiment. *Jurassic Park* had yet to be written, yet there he stood before us: the Cretaceous Candidate.

Once the crowd settled down and he started talking, "prehistoric" applied to his proposals as well. Indeed, part way through the speech, when two women behind the dais hoisted up a G.O.P. Elephant banner, it struck me that the Party should change its mascot to the mammoth.

Which brought to mind Atwater Beach and the day I'd met Stef. . . .

I glanced again at Cheryl, then told myself: *I've done nothing wrong.*

He was speaking now of the American hostages still being held in Iran: "Well, where I come from, you don't ask for your people back. You say, 'Give them back, now—*or else!*'" The line drew a rollicking response. And understandably: we'd all grown sick and tired of the months-long stand-off. Yet, as a *Journal* op-ed piece I'd just read pointed out, the situation was complex: when dealing with people who venerate martyrdom, threats of attack can be counterproductive. Even dangerous.

But complexity be damned. Back in 1980, America craved simple solutions. And in Ronald Reagan—a staggeringly simple man—our weary, bedtime-story-craving nation found its genial if doddering Grandpa-in-Chief.

Who turned, next, to domestic affairs. "Well," he said wistfully, "I can recall a time when America didn't even *have* a race problem."

At which Danielle murmured to me: "I'm guessin' the *slaves* were aware of one."

". . . and as for my opponent's so-called 'alternative' energy program—if elected, I'll scrap it! The answer is to get the government *out* of energy and the environment, and leave those matters to the marketplace. That's the way to a bright, clean future!"

I ask you now, dear contemporary reader: how'd *that* work out for ya?

Anyway, at speech's end, Reagan paused and looked down. Below him, the Polish Princess was fussing with the frilly cuffs of her dress. The Governor bent low, swooped her off the stage and tucked her close to his chest. He gazed into her shining, white face for several seconds before turning, misty-eyed, to the crowd. "You know," he said, head a-tilt, "it's for her sake that I'm, well, in this race at all."

"Then why do you oppose the E.R.A.?"

It was the perfect rejoinder. Many of us in the dissenters' section must have been thinking the same thing, or something like it; I know I was. Yet it wasn't I who dared say it—dared *shout* it—nor was it Danielle, nor any of the women from N.O.W.

It was Cheryl Jantz.

Having pointed out, in effect, that the would-be Emperor had no clothes, she stuck her cigarette back between her lips, folded her arms and stared up at the podium, waiting: a pretty, petulant study in stoner-girl pluck. As those of us near her applauded, Reagan stiffened; his big Mardi-Gras-puppet head swung toward us, eyes wide, mouth open and aghast. *Wait*, I thought. Hadn't I seen that expression before?

Of course: Mr. Varland!

But unlike Mr. V. (who'd have made a piss-poor politician), Reagan regained his composure. He lifted his gaze to some spot far out in the crowd, spread a smile over his crinkly crocodile face, canted his head and responded to Cheryl's query in the only way he knew how:

"Thank you very much. God bless the state of Wisconsin, and God bless America."

Carter, I knew then, was a goner. For you see, the crowd went wild.

*　*　*

It's a quarter to 9, Saturday night. I'm in my bedroom, standing in between two pieces of furniture, hopelessly conflicted.

To the left: my desk. Upon it, three items: some clay I've been molding into the Proof Positive *plesiosaur; a note I wrote to myself after the rally; and my second letter from Stef.*

To the right: my dresser.

I could return to the desk and work on my sea-beast . . . then re-read Stefanie's sweet missive (addressed to "Phil Corcoran, Philm-Maker Extraordinaire") and write her a reply.

Or I could open the dresser.

I look over at the envelope, recalling what my girlfriend wrote: how impressed she was by the script I sent; how eager she is to portray my resourceful yet reckless traveler through time; how much she's learning from the improvisational exercises; how huge and loud and alive Manhattan is; how lonely she sometimes feels in the midst of it all without me. And throughout, not a mention of any cowboys—or boys of any other *type. It's a lovely, loving letter penned with casual intimacy; reading it in bed is practically pillow talk.*

Again, she signed off with "KENTUCKY"—Damn! I forgot to check that motto.

I turn to the right and glance at the dresser . . .

. . . then shift back to my desk and the note I wrote: CALL DANIELLE! Right. I have to set her straight on just who my "lady" is. And on who Cheryl Jantz is—and isn't—in my life.

But four days have passed, and I've yet to make that call.

I could make it now. Then I could call Cheryl and cancel our plans for tonight. Then return to my desk and finish that model and write that letter to Stef. I could. . . .

But I don't. Instead I head for the dresser, open the top drawer and reach under my socks and jock straps for the object I stashed there eight weeks ago. I slide the drawer shut, grab my keys to the Pacer and step out the door—air freshener in tow.

* * *

When I pulled up outside her home, Cheryl was sitting out front, smoking away. (I mentally applauded myself for remembering to bring the Summer Breeze.) She rose, and as she headed for the car I saw a small, timid face peeking out one of the townhouse windows. Cheryl opened the car door and plopped herself down. "How goes it."

I pointed. "Is that Gabby?"

Cheryl glanced back. "None other." Then she stuck her arm out the car window as if to wave . . . and raised her middle finger.

The face withdrew.

Pulling away from the curb, I found myself empathizing with Gabby. After all, I too was someone's younger sibling, and Cheryl's behavior struck me as distressingly Todd-like. "What's your problem with her?"

"She sucks." Cheryl turned on the radio: it was Pete Townsend's catchy pop ditty, "Let My Love Open the Door." She reached into her pocket for a cassette—"Man, everything on the radio's so sugary"—and stuck her tape into the deck.

"It's from all the punk we've been listening to."

"Likely." The X song "Nausea" began to play. "Better."

"Seriously, though, what's your beef with Gabby?"

Cheryl lit a new cigarette off the old. "She gets between my mom and me."

"When'd that start?"

"Before she was born."

"Yeah? How'd she manage that?"

Cheryl took a long drag. "Mom got pregnant with Gabby when we were livin' on Brady. And when Annette got pregnant, she got *huge*. I'd go to sit on her lap, but her lap kept shrinking 'cause her stomach kept gettin' bigger and bigger. 'No room,' she'd say, and kinda push me away. And Clyde—her boyfriend at the time, Gabby's dad—he'd laugh his shaggy-ass hippie head off. Like it was all a big joke."

I turned south, heading downtown. "Sorry."

"Then, after Gabby was born, *everything* was about the god-damn baby. It was like I didn't exist. The only time my mom paid me any mind was when I fucked up. So . . ." Cheryl shrugged.

So you started fucking up a lot. "She should have made room for you," I said, looking over. "On her lap . . . in her life. . . ."

"Yeah, well. . . ." She looked away; her voice dropped. "Clyde did."

I returned my eyes to the road. "Um. . . ."

"Can we change the subject."

"Sure." Finally, I got it. And while it was in no way fair of Cheryl to blame her kid sister, it was perhaps understandable. "Hey. You rocked at that rally."

"Someone had to say it."

We parked a block shy of the Starship Club and headed up to the entrance. The doorman—a pallid young tough whose green hair resembled a bug-infested lawn—glanced at my fake ID, then at Cheryl's, then took my $10 and pressed two moist singles into my palm. His touch was cold; on reflex, I glanced down. The retreating hand was half-hidden in shadow, but I glimpsed broken nails encrusted with dirt. As if, I thought, he'd dug his way out of a. . . .

"What the fuck you lookin' at?"

"I just . . . I thought you were someone else," I lied. "You remind me of a friend."

He sneered. "I ain't yer 'friend.'"

I grabbed Cheryl's arm and led her quickly inside.

If punk rock was the opposite of disco, then the Starship was the anti-Park Avenue. Instead of burnished chrome and glistening glass, here were cracked plaster and crumbling brick. Instead of a flashing, under-lit dance floor, here was a dank concrete pit. The music was louder and faster here, with nary a harmony, string section or synth. And while there was no mirror ball sending a cascade of light across the room, I did spot a girl balled up in one corner sending a cascade of puke across two unfazed companions.

Which brings us to the denizens of this Dantean domain. To begin with, all looked to be in their late teens or early 20s; were a 30-plus to wander in, he or she might well have been given the *Logan's Run* treatment. Indeed, an aura of simmering hostility pervaded the place, as if the slightest misstep (say, by a couple of first-timers) could result in a riot. Still, Cheryl and I made our way deeper inside.

There were as many women as men, and though none were what I'd call "cute," some were sexy in a have-ya-for-lunch-and-spit-yer-bones-out way. Others—male and female—were just ghastly. Many appeared to be suffering from, or aspiring toward the look of, radiation sickness: sallow complexions, patchy hair, sunken eyes with drooping lids and an overall aspect of dissipation. Truly, this was the Night Club of the Living Dead.

Their clothing was black or, nearly as often, involved garish, fake animal prints: a miniskirt with black and blue zebra stripes; a sleeveless, snake-scale T. Safety pins were ubiquitous, stuck through sweat-soaked bandannas and panty hose, through ears and eyebrows, cheeks and lips. A couple at the bar slouched over their drinks, connected by a three-foot *chain* of pins; one end led to his nasal septum, the other to her left tit.

Cheryl nudged me. "Let's get a drink."

We headed for the bar, where I bought her a vodka-rocks and got a beer for myself. I was, back then, only a sporadic drinker—for me, the fake ID was more about access than alcohol—but was loath to order pop in a punk bar.

Sipping our drinks, we gazed up at a nearby TV screen, where a wrinkled and Reaganesque Bert Parks was crowning Miss America. *A rerun*, I noted; I recognized her cleavage. In fact, they must have been showing it on videotape, for the scene had been augmented: the crowning was pre-empted periodically by brief shots from slasher films. First runner-up hugs weeping winner . . . maniac strangles teenage girl . . . winner beams as bejeweled tiara is placed on her head . . . screaming blonde takes a hatchet to the skull. And all the while, blasting out of the megawatt sound system, was a mile-a-minute thrasher whose lyrics consisted entirely of the word "Fuck," over and over, followed each time by a different target:

> Fuck Ann! Fuck Stan! Fuck Lee! Fuck me!
> Fuck Clem! Fuck them! Fuck Lou! Fuck *you*!"

"I wonder," I mused to my companion, "if anyone in here is snuggling up to their sweetie right now and saying, 'Honey, they're playing our song!'"

"Unlikely. Plenty of couples, but no P.D.A.s."

She was right. I saw no arms slung around waists, no kissing or hugging or hand-holding. Indeed, the safety-pin-linked couple was the closest anyone came to tender contact.

Down in the pit, though, contact of an *un*-tender sort was running rampant. I'd heard of slam-dancing, but had never seen it; the reality did not disappoint. Each punker made of himself a human missile, propelled toward the rest—who themselves were hurtling forth from other parts of the floor. The music covered the sounds of impact, but many a collision appeared severe.

A brawny blond man stood shirtless at the periphery, leaning against a pillar and glowering like an albino ape. Massive arms crossed, he scanned the slam-dancers with simian eyes and watched the unfolding carnage, his look bordering on boredom. But when anyone came near him, he extended one gargantuan hand, caught the offending punk and flung him back into the fray—toppling all those in the way. This man, I came to realize, was the bouncer.

The slammers were mainly male, but I spotted three girls out there, too. Then I caught Cheryl's eye, saw the glimmer therein . . . and knew there would soon be four. She downed the rest of her drink, stood—"C'mon"—and headed for the pit, pulling me along behind.

Within seconds, I was glad she had. I'd always loved scary amusement-park rides, but this was even better, for more was at stake . . . namely, life and limb. I learned quickly and well, and, oh, the *rush!* Although it was with several bruises that I eventually departed, I wouldn't have traded the experience for anything. What had seemed so alien turned out to be so right; there was just no way to know it from the outside.

As for Cheryl—the smallest slammer there—she was a natural. Her low center of gravity helped her stay on her feet, and her shortness let her duck under most every onslaught. High on a quite legal substance called adrenaline, she spun about at lightning speed, bobbing and swerving like a girl on fire.

She spun toward me—I caught her—and grinned a dazed grin. "Wow."

I grinned back. "It's awesome."

"Gotta use the can."

I accompanied her out of the pit and walked her as far as the bar, where I ordered a Schlitz for us to split. Not a second vodka, though; I was, after all, supposed to be helping her out. I returned my attention to the slammers, whose collisions now proved oddly hypnotic. At one point, a gangly girl fell to the floor; a man with stiff, orange hair-horns lurched toward her but, instead of helping her up, began dancing on her back. It was then, at last, that the bouncer burst into action. With one sprawling step he was there in the pit, lifting the girl to her feet. Then he swung a bicep around the spiky man's neck and dragged him off, kicking and hollering, into the dank nether-regions of the Starship Club.

I never saw Spike again. It's possible that no one did.

A tap on my shoulder: I turned, and there was . . . Cheryl?

Her hair was cut short, jutting out every which-way with sassy pizzazz—and a sizable safety pin occupied her left lobe. The music drowned out her voice, but she seemed to say, "Hey."

I shouted over the clamor: "What'd you do?"

She shouted back: "Chick in the bathroom lent me scissors." As she ran a hand through her hair, the short-cropped locks sprang right back up; not a follicle was more than two inches long. "Go on," she said. "Feel it."

I wavered. The haircut did showcase her slender neck. And the safety pin, well, it looked pretty hot . . . but was it safe? "That lobe wasn't pierced, was it?"

She shrugged. "Is now."

I reached out. "It's bleeding."

"Only a little. Chill, Phil."

"Did you sterilize it?"

She nodded—"With gin"—then grabbed my hand and placed it on her scalp.

I went ahead and petted her punky new scare-'do. No denying it: her jet-black hair—soft yet bristly, poking into my palm—was as enticing to the touch as to the eye. So I just kept stroking her head and looking into her eyes and thinking about this freaky little friend of mine and all I'd learned about her in the past two weeks.

I saw her hanging upside-down from our basement couch; then dancing, drumsticks a-whirl, behind her kit; then toppling slammers twice her size in the pit. I heard her giggling as she puffed away on a doobie of dill; then calmly assuring me that I, not Varland, had the upper hand; then shouting her gutsy question at a bewildered "Gipper." I recalled watching in shock as she knocked the cassettes out of that hippie's hands—then remembered her reference, earlier tonight, to a different hippie from her past.

Which is probably what had made her swat at those tapes in the first place . . .

One thing was clear: she was like no one else I'd known. She'd come up hard, all right—a lot harder than me. But damned if she hadn't made it.

"Well," she said. "Whatcha think."

I bent down and kissed her, hard; her tongue fondled my own. Her hands on my waist, she held me in place—as if that were needed! I wasn't going anywhere, wasn't thinking about anything else or any*one* else. At that moment, all I wanted was Cheryl Jantz.

And here she was.

* * *

The next afternoon, I crouched on the ground by the 17th sapling on Mr. Ruskin's acreage, an overturned milk jug in hand. As the water surged out, saturating the dirt, I listened to the *glug, glug, glug* of the jug—the sound of emptying, of depletion—and stared at the word on its side: KENTUCKY.

The gush dwindled to a stream and the stream to a dribble. As the last drops fell earthward, I gave the jug a shake and dropped it, quite purposely, KENTUCKY-side up—but a breeze flipped it over en route to the ground. What faced me now was the container's adverse side. Though I knew, by then, the motto written there— had read it and cringed while filling the jug an hour before—that fact made the words no easier to bear. I gazed down at the familiar script for a full minute as birds sang, clouds inched across the sunny sky and the six words hit me full-force. Then, with a plum-sized lump in my throat, I labored to speak them aloud:

"United, we stand; Divided, we fall."

CHAPTER 14

Best Intentions on the

Planet of the Dates

I spent the rest of that weekend strenuously beating myself up.

Stef and I had said our fond farewells a grand total of, what, 20 days before; I couldn't keep my nose clean for three lousy *weeks*? Plus, this wasn't one quick, impetuous kiss: it was a marathon session of saliva-swappin', tonsil-ticklin' tongue-hockey—first in the bar and, later, in my car. I was justified in kicking my own sorry ass all the way up I-43 and clear into Ozaukee County.

Following a near-sleepless Sunday night, I rose to find that a solitary elm leaf had blown through my open bedroom window to land on the sill. This discovery gave me a glint of hope, reminding me that with the new week came my chance to turn over a new leaf. It *wasn't* too late, and what I had with Stef was surely worth saving. All it would take was a little self control, a distraction or two . . . and the absence of Cheryl Jantz.

I picked up the leaf and, turning it over, set it on my desk.

Then I turned on the stereo (playing pop, not punk), sat down and spent a couple of hours readying my *Proof Positive* plesiosaur for its proverbial close-up. The clay model turned out bigger than I'd planned (about 16" long) and better than I'd hoped, a result that boosted my morale. I even topped off the ancient sea beast's head with a pompadour-like crest in "tribute" to a certain primeval politician. And why not? On the *Jaws* set, they'd nicknamed the robotic shark model "Bruce"; this, then, would be "Ronnie."

Around noon, I took Ronnie down to the basement, where I'd built a miniature table-top Loch Ness using a discarded windshield from the village dump. Laid flat, the glass sheet made a plausible lake surface, especially when bordered by sand from the beach and some little plastic trees from Kay-Bee Toy & Hobby. I grabbed a putty knife from my Dad's work room and sliced through Ronnie's long, sinuous neck. Then I stood the upper portion atop the glass and positioned the rest below, creating the illusion (or so I hoped) that the creature had swum up to the surface and thrust its head out into the chilly Scottish air. I reached to make an adjustment . . .

"Hey."

. . . and knocked Ronnie right over, for there at the bottom of the basement stairs was 64 inches of pure punkette. She looked tough as nails in a tank top, mini skirt, combat boots and tights, all black as her hair and accessorized throughout with the requisite safety pins and lengths of chain. I looked her up and down, then waxed eloquent: "Jeeez!"

She stepped toward me. "Been years since I wore a skirt."

"You're . . . barely wearing one now."

"Yeah, I guess it *is* a little short."

"An observation, Cheryl. Not a complaint."

Flattered, she shot me a crooked smile.

I smiled back but reminded myself: *New leaf.*

"Got it at Sweet Doomed Angel, on Farwell. . . ."

"I know; I saw the ad in *Head on a Post.*"

"We should get you over there." She stared blankly at my silly little "lake," then grabbed the putty knife and sat down on the couch, left knee raised. "These tights look like shit," she said, and set about "fixing" them by ripping holes into the fabric.

"Uh . . . did my Mom see you?"

"I don't think she's home."

"You ever hear of a doorbell, Cheryl?"

She shrugged. "I phoned an hour ago. It just rang 'n' rang."

I *had* cranked up the Kenny Loggins pretty loud. "Uh, I had tunes playing. Sex Pistols."

"Right on." Cheryl stopped to inspect her work: the tender flesh of her left leg peeked provocatively from a dozen gashes of varying shapes and sizes.

I imagined tracing each one with my tongue . . . then made myself look away.

She switched legs and nodded toward the table. "What's goin' on there."

"It's for a film." I walked over to my "set" and stood the model's neck up again on the glass. "See, this sea monster's supposed to be sticking its head out of Loch Ness," I said. And felt, as I said it, all of nine-and-a-half years old.

Cheryl stared at the model for a moment, then offered, "If ya hollowed it out, it'd make a killer bong." She checked her leggings (which now matched), set down the knife and stood. "Still makin' movies, huh."

"Off and on."

She reached into the top of her boot—"The one you showed me, that *Curse of Dr. Jekyll*"—and pulled something out. "It was pretty good."

"Thanks!" Taken aback by the compliment, I didn't grasp what Cheryl was doing at first. But then it registered: she was lighting up. "Hey, I told you: no cigarettes in the house!"

"Ish not a shigarette," she said, puffing, then retracted her hand to reveal a pipe. A large, rather expensive-looking pipe. My *father's* pipe.

"Cheryl! What the *hell*?"

She took a drag, and a thin line of smoke snaked up to the ceiling. "You said he doesn't use it. Seemed like a waste."

I grabbed the pipe out of her mouth—"Ya wanna get me *killed*?"—and ran it upstairs. I took it into the bathroom and drenched it in the sink, then dried it with a hand towel and rushed to my father's study. I opened the Lucite case and placed the pipe back in its spot. I closed the lid and wiped the fingerprints off the box. And all the while, one phrase kept running through my head: *This girl is trouble.*

As I headed back to the basement door, my mother came bustling into the house, four jam-packed Sentry Foods bags worming their way out of her arms. "Help!" she cried.

I rushed to comply. "They're falling apart," I said, taking what I could from her and hoisting it into the kitchen as she followed with the rest.

"These new plastic grocery bags are sheer lunacy." She dumped her purchases onto the table. "What good's a handle if it can't hold the weight?"

I surveyed the literal mother lode of Popsicles and Pop-Tarts, Hungry Man dinners and Honey-Nut Cheerios sprawled before me. It seemed like an awful lot of food, what with my folks' imminent anniversary trip. Unless . . . *uh-oh.* "Aren't you and Dad . . . I mean, you *are* going to New Orleans, right?"

"Stocking up for you, dear."

"Oh. Thanks."

The grocery crisis now contained, my mom segued into investigate mode. "I see there's a bicycle parked out front."

"Yeah."

"That Cheryl girl?"

"My friend, Cheryl. Yes."

"Where is she?"

"We're hanging out in the basement."

My mother raised one eyebrow—her Mr. Spock look.

"Mom, we're just. . . ."

From below came a drum roll and cymbal crash, then a steady 4/4 beat.

Thank you, Cheryl. "We're jamming. Y'know—rockin' out."

She grimaced, but I could tell she was relieved: playing instruments would divert our hands from each other. "Just keep the door closed."

I returned to the basement to find the Little Drummer Girl standing behind her kit, pa-rumpa-pum-pumming away. Seeing me, she slowed the tempo but continued to play.

"I can't believe you took that pipe."

"*Didn't* fuckin' *take* it," she rapped to the beat, "I was *gon*-na put it *back*."

"Well, it was a close call: my mom came in and nearly caught me."

"Is she comin' . . . down here."

"Not if we're jamming." I reached for my Fender.

Cheryl stopped—"Hold up"—and set down her sticks. She stepped out from behind the kit and headed for the stereo.

"What are you doing?"

She crouched beside the tape deck and hit REWIND—but what tape was she rewinding? "Just a sec'."

I folded my arms. "You could've gotten me grounded."

"That'd suck."

"Y'know, my folks are supposed to be leaving town . . ."

She looked up.

". . . and I don't want anything coming along to change their minds."

The cassette stopped rewinding. "When do they go."

"Saturday. For a week."

She hit PLAY, and I heard my own voice: "It's just a little condenser mike; it'll sound like shit"—followed by Cheryl's: "Right on"—then recognized the sound blasting from the speakers as our first cacophonous jam session, recorded more than two weeks before. This was the tape she'd said "could come in useful."

Cheryl raised her voice over the noise: "Sounds just like we're playin' live, huh."

"Well . . . yeah. It does."

She stood. "Sorry 'bout the pipe, Phil. I was only messin' around."

I looked at her.

"Guess I was outta line."

"I . . . appreciate the apology."

Cheryl walked over to the couch. "Give ya more'n that." She plopped herself down, drew her boots up onto the edge and—and *man*, that skirt was short.

I stepped up beside her. "You . . . didn't nab anything else up there, did ya?"

She raised her arms. "Frisk me."

I sat. And pictured the new leaf on my desk bursting into flames.

And as Cheryl leaned toward me—the cathartic clamor we'd made together echoing off the walls—I warned myself again: *This girl is trouble.*

Then added, as her mouth met mine: *Bring it on.*

* * *

I spent the rest of that day strenuously beating myself up. Again.

So much for self-control. Where was my fidelity; where was my resolve? These ideals proved solid in solitude . . . but elusive when *she* was around.

What's more, my relapse had been no mere rerun: we went further than before, engaging in some aggressive through-the-clothes petting. Then, just as I started to take off her top, the tape ran out; moments later, we heard someone tromping down the stairs. It was all Cheryl and I could do to scramble back to our instruments before my mom appeared, clothes basket in hand. (Fortunately, the body of my guitar covered a key region of my own.) When she saw Cheryl's new look, my mother froze, her expression that of a character in a disaster movie. Then, without a word, she veered off into the laundry room.

I walked Cheryl upstairs and saw her off, then retreated to my bedroom for a round or 12 of psychic self-flagellation. I forced myself to re-read Stefanie's letters from camp; I held up her picture and stared into her eyes; I imagined her reaction if she ever found out. Then came the day's mail, and with it a mid-sized package handed to me by my tight-lipped Mom. A package from New York City; a gift from Stef. It was addressed to "Philip Corcoran, Birthday Boy" with the admonition "Don't Open Till You're 17!" written inside a heart.

I placed the box on my desk, right over the leaf, and stared at it in silence. Whatever was inside, one thing was certain: I didn't deserve it.

My guilt was a being, a living thing the size of a pubescent bear, that clung to my shoulders and mewled in my ear that whole afternoon—then joined me for my evening commute and shadowed me at work as well. Waxing the front-lobby floor, I recalled something we'd read in World Lit the year before. From the play *No Exit*, by Sartre: "Hell is other people."

No, it's not, I countered now. *It's letting other people down.*

On the bus ride home I hunched over, elbows on my knees, listening to the curler-coifed woman beside me coughing up God-knows-what, and struggled to think of a way out. Stef would be back in two weeks; I just needed to stay clean till then. That seemed feasible, for this was no addiction—I did fine when Cheryl was gone. It was like my relationship with Cheetos: I never went out and bought them . . . but when they were around, I was powerless to resist.

The key was to keep my distance. But how? I could call her up and break it off, but I doubted she'd take "no" for an answer; almost certainly, she would stop by some time and try to change my mind. And almost certainly, she would succeed. So, how the hell. . . ?

"Hok, Hok, *HOK*," the woman beside me coughed, spraying the vile contents of her respiratory system throughout the vicinity. I turned to glare at her—but as I did, the answer came to me, and I nearly gave her a hug.

She looked over, a yellowish dribble hanging off her chin.

I gave her a Kleenex.

As soon as I got home, I called Cheryl. It was nearly 11, but I knew she'd be up. And indeed, it was she who promptly answered: "Yeah."

"It's Phil," I rasped.

"What's with your voice, man."

"Strep throat." I coughed, twice. "I'm sick as a dog: fever, chills. . . ."

"Drag," she said. "When'd it start."

"A couple hours after you left."

"Shit. Hope *I* don't catch it."

"Take some Vitamin C."

"Uh. . . ."

"You got any fruit juice?"

"Hold on." I heard her rifling around in the fridge. "Uh . . . got some margarita mix."

"That'll do. Anyway"—cough—"I'll be out of commission for a while."

"Well, when ya feel better. . . ."

"I'll call you; I will. And, Cheryl. . . ."

"Yeah."

"Stay out of trouble."

As I hung up, a weight lifted—well, partly. It was as if that young bear had climbed off me and moved to a spot across the room . . . a spot from which it now stood, watching. Maybe this wasn't a permanent solution, but at least I'd bought some time. Plus, it should get easier day by day. Out of sight, out of mind.

I went to the kitchen and opened the fridge: blueberry pie! My folks were in bed, so I sat down right on the counter and began eating it out of the tin—

. . . then recalled Cheryl seated on her own kitchen counter, smoking her way from spice to spice to . . .

"Christ!" I pushed the pie aside. Why was I still thinking about her? What was wrong with me? If memory served, the plan had been to help her out—nothing more—while awaiting Stef's return . . . but things had gotten murky. What, precisely, were my motives now? Staring down at my dessert, I envisioned a pie chart divided into three sections: Altruism, Friendship, and Lust. But which one was the biggest? And why was Cheryl's pull so strong?

And what if *she* was the one I was supposed to. . . ?

"No," I said aloud, "I'm supposed to be with Stef." Then I put the damned pie back in the fridge and slammed the door for emphasis.

Up in my room, I reached for my birthday package—I was dying to see what she'd gotten me—then read, again, the message inside the heart. I paused, chewed my lip; I let my hand fall. *Self-control. Resolve.* I would do as my girlfriend had asked. I wouldn't open her gift just yet; I'd take the time to thank her for it instead.

I turned on the radio and sat down at my desk. I pulled out a sheet of "Star Trek" stationery and picked up my favorite pen. I began to write—then stopped, the bear's breath hot on my neck again, and stared at the string of letters below:

Dear Ch

* * *

I spent the rest of that week strenuously beating off.

That's an overstatement, but not by much. Consider: Stefanie and I had come tantalizingly close to going all the way, and then she'd left. I had responded to her departure by taking up with another girl and coming tantalizingly close to going all the way with her as well. So, yes, there was a fair amount of self-gratification that third week of August—all focused, I might add, around thoughts of sweet Stef.

My night-janitor job provided little distraction. If I haven't written about it much lately, it's because there wasn't much to write. To wit: on Wednesday of that week, the big white vending machine in the employee lounge gave me two Baby Ruths for the price of one. When I mentioned this to Mr. Puckett, he raced down to try it himself, as if we were in Vegas and he'd gotten word of a "hot slot"—but the machine only gave him one. "Thing must be racist," he had joked.

That was the highlight of the work week. For building services and property management was, in the end, a colossal yawn: the same old chores and the same old floors, over and over, *ad nauseum*. Even the complex fantasy games I'd developed had become monotonous—or, perhaps, had been eclipsed by the reality of my ever-more-complex life. Whatever: I showed up, did the work, collected my check and left.

During the days, I continued pre-production of *Proof Positive*: viewing and indexing my Scottish location footage; modifying a bathysphere model kit into a "hydroponic time machine"; storyboarding key scenes from the script. I even found and purchased a kilt (well, a big plaid skirt) at the local Salvation Army store; all I needed now was someone to wear it. Avery was off camping with his dad, so I called up Craig in Indiana and, to the strains of his booming Black Sabbath, offered him "a really cool role in the final scene."

"Any lines?" he asked.

"Just one, but it's a great one: 'Ach! Ther-r-re be a *Monster-r-r* in *Loch Ness!*'"

"Thought you said this guy was Scottish"—a swipe at my accent.

"I suppose you can do better?"

Craig tried the line himself, bellowing it back to me over the music.

I hastened to praise his brogue: "That's perfect! Craig, man, this part is for you."

"OK, I guess I could . . . wait a second. A Scottish fisherman? What's he wear?"

"Well, of course, in the interest of, uh, cultural authenticity. . . ."

Thus ended the telephone audition of Craig Starling. *Fine*, I thought while hanging up. *I'll wear the damned thing myself.*

I didn't shoot hoops at all that week; how could I explain my presence on the court if Cheryl happened along? I likewise mowed our lawns at dawn, minimizing the chance that she might bike past and see me. Though in fact, to my knowledge, she did not stop by at all.

She did, however, call—once. When I returned home from work on Thursday night, I found a slip of paper taped to my bedroom door:

Cheryl phoned and asked if you were "still sick."
I told her you were.

I tore off the note, crumpled it in my hand. *Thanks, Mom*, I thought—and mostly meant it.

It wasn't easy. But I was doing it.

* * *

My final week as a 16-year-old, presented day by day:

Friday

My father came home early and called me into his study for "a little chat." I sat down opposite him and immediately focused on the pattern of his tie, the pen in his shirt pocket, the still-life painting on the wall beyond. In view of his pipe's recent adventure, I was trying like hell not to look at it . . . and so drew his attention straight to it.

"Awful habit," he said, eyeing the box. He squinted a bit, as if something were amiss; he leaned in for a closer view. . . .

I held my breath.

He looked back up. "Don't ever start."

Whew. "I won't."

My father folded his hands. "Phil, I'm sorry we won't be here for your birthday."

"Hey, I don't mind."

"Of course, this won't be the first time we've left you on your own. But it will be the longest. You'll have our number at the hotel, just in case. And you have Todd's number in Lauderdale. But I trust you'll be able to deal with whatever might come up."

"I'm sure I will."

He looked at me, long and hard. "Is there anything you'd like to . . . ask me about, son? Anything at all?"

My rote response was "nope," but this time I actually stopped and considered. He knew I had a girlfriend; undoubtedly, my mom had filled him in on "that other girl," too. At any rate, he seemed to grasp that I'd been struggling. And while J. Theodore Corcoran, MD, was in some ways a distant figure in my life, that distance made him no less substantial. From his thriving cardiology practice to his prescient blue-chip investments to, 25 years ago, his choice of whom to wed, his decisions had proved sound . . . at least, outside the voting booth.

I noted the scar beside my father's mouth—a souvenir of his hard-scrabble boyhood—then pictured his whole life in capsule. I pictured him growing up on a struggling, Depression-Era dairy farm . . . going to boot camp at age 18—barely older than *me!*—then shipping off to the Pacific Theatre and earning a Bronze Star . . . attending college on the G.I. Bill . . . working his way through medical school . . . joining a small group practice on the bottom rung and rising, over the years, to make it huge—and make it his own. The same hands that had gripped Guernsey udders and then grenades now grafted arteries, opened up ventricles, repaired and re-started ailing human hearts. It was a hell of a story; it was the American Story. And I guess that was the problem: it intimidated me.

He may have been able to help me; I'm sure he'd have offered good advice. But therein lay the problem. Call it the Paragon Paradox: the example he set loomed so large, I dared not share with him my conflicts, my dilemmas, my own flawed and faltering self.

The wall clock chimed three times; my father cleared his throat. "Son?"

"Nothing, Dad. Nothing at all."

Saturday

At 10 AM, I drove my folks down to Mitchell Field. I pulled up outside Departures, hit the blinkers and helped my father heft their luggage out of the trunk. "Anything you want from New Orleans?" my mom asked.

I thought about it. "Stop by the Voodoo Museum."

She stared at me. "I beg your pardon?"

"Look it up; it's there." I handed her the smallest bag.

"What on earth would you want from a voodoo museum?"

"Candles, dolls, potions—whatever. Just for fun." I was hoping there might be, among her purchases, a fitting gift for my own high priestess of the Super-8 screen.

My mother shook her head. "It's *your* birthday, I suppose."

I half-hugged my father, who said, "Take care."

My mom kissed my cheek. "Have a good time," she instructed, with a tone that meant, "Not *too* good."

"Hey, you too. Happy anniversary!"

They began walking toward the terminal; the automatic doors slid open. My father glanced back. "No parties."

"None," I promised.

The doors were closing, but I heard my mom's last words loud and clear: "That includes parties of two."

I drove straight home and spent the day in the den, eating Quisp cereal and Fritos (but abstaining from Cheetos), watching baseball and "Bonanza," wearing my Brewers cap—and nothing else. Why? Because I could.

Sunday
More junk food; more TV in the nude.

Monday
I'd made it through the weekend—and one week away from Cheryl—without a lapse. After all that time indoors, though, I felt like one of those underground cave fish that turn dead white and lose their sight. It was time to venture back into the sun, so I started with something that sounded safe: a birthday week visit to my good ol' birth tree. I slid into cut-offs, filled my thermos, pulled my bike out of the garage and hit the road.

My route took me, as always, right past the high school. And wouldn't you know it: seated there on the concrete stairs, leaning back against the building's locked Door 3 with a Marlboro in hand, was Cheryl Jantz.

She was slouched by her bike and decked out, again, in her black-on-black ensemble; she'd left the hole-ridden hose at home, though, her legs bare and white and folded beneath her. This punk persona really suited her; she looked sinister yet sweet, like little Wednesday Addams a few years on. I was about to veer away, but Cheryl glanced up and saw me and—and then it was too late. "Hey."

I angled toward her, brought my bike to a stop. "Hey, Cheryl."

She took a drag. "What's new in Philsville."

Déjà vu, I thought. For, her attire aside, this was playing out much like the first time we'd hooked up, back at the start of summer. "Well," I said, "I'm feeling much better."

"Some nasty-ass bug, huh." She sounded dubious.

"Yeah, it was. There were . . . complications."

"Likely." She pursed her lips, blew a smoke ring. "Funny *I* didn't catch it. I mean, considering. . . ."

"Whatcha doin' here?"

"Meetin' a guy from Madison."

"What for?"

"Conducting a little business."

That was the last thing I wanted to hear. "Hey, didn't I tell you to stay out of. . . ?"

"Yeah. And then you disappeared."

"Cheryl."

"You weren't around, man. What the fuck *else* I'm s'posed to do."

Maybe it was the way her voice cracked on the word "around," betraying the emotion behind her blasé delivery. Maybe it was the wounded look that passed, just for a moment, over her gray eyes. Maybe it was the realization that now I, too, had let her down, as had so many others. Or maybe it was her seriously flawed grammar. Whatever the reason, I leaned over and offered her my hand. "I'm around now."

She looked at me.

"You don't need . . . that kind of business."

She wavered, glanced about . . . then tossed away her cigarette and reached up.

I lifted her to her feet. "C'mon."

"C'mon where."

"Let's ride."

For lack of a better idea on short notice, I led her to my original destination. We got off our bikes, and Cheryl stood staring at the plaque on the rock while I explained to her my curious bond with this seemingly normal tree, this unassuming maple out of many. I opened my thermos and gave the tree a drink, then handed the vessel half-full to Cheryl.

She took a sip, swallowed. "Kinda cool."

"It's . . . a good thermos."

"No—I meant, you and the tree."

"Oh. You don't think it's silly?"

She shrugged, handed the thermos back—"It's both"—then looked again at the plaque. "So, your birthday was. . . ."

"It's the 29th—this Friday."

Cheryl pulled her trusty Magic Marker from her skirt pocket and scribbled "Phil—FRI" on her forearm; never had an act of self-defacement so touched my heart. She capped the pen and put it away. "Your folks are outta town, huh."

"Till Saturday night," I slowly replied. Then nodded. Then added, "Yeah."

She stepped toward me; as the bottom branch of my birth tree swayed, its shadow fluttered over her face.

"Cheryl. . . ." This was the hard part. For how could I tell her; what was I to say? How could I explain that, as much as I thought of her and cared for her and wanted her, I simply couldn't see her any more?

"I'm glad you came by," she said.

"Yeah?"

"Yeah. Last fuckin' thing I need's another arrest."

I nodded. "That's right."

"Besides, I . . . kinda missed ya."

I took a breath. "Missed you, too."

She placed her tiny hands on my waist. "Ya wanna hang out this week."

I placed my hands over hers. "I do."

Tuesday

We strolled the cluttered aisles of Sweet Doomed Angel, my personal wardrobe consultant and I, to the accompaniment of the Roxy Music song playing behind the counter:

> Oh, whoa-oh, catch that buzz,
> Love is the drug I'm thinking of

I scooped a hanger off the nearest rack and held the shirt aloft: a sleeveless black terry-cloth T, festooned with six functional if superfluous metal zippers—four on the front, two in back. "Hey, Cheryl, check this out."

She stepped over to join me. "Wicked."

I positioned the shirt in front of my chest. "Well, it *is* my size. . . ."

"I could have fun with these." She reached toward me—I could still make out the letters scrawled across her arm—unzipped a zipper and poked a finger through the gash. Then, spotting something on the next rack, she swept past me. "Black leather pants!" she all but cooed, stroking the leg of the nearest pair as if it were a living creature. "These are *so* for you."

I joined her, zipper-shirt in hand, and examined the pants. "Think I could pull it off?"

"Think it'd be me pulling 'em off."

Blushing, I looked away.

She checked the price tag—"Whoa, pretty steep"—then showed it to me.

"I can swing that."

"On a janitor's salary."

"Sure. Other than records, I haven't bought much this summer. Besides, I kinda have this second job. . . ." I gave her the scoop on Ruskin Ranch.

She listened attentively, then shook her head. "Man, what is it with you and trees."

She had a point. "I don't know. Anyway, it's not a ton of money, but it adds up."

Cheryl turned back to the leather pants and gave them another stroke. "Mmmm."

I had yet to buy them, let alone put them on . . . yet already could feel her touch.

"You oughta take me with, some time. Up to that guy's land."

"I'm going on Thursday, so if you want. . . ."

"Private beach, huh."

"Private beach."

Cheryl nodded.

I nodded back.
"Right on."

> Oh, whoa-oh, can't you see?
> Love is the drug for me.

Wednesday
After work, I changed clothes in the car and hooked up with
Cheryl for Live Music Night at the Starship. A local group called the
Oil Tasters was scheduled to play a late gig; we'd both read about
them in *Head on a Post* and were eager to check them out.

As soon as the band appeared, punkers poured into the pit,
filling it in a heartbeat; fortunately, Cheryl and I were among a
modest crowd standing there already, pressed up against the stage.
We thus were ideally situated to witness—and join in—whatever
was to come.

The Oil Tasters consisted of three surly members: a drummer,
a sax player and a bassist/vocalist—but no one on guitar. The sax
player's squawks and bleats burst into the air like pipe bombs; the
drummer *attacked* his kit, pounding it into submission; the bassist
ground away at low E as if tunneling into Hell. As he strummed, he
bellowed out a livid refrain:

> What's in your mouth? What's in your mouth?
> Keep it to yourself! *Keep it to yourself!*

The style of "dance" this murky, malevolent sound inspired was
just shy of slamming and seemed sure to get there soon. Like those
around us, Cheryl and I jerked and hopped, lurched and spun,
our bodies in constant, chaotic motion. I even threw in—to my
date's amusement—a couple of disco moves, albeit in a decidedly
sneering, mocking way. Call it "tripping the light sarcastic."

Unbeknownst to us, in a scant few years the city would raze the
Starship to build the gleaming Grand Avenue Mall. Trendy stores
and a food court would supplant the dank bar; not a trace of punk

squalor would remain. But on that crackling night in the club's heyday, it was a place of purest black magic.

Our eyes flitted between the band and one another—though not until song's end did our gazes meet. Cheryl was wearing a blissful grin, and I had a good idea why. I started to speak: "They're real—"

But the Tasters came tearing back, upping the tempo for "Get Out of the Bathroom." The crowd was dancing more wildly than before and Cheryl whirling madly in front of me, spinning and spinning around and around and *BAM!*—into my chest. I was braced for it, though; I'd seen her coming. She looked up, blinked . . . then yanked at my top shirt-zipper.

I grabbed her shoulders, gave her a shove.

She stumbled, found her footing. Reeling back, she laughed.

The saxophone shrieked.

She gripped another zipper, yanked—*ow, my nipple!*—then spun away.

I chased her, gave her ass a *WHACK*.

The speakers squealed; the singer roared.

She dug into my shirt and *tore*.

We flailed at each other like bloodied sharks as the drums crashed and the punkers thrashed and I saw my brand-new $18 zipper-shirt ripped to ribbons before my eyes—not that I cared. By song's end, Cheryl and I were beaten and battered and standing in a pool of fabric scraps, hanging onto each other out of sheer self-defense.

"Truce!" she cried, panting, and squeezed my bare torso tight. "*Truce!*"

I nodded—"Truce"—and released her. Then touched the stanza of scratches her nails had etched on my chest.

She kicked at a shirt scrap. "I'll go back to Angel and getcha another." By which she meant, "steal."

As the band resumed, I looked down at my date: sexy, sweaty little Cheryl, all bruised and bedraggled and breathing hard before me. And I thought:

How the hell am I supposed to keep my hands off you?

Thursday

In southeastern Wisconsin, summer storms can sweep in without warning.

So it was that afternoon. For though the sky had been clear when Cheryl biked over to my place, by the time we arrived at Mr. Ruskin's property, the sun was but a memory, and a glowering cloud bank was gathering force above. I stopped the car at the bluff and looked out. "It's comin' in fast from the northeast—see? It's raining over the lake."

Cheryl gestured toward the water jugs behind us. "Not gonna need these."

"Guess not." Distant thunder rumbled.

"Private beach's down there, huh."

"Yup."

She opened her door and darted out. "C'mon."

I cut the engine and got out of the car; the air was unseasonably cool. With an anxious eye on the darkening sky, I followed Cheryl. By the time I reached the edge, she'd already made it halfway down and was navigating the foot path with relative ease. I charged down myself and, knowing the path well, caught up with her by the time she arrived at the bottom.

Collecting our breath, we stepped side by side onto the sand. Cheryl yanked off her boots, proceeding barefoot; I pulled off my sneakers and did the same. Mammoth storm clouds were ballooning out over the water, stretching toward us from the north. The horizon line looked like the trembling blade of a great, serrated knife; the frothy whitecaps were high and alive. "Wow," I said. "Wish I'd brought my movie camera!"

Over the lake, a mile out, lightning crackled down to the surface. "Wicked!"

I raised my voice over the *BOOOM* that followed: "So much for swimming."

She smiled—"Sounds like a dare"—and pulled up her tank top, yanking it off.

No bra!

Without a hint of self-consciousness, she took off her miniskirt and dropped it by her shirt; she wore nothing, now, but plain white panties.

Which she then removed.

I stood and stared. Her pubic hair was dark but spare—a mere down payment for the bush to come. Her broad, flat nipples made her breasts look even smaller than they were. Her knees were knobby, her legs coltish and thin; her hips were narrower than mine. She was no hot babe, no Playmate of the Month; she was too skinny, too straight, too inchoate for those glossy pages. Her jaded history notwithstanding, Cheryl was no grown-up woman; she was just a girl.

And oh, what a girl.

She was also charging full-speed into the surf.

BOOOM.

"Cheryl, wait!" I pulled off my shirt and tore in after her, chasing her pale butt into the roiling swells. "Cheryl!"

She bounded out deeper, screaming in glee as a six-foot wave raced right toward her. She dived, sleek and seal-like, into its crest; the wave rose and rushed forward, carrying her toward shore. I hurtled sideways and caught her, Cheryl's cold, puckered flesh slick against my chest. She spat out some water, then burbled, "Right on!"

To the left, a flash; my head swerved. "Jesu—" *BOOOM!* That one was *damned* close—and sounded, I thought with sudden shame, like Fourth of July fireworks on Atwater Beach. . . .

Cheryl squirmed, hopping in my arms. "Body surfing's the *best!*"

"I know, but. . . ."

"Try it!"

"I have! But. . . ."

She pressed her mouth to mine. As we kissed, her nipples poked into my ribs; the danger, evidently, was a turn-on. But . . . was she as wet inside as out? I lowered my hand. . . .

She bolted away and headed out for more. *BUH-BOOOM.*

I started after her again, then slowed, halted; I stood waist-deep and watched.

She stopped on a sand bar, looking out, the lake lapping up at her buttocks. I saw her back-lit against the inky, surging sky: legs apart, feet planted, stubbornly standing her ground. Thunder echoed over the lake, and rain streaked down like darts from the sky. A jagged vein of light hit the surface in front of her: *BOOOM*. Cheryl didn't flinch—just raised her arms to the heavens and shrieked out a battle cry. Then she looked around, found the next monster wave . . . and splashed off in pursuit.

I stayed right where I was. If she got into trouble, I'd try to rescue her—but there was no point trying to stop her. In her restless, reckless mind, Cheryl didn't think herself in peril. If anything, her presence here was redundant, for she herself was a naked force of nature. She too was electric; she too was storm.

A few minutes later she stumbled, dazed and dripping, toward me. I took hold of her with both hands and led her quickly to shore.

We donned our now sopping-wet clothes, and I helped her up the bluff. Then we got into the Pacer and headed home, both of us soaked to the bone. We didn't talk much on the ride back. But the silence wasn't awkward, as on our initial, ill-fated date more than two months before; no. This time, it felt right.

I took Cheryl to my house with the intention of getting her dry and dressed and on her way so that I could head to work. That said, when she proposed that I phone in and play sick—"You know how to do *that*, right"—I wasted little time in obliging.

While she showered, I made the call. Then I went up to my bedroom, changed into gym shorts and a T, and picked out dry clothes for Cheryl as well. I found something else in my dresser, too . . . something that, like the air freshener, I'd kept hidden under my socks: the dozen-count box of Trojans from Todd.

I stared down at the box for a while, heart pounding.

Then told myself: *These are for Stef.*

When I returned downstairs, Cheryl was wrapped in a towel, casing the liquor cabinet. "Hey," she said, "you want a drink."

"How generous of you to offer." I held out the spare shirt and shorts. "Here."

She grabbed them and handed me a bottle of Chianti—"Trade ya"—then dropped her towel and got dressed in front of me.

"You don't embarrass easily, do you?"

She shrugged. "I don't embarrass at all."

I went into the kitchen and turned on the oven, then pulled a pizza out of the freezer and popped it in. I located a corkscrew, and we took the wine into the den. I turned on the TV and turned off the lights, and we sat down side by side on the shag, leaning against the sofa. We handed the Chianti back and forth, gulping it straight from the bottle. We spent the night eating pizza and Cheetos and drinking and talking and listening to the rain and necking and laughing and opening another bottle and drinking some more.

Then fell asleep on the floor.

* * *

I'm not sure which one woke me—what I heard, or what I felt—for they were simultaneous. What I heard was the clock in the study chiming: one, two, three. What I felt was my shorts sliding down my legs, then off . . . then a moist little mouth closing around my—my—

—my eyes opened:

I saw the TV test pattern. Saw the top of her head. Watched it start to bob.

Closed my eyes again.

Heard the thunder. Heard the rain. Saw her in the water, reveling in the lake. Reached down. Stroked her hair. Told her, "So good. . . ." Felt her swirl. Let out a moan. Lifted my hips. Felt her quicken. Fought the surge. Trembled. Shivered. Spoke her name. Shuddered. Groaned. Let go—

Came

. . . felt her rise and move away.

Heard her say:

"Happy birthday."

CHAPTER 15

Not-So-Sweet Seventeen on the

Planet of the Dates

So began my 18th year—and the longest day of my life.

I opened my eyes and saw her in silhouette, a dim figure in an unlit room. She was up on her feet but bending low, searching the carpeted floor. "Shit! I can't believe it's after 3."

I sat up and held out my hand. "Cheryl."

She moved away. "I'm s'posed to be watching Gabby. Now I gotta beat my mom home, or there'll be fuckin' hell to pay." So much for the cozy pillow talk I'd sought; Cheryl had neither the time nor, it seemed, the inclination. She found her sandals and, slipping into them, stood up straight. "Was worth it, though, either way. Later, man."

"Wait." My throat caught. "Don't you want me to . . . do something for *you?*"

"Like you haven't already." She headed for the door.

"I mean. . . ."

She turned back. "I know what you mean." I started to get up, but she motioned me to stay. "Take a rain check. I really just wanted to getcha off. For now, that's enough." Something occurred to her, and she snickered. "Guess you could say I've 'had my Phil.'"

I looked for her face but could see only darkness.

Cheryl grabbed her Marlboros off the end table. "I'm outta here." And she was.

I heard her step into the garage, lighting up as she went. I heard her open the automatic door. I heard the quick *tik-tik-tik* of the wheels as she walked her bike out to the driveway. By the time the door had finished descending, not a sound could be heard but the gentle tapping of rooftop rain.

I stared up at the wall and, eyes adjusting to the darkness, spotted my mother's cat clock, its tail and eyes swinging left, right, left, right. The room felt mucky, and the top of my skull throbbed: too much wine the night before. I became quite conscious of my own respiration—deep breath in, deep breath out; deep breath in, deep breath out—as if I were in imminent danger and needed to . . . to what? Steel myself? Heal myself? I didn't know.

As I rose and walked, I felt buoyant, insubstantial, as if in zero-gravity. I drifted into my father's study and turned on the overhead light. Eyed his pipe—a trophy of one man's triumph over temptation. Scanned the book shelves: row upon row of *JAMA* back issues, musty medical texts and cardiology tomes. Half a million pages on the human heart, yet nary a word that'd be of use to me now.

I went up to my room, grabbed the package off my desk. Stef had said to wait till today, and I had; wasn't I the model of fidelity and self-control? I tore off the brown paper, and there was my present: a handsome hardcover book—a comprehensive volume on Greek mythology. I paged through it, touched by the gesture and impressed by the lavish, full-color illustrations of gods and goddesses, Muses and Monsters. Near the center was a "Happy Birthday!" bookmark; I turned to the indicated page, where she'd circled a passage in red:

Styx was the river of the unbreakable oath, by which the gods all swore. It was said that only a winged creature could safely approach it, so slick and steep were its banks and so forceful the rush of its current. But if a mortal succeeded in reaching its slippery shore, then a coin paid to Charon, the ferryman, would purchase the traveler's safe passage.

It was then I noticed a penny taped to the bookmark's other side. Below the coin, Stef had written:

If you should be inclined to find your way there, well . . .
"that'll work." (Soon as I get home!) I love & miss
you, Philip. HAPPY BIRTHDAY!   ♥, S

I stood in silence, holding book and bookmark before me. I re-read the excerpt. I re-read Stefanie's note. I ran my fingertip over the coin. At some point, I sensed that I was no longer alone. But for once, it wasn't Cheryl who'd slipped in on me—*onto* me; it was my nagging inner nemesis, the pubescent bear of guilt. I couldn't see but surely felt him: his warm, gamy breath on my neck, his ample weight on my back. A greater weight, actually, than before. He had grown.

I sat down on my bed, shoulders rigid, the open book still clenched in my hands. Out of nowhere I thought of the Oil Tasters, heard in my head their opening number from two nights before: "What's in your mouth? What's in your mouth? / Keep it to yourself!"

I stared at the pages below, the words blurring as my eyes began to fill. I'd have given my sight to take it back: the blow job, sure . . . but also the beach, the basement, the whole damned month. Too late, I understood that Cheryl was not, would never be, the one for me. I needed the girl who sent me sweet, flirtatious notes about the River Styx, not the one who substituted a crude quip for a good-bye kiss. I needed the girl who, after coming, curled herself into me and hung on for an hour, not the one who sucked me off and split. I needed the girl who'd just written that she *loved* me—as, God help me, I loved her, too—not the one who'd said, "I'm outta here."

I touched my chest. "Outta here, too," I croaked as a tear fell down to the page below, into the river of the unbreakable oath.

I should have focused on my film; for all the pre-production, I hadn't yet shot a frame. I should have hung out more with my buds: gone to more movies with Avery; invited Craig to come help me with *Proof Positive* . . . and if I had to spend time with a female friend, then it should have been Danielle, who'd recused herself from romance with me. I should have heeded the words of my mom; I should have leveled with my dad. I should have done more reading: I glanced over, spotted the seven sci-fi paperbacks lying in a dusty stack by my bed; my time would have been far better spent with Beaumont and Nolan and Knight than with Jantz. I should have played more hoops, done more running and swimming. I should have practiced guitar—solo. I should have spent more time, alone, on Mr. Ruskin's land, communing with nature in a place of safe retreat. Most of all, I should have steered clear of Cheryl and *embraced* my yearning for Stef, nurturing the ache . . . and paving the way for a glorious reunion.

I should have waited.

"Shoulda, shoulda, shoulda!" I fell with a whimper onto my bed, closed my eyes and retreated into science fiction. Given the means, I told myself, I'd zip back in time—not to abduct some *new* serpent, but to keep my own out of trouble. Or I could go into suspended animation, like a space traveler on an interstellar voyage. I'd buckle myself in, fold my arms over my chest—*like this*—and suck in the astro-ether as the curved glass lid slid down around me . . . then wake up in 20 centuries or so, when my adolescent problems wouldn't matter a whit. I'd have done it, too, if I could—but for one fellow adolescent here on earth. . . .

Stef would be home in three days. And while I longed to see her, to take her into my arms, kiss her sweet lips and do my damnedest to get back on track, I wasn't even sure I could look her in the eye. Yup: some form of cryogenics was definitely the way to go.

I held up the "Happy Birthday" bookmark, read her note again. Studied the penny: 1963—the year of my birth. My God, she'd thought of everything. The coin was covering some text; I peeled it off, revealing the logo of some book store in Manhattan.

Manhattan. . . .

I stared at the logo, and as I did, the answer came to me. *That's it. Yes, that's it!*

"I'll fly to New York!"

I had her address—it was on every envelope she'd sent. Hell, it was on the wrapping paper right there at my feet! I'd track her down and tell her I loved her. And . . . I would come clean: I'd go ahead and confess to, well, at least *some* of what had happened with Cheryl. But my presence in Manhattan, the lengths I'd gone to—

surely, that would win us a brand-new start. My bold action would convince her that I was serious now . . . and it would convince me, too. It would allay my guilt, keep that goddamn bear at bay until I could drive it out in the only way I knew how: by loving Stefanie faithfully and well.

I leapt off the bed, dashed to the den and flipped through the Yellow Pages to "Airlines." I called the first one and booked a seat on the first flight to La Guardia, departing from Mitchell Field in a few hours and returning tomorrow afternoon. (I had to get back before my folks!) "How will you be paying?" the agent asked.

"Cash." I'd stop at the bank when they opened at 8.

"You can pay at the terminal when you pick up your ticket. Are you . . . 18 or over?"

"Yeah!" Did I sound *that* immature? I nearly began explaining myself as I had at the motel with Stef—"Y'know, ha-ha, I get that a lot"—but caught myself. "Yes, I am."

"Be sure to bring proof of age."

"Will do." I hung up and set about clearing the den of the detritus from earlier that night. I should have been rife with regret, I suppose, as I picked up the pizza crusts and Cheetos, wine bottles and cigarette butts; as I sprayed Summer Breeze throughout the vicinity; and especially as I scrubbed at the carpet stain in front of where I'd lain. But I felt fine. Chalk up another victory for the human spirit: the knowledge that I'd turned the corner gave me solace, as did my faith in the plan ahead. It was as if in cleaning up the den, I was cleaning up my act—this time, for good.

I showered, dried off, brushed my teeth. I shaved (it was that time of the week). Then I returned to my bedroom and grabbed the canvas backpack from my closet. The first thing I packed was the mythology book. From the bathroom I retrieved toothbrush, toothpaste and deodorant. From my dresser I took a change of socks and briefs . . . and spotted, again, the Trojans. This time I picked up the box, and there, taped to the back, was my brother's prescient note from so many weeks ago:

Don't fuck up.

Too late, I thought—then caught myself. "No," I declared. "It's not."

I left the condoms in the drawer. In light of my actions, it would have been presumptuous to take them to New York. But I was determined to earn my way back: into the rubbers, yes, but first into her heart.

Although I wasn't hungry, I knew I'd need energy for the day ahead, so I gulped o.j. from the carton and reached for the Quisp—the last box from our stockpile, and itself nearly cashed. There was but one serving left of my favorite cereal, discontinued two years before. I snarfed the sugary saucers straight from the box, then tossed it into the trash. *Childhood's end*, I told myself. *Step up and be a man.*

Jaw set, I grabbed my backpack and keys off the table, then walked decisively into the garage, locking the door behind me. I'd spent my summer weeknights mopping up other people's messes; now, goddamn it, the time had come to clean up my own. Brimming with determination, I opened the garage to the mellow half-light of dawn and slid into the Pacer, its rain-soaked upholstery damp against my ass. My—*bare* ass. . . ?

A bit preoccupied, I had neglected to dress.

I got out, unlocked the door and went back inside. I donned a rust-colored T-shirt and my raggedy tan "Tarzan shorts"—the ones Stef had said were her favorites. I returned to the garage, closed the door . . . and found I'd locked my keys in the house.

"Oh, for God's sake. . . !" I walked around to the side, crawled up the storm drain, jimmied open the kitchen window (not for the first time) and slipped in; I nabbed the keys and headed back to the car.

Pulling out of the garage at last, I gazed in dismay at our front lawn, then at the lawns of our neighbors: the area was a veritable wood pile of broken limbs and branches. That had been one hell of a storm, and as I surveyed the damage, I couldn't help but brood. What had happened outside the previous night seemed an apt reflection of all that I had broken within.

I knew the song playing on 'KTI—couldn't quite name it but recognized the bass line. *Oh, right*: that new single from Queen:

"Another One Bites the Dust."

I sped to the spot where my birth tree stood. Slowing, I heaved a sigh of relief: the stolid maple was largely unscathed, the ground below it littered with twigs and leaves but nothing more. My gaze lingered; I bit my lip. Would that *I* had shown such resistance.

I hit the accelerator, picked up speed. Told myself: *I'm showing it now.*

I steered straight to Lake Drive, headed south and soon found myself driving past Atwater Park. With time to kill before the bank opened, I decided to pull over and take a wistful walk down the bluff. For Atwater Beach was where Stef and I had met—and where, four years later, fireworks had commemorated our first kiss.

Before I'd reached the bottom, though, I noticed two differences between the beach of July 4th and the beach this morning. For one thing, the water level had risen, so the jetty on which we two had sat was largely submerged. More pressing, though, was the smell: the sand was laden with uncounted putrefying alewife fish, the "Lemmings o' the Lake" that annually beach themselves along its western shore. Alewife season had come late that year, but it had come with a vengeance. I did an about-face and, holding my nose, charged back up the bluff.

Shepard Avenue is only a few blocks south, so I drove there next. Given the way Stop #1 on the Phil & Stef Memory Tour had turned out, I half-expected to find the Slocums' two-story brownstone burnt to the ground . . . but there it was, very much intact. Looking up at the front entrance, I recalled the night we'd returned from *The Shining* to find the door slightly ajar. I grinned at the memory of the hoot-owl we'd heard while circling the house . . . the turkey baster Stef had accidentally grabbed from the knife drawer . . . our room-by-room robber hunt. That was the night she had said she'd be spending August at camp:

"It's not like I'm moving; we have our whole senior year ahead of us."

And perhaps we still would. For a while there, I'd lost my way. But surely the girl from Shepard Avenue would step in and shepherd me home.

I could have driven to the Magic Pan; there was plenty of time. But Stef had said the place was closing, and I wasn't sure when. Already, this new day seemed rife with omens; the last thing I needed was to stop by the restaurant where we'd reconnected, only to find boarded-up windows and bolted doors.

So I drove straight to the First Wis, parked on the street and grabbed my wallet from the backpack. The bank hadn't opened yet, but I'd be first in line when it did. As I reached the building's front steps, a female voice beckoned from my left: "Good morning. Would you like to save someone's life?"

I turned. Smiling at me from a dozen feet away was a bronze-skinned woman of 22 or so—a Filipina?—in a long white lab coat. Parked behind her was a white van, its side festooned with the words "Blood Center of Greater Wisconsin" and a valentine-style heart with a big red drop inside. "Well," I began, "I'm, uh. . . ."

"Do you have *half an hour* to save a life?"

In point of fact, I did. And as I stood there looking at the nurse, or whatever she was, I struggled to recall the last time I'd done anything for purely altruistic reasons. Of course, the Cheryl Episode had *begun* that way, but. . . .

"Sure," I blurted. "Let's go."

She led me into the back of the van and had me fill out a form. She pricked my fingertip to check my iron, then took my blood pressure and pulse. Speaking with pointed precision, the nurse strained to make conversation. "The supply is low statewide," she said, ushering me to a recliner. "It is especially bad here in town." She tightened a rubber strap around my bicep. "That is why we are out in these mobile units, 'taking it to the street.'"

I could have replied in kind—"I let the wrong girl blow me, and I'm wracked with guilt; that's why *I'm* out in this mobile unit"—but she'd secured my arm and was taking aim, so it seemed wise not to jar her. Instead, for the second time that morning, I lay back, closed my eyes and let a skilled young woman drain me. I suppose I was hoping that, on some karmic level, this second fluid-donation would begin to atone for the first.

Afterward, she offered me cookies and my choice of juice; I selected tomato. As she poured it, though, I noticed the drink's resemblance to what had just left my body, and for the first time I felt woozy. "Uh, on second thought," I said, "could ya make it apple?" She obliged, and the spell soon passed; I made quick work of the refreshments, then hurried off with the nurse's thanks.

There was no line inside the bank, and three of the stations had tellers waiting. As luck would have it, one of those tellers was my erstwhile disco-dancing partner, lookin' good in a low-cut lilac blouse. I'd forgotten that she worked at First Wis. I'd forgotten how lovely she was, too—but as I stepped toward her, it all came rushing back. "Hey, Cassie."

She squinted at me with glistening green eyes. "Uh, it's . . . Paul?"

"Phil."

She nodded. "Right. Phil."

"How's it going, Cassie?"

"OK." She gave me a look. "Listen. If you're back again to try and convince me . . ."

"No," I assured her, "not this time. I have to take some money out of savings. Better make it. . . ." I'd need enough for the ticket, then cab fare from LaGuardia and back, plus other expenses—whatever those might be. ". . . seven hundred dollars."

"That's a lot of cash, Phil." She glanced down. "You in some kind of trouble?"

I followed her gaze to the bandaged crook of my arm. So she thought I was, what: a junkie? "No—well, not *that* kind of trouble. I just gave blood, is all." I leaned in close, confiding. "I need to take a trip. To go see my girlfriend."

"Your girlfriend? Hey—good for you!" All of a sudden, there she was before me: the big sister I'd never had.

"Her name's Stefanie; she's in New York." It felt good to share even part of the story with someone, so I went on: "I kind of screwed things up after she left. Now I have to fly out there and, y'know, try to make it right."

"I'm not supposed to let a minor take out that much cash."

I handed her my ID. "Who says I'm a minor?"

Cassie looked the card over, smiled—she knew it was a fake—and returned it. "Birthday boy, huh?" She gave me a slip of paper. "Here's a present."

I filled out the withdrawal form and handed it back. She processed it, then counted off my currency and slid the stack to me. Stuffing the bills into my wallet, I thought, *There goes half my summer wages.* I began to thank Cassie, but she cut me off:

"Just doing my job, Phil." She raised a hand, flipped her bangs out of her eyes. "Now . . . do yours."

I nodded slowly—my *God*, she was a fox!—then turned and hurried away.

From there I drove to the highway; I exited onto College Ave. and headed east to Mitchell Field. The route was certainly familiar: I'd taken it six days ago to drop off my folks. And I would take it again tomorrow night, three hours after my return, to pick them up. For a moment, the utter madness of my plan registered in my brain. But only for a moment.

I parked in the long-term lot, grabbed my backpack and jogged to the terminal. Once there, I found the ticketing counter and stepped right up. Yes, the sales agent asked for proof of age; yes, she examined the card closely; yes, she wished me a happy birthday. But she also did what I needed her to do: she sold me the goddamn ticket.

The jet boarded right on time. I took my seat—a window on the left—and buckled up. The flight was undersold; many seats were empty, including the two to my right. Thank God for that: I was in no mood for chit-chat. I half-listened as the flight attendant recited her safety speech with android-like efficiency. Soon we were trundling onto the runway, then speeding up, then lifting off. At which point it struck me: never before had I flown alone.

I could have amused myself, as usual, with the safety-instruction card, drawing sizable shark fins next to the passengers floating in their vests. I could have made a list of the ways in which I would have to cover my tracks when I got back. I could have pulled out the mythology book and distracted myself from my own situation— that stale old tale of betrayal and remorse—by reading the oldest tales of all. For that matter, I could have given some thought to what the hell I'd say to Stef when I found her. But I didn't do any of that. What I mainly did on the two-hour-plus flight was think about "The Munsters."

Yes, "The Munsters," that old, black-and-white sit-com about a family of monsters living the suburban-American dream in a haunted mansion at 1313 Mockingbird Lane. I'd watched the syndicated reruns daily on Channel 18, half my lifetime ago. Years before I knew what girls were for; long before lust or love.

Sitting, today, in seat 11-A, I closed my eyes and recalled an August afternoon when all of Milwaukee County had been under a tornado watch. The wind picked up, the temperature dropped and the sky turned that eerie off-yellow that you see once, maybe twice a year. I was indoors, lying on my stomach with a sketch pad and some crayons; Channel 18 was holding a "Draw Herman" contest for kids, and I intended to win. Propped up on my elbows on the TV room floor, I tracked the antics of the Munster clan while working away on my entry. I don't remember where my mother was; maybe out, or else just upstairs. But I—adding the silver neck bolts, filling in the face with green—was happy to be alone.

On the screen, Herman moped, and Lily consoled him. Grandpa goaded him; Herman stomped his feet; half of the ceiling fell down. A corny gag, but I laughed. Tornado or no tornado, I had never felt so cozy, so contented and secure.

Quite possibly, I haven't since.

The plane hit some turbulence, and my eyes flicked open. I looked through the window: spread out below was a mantle of fleecy white. On previous flights, I'd enjoyed the aerial perspective—viewing the heavens from within—but this time I felt unnerved. Time bent; space seemed boundless. *It squashes a man's ego*, I thought . . . then wondered what movie I'd gotten that from.

I felt lonely. Yet when I turned to my right, the aisle seat was no longer empty: the pubescent bear was sitting there. It was facing forward, stumpy legs dangling, just as a child would sit; Christ, it was even wearing its seat belt! I glared in the beast's direction. *Who let you on board?*

It turned its head to face me, staring over with doleful eyes.

I leaned in—*I'm doing everything I can*—then decisively turned away. The bear had made its point; I was here, wasn't I? Enough: I would leave my regrets on the plane. From that moment forward, guilt could only get in the way.

About the time the "No Smoking" light blinked on, Manhattan came into view. It was a staggering sight, this sprawling island metropolis, this strange and somewhat foreboding land that I'd seen all my life in movies and on TV but never in reality. The skyline was bracketed by the buildings King Kong had climbed—Twin Towers on the left, Empire State toward the right—with myriad lesser skyscrapers packed around and in between. I tried to picture the First Wis among them, but here, Milwaukee's 40-story standout would scarcely have registered.

So, this was New York. But what would I find here? What did it hold in store for me?

My destiny.

The runway landing was bumpy and abrupt, as if we'd set down on water. A woman behind me let out a scream, but the flight attendant was unruffled: "Uh, sorry about that, folks! Slight issue with the landing gear, but we're on the ground now, and we're fine. Welcome to New York." Welcome, indeed. Again, I was thinking of omens.

An offsetting one arrived, though, as the plane continued to taxi and the attendant continued to talk: "For those of you traveling to Norfolk, to Wilmington, or to our terminal stop of Columbia, South Carolina. . . ."

South Carolina. I hadn't memorized every state motto, but that one I knew—and whispered to myself as we came to a stop: "While I breathe, I hope."

The gate was noisy with joyful-tearful reunions (intensified, no doubt, by that quasi-crash-landing). As my own reunion was an hour or more away, and its outcome uncertain, I beat a quick retreat. Following the "TO TAXI" signs, I made my way through the labyrinthine La Guardia—into which several Mitchell Fields could have fit—and eventually reached a revolving door that led outside.

It was hotter out than back home. I waded through the steamy air toward a sign that read "Cab Stand." Yes, there was a line for cabs; as I was to discover, in New York there was a line for everything. When my taxi came, I opened the back door, tossed my backpack onto the seat and sat. *Shit*—no a.c., and I was sweating already.

The driver, a durable-looking middle-aged woman, eyed me in her mirror. "Where ya headed?"

I closed the door. "Manhattan."

"Got an address?"

Then it hit me: I didn't. Sure, it was on every envelope Stef had sent; yes, it was on the paper wrapping that had lain there at my feet. But at no point had I actually bothered to grab that address from any of its many locations and take it with me. "Fuck!"

The cabbie turned her head.

"Uh, sorry."

"Fuggedaboutit," she said, "that's the native tongue."

Maybe I could call the address to mind. "Can you give me a second?"

"Take ya' time, kid; meter's runnin'."

"For now, just . . . head for Manhattan, all right? I'll let you know."

And so, we set off. I seem to recall crossing a bridge and going through a tunnel, but I wouldn't swear by it; I spent the trip hunched over a scrap of paper I'd found on the floor, scribbling out numerical combinations. Was she at 40 W. 16th Street or 40 W. 116th? I was sure a 40 and a 16 were involved . . . or possibly a 400 and a 6. I was, however, just as sure that New York City was not a good place for navigation by process of elimination.

"What's it gonna be?"

"Just drop me off somewhere in the center; I'll figure it out from there."

She took me to Grand Central Station, perhaps to facilitate my grabbing a train back to the family farm. I paid the fare (*yikes!*), then found a pay phone—or, rather, a line of people waiting for one. As I stood there under the beating sun on Park Avenue, it occurred to me that I was about a block from the offices of *Starlog* Magazine. And I thought: *Sure, that address I can remember!*

Commuters were filing in and out of Grand Central in silent-movie fast-motion. The pace was far quicker than back home; the only people moving at normal speed were the tourists. Gazing at the station, I recalled a joke my dad had once told:

"A Milwaukee businessman arrives at Grand Central Station, steps outside and hails a cab. 'The Such-and-So Hotel,' he says. Now, the hotel is right across the street, but the cabbie figures he's got a live one, so he drives all over town: down Broadway, past Chinatown, up to Harlem, around Central Park and through Times Square—the whole shebang. Finally, an hour and a half later, he pulls up in front of the hotel and says, 'That'll be $125.' The businessman folds his arms and says, 'Ha! You think I was born yesterday? Last time, that trip was only a *hundred*!'"

I'd always liked that joke. Though now, as I peered into my gravely depleted wallet, it seemed less funny than before.

When my turn came, I dialed Directory Assistance and got the address of the acting camp—on Greenwich, as it turned out. Though it didn't sound familiar, I figured it had to be right.

I hailed another cab, and down I went toward the south side of Manhattan—only to find an arts alliance that housed the camp's administrative office, but not the camp itself. "Oh, it's nowhere *near* here," the haughty office manager said, as if she were stating the obvious.

"No?"

"Of course not! Camp's on the other end of the island." She turned away, waving a hand dismissively. "Up north, on the Columbia campus."

Another cab; another, even longer trip; an even bigger dent in my crash-dieting wallet. But by mid-afternoon there I was, striding toward a stately old dormitory whose front signage bore a banner reading "Northeast Youth Acting Camp." Was Stefanie in that dorm even now, sprawled across her bed with a script in hand, practicing her lines? Or was she in an auditorium somewhere across campus, delivering a poignant soliloquy to her admiring classmates?

The dorm lobby was empty, and no one was manning the front desk, but upon that desk sat an "N.Y.A.C. Student Body" ringbinder. I picked it up and, flipping through, found an alphabetical roster of names. I turned to S, and *yes!* There she was (albeit misspelled): Slocum, Stephanie, Rm. 309.

I bounded up to the third floor, where I was greeted by silence. The room doors were closed, the students surely absent; it was, after all, the middle of the day. Each door was decorated with a pair of construction-paper name signs the kids seemed to have made themselves: "Hannah" and "Becky" here, "David" and "Martin" there. Boys and girls on the same floor? At least they weren't in the same room!

And then, there it was, Room 309: "Erin" and "Stefanie." She'd drawn the "S" as a loop of movie film, a cartoon sketch of her own face inside each frame. (Nice touch.) I knocked: as expected, no answer came from within. The door to the next room swung open, though, and a pajama-clad girl peeked out, a wad of Kleenexes in her hand. "Hello?"

"Hi. I'm looking for Stefanie Slocum."

"She's gone," the girl said, and hacked a rattling cough. "They all are, till . . . pretty late tonight, I'd guess."

"Are they on campus?"

She shook her head. "Our one day *off* campus, and I'm stuck here."

"Where'd they go?"

"Sightseeing." She raised the tissue-wad to her face and blew her nose, hard. "By now, they should be on their way to, uh, whatchacallit . . . Liberty Island. Then dinner, then a show."

"Dinner—where? What show?"

"Dunno." She sneezed mightily, as if for emphasis.

It occurred to me that, this being Acting Camp, the girl might have been in perfect health and merely practicing for a role. If so, she was good; I'd have cast her in a New York minute. Regardless, she undoubtedly was telling the truth about the whereabouts of the group. "Thanks," I said as she shuffled back into her room. "Uh . . . you OK?"

"Death," she intoned miserably, "would be a sweet release."

Liberty Island is accessible only by ferry—specifically, one that departs from Battery Park at the tip of Manhattan, clear on the other side of town. As I climbed into the latest in my ongoing series of cabs, I thought again of that businessman at Grand Central. My father had told the joke, but I was living it.

What's more, between the hangover, the heat, my blood donation and insufficient hydration, I was wiped. Disoriented, too; was this my second ride south, or my third? Already, I'd lost track. I spent the long ride slumped in my seat, caressing my precious book through the canvas and gazing out the window.

The streets were bathed in a greenish haze—not the lush green of foliage, but a pale hue reminiscent of aquarium algae or infected piss. Tinted thusly, the gargantuan structures of lower Manhattan loomed all about, forbidding and still, while at street level the rat race continued apace. I was overwhelmed. As the taxi screeched and weaved through this sickly Emerald City, I looked down at my backpack and imagined not a hardcover book but a small Cairn terrier within. *Toto, I have a feeling we're not in Wisconsin any more.*

Then, on Broadway, disaster hit: a New York City traffic jam. It wasn't the first, but was easily the worst I'd yet encountered. "Come *on*," I seethed, glaring in turn at my wristwatch, the meter, the cabbie, the street. After five minutes of waiting (and four feet of forward progress), I paid the fare, grabbed my bag and took off on foot. What choice did I have? It was getting late; if I didn't catch Stefanie now, it'd be way back up to the camp for me, sitting on my hands till midnight, making awkward small talk with Miss Sweet Release.

So I ran. I ran past souvenir stores and street vendors, past brokers and bums and boutiques; I sidestepped a trio of Krishna musicians, hurdled a vast trash-heap. I ran a red light and, somehow, lived. At the curb, a well-meaning stranger grabbed my shirt: "Yo, kid, *watch* it!" The fabric tore down the middle but stayed on, my backpack holding the pieces in place as I charged forward, unimpeded. The extra ventilation was a relief.

Abruptly, Broadway ended; I'd reached an open area, a public square by the bay—Battery Park? This was it! I passed a few statues, then spotted a sign up ahead: "Ferry to Liberty Island!"

Chest heaving, I got in line. Reached into my backpack for my now-emaciated wallet. Paid my $5. Walked to the embarkation point and joined yet another line. Harborside amongst the happy tourists, I stood panting and held out my ticket, my talisman. *Please take me to her. Just get me there.*

A few feet ahead, a Jamaican woman wearing a tie-dyed sundress, a rainbow wig and an acoustic guitar was working the line: asking people their nations of origin and what had brought them to New York, then singing songs from their native lands—all to a reggae beat. The bemused Swedes gave her a $5 tip; the Japanese couple had their picture taken with her. To the Englishman she said, "I'm goin' to your country next summer, mon, to marry into the Royal Family. That's right: me and Prince Charlie." Then, to the crowd: "So, when you see your Mr. Cronkite talkin' 'bout it on the tee-vee, remember that ya heard it here from me!" She proceeded to strum a bar or two of "God Save the Queen."

She was funny, but I wasn't in the mood; what's more, she was quickly working her way toward me. I was tempted to go ahead and tell her my story—"Got any numbers about fellatio?"—just to see how she'd handle it. (The Blondie song "Eat to the Beat"—?) But fortunately for everyone, a call soon sounded from the speaker above: "All aboard the *Miss Freedom* to Liberty Island, our final outbound of the day."

Once I'd boarded I made straight for the top, ran past the wooden park benches bolted to the deck and positioned myself at the bow. I grabbed the guard rail with both hands and looked out to sea: to the island . . . to Lady Liberty. Was Stefanie on that island even now? Was she within the Statue itself: standing in the crown, staring up at the torch of freedom and—dare I hope—recalling how she and I had marked Independence Day?

The whistle blew, and the ship left port. Then a voice came over the intercom, and for the second time that day I was welcomed aboard and given safety instructions. The announcer pointed out the life vests and preservers, then assured us, "This equipment is for emergency use only. We do not anticipate trouble of any kind."

No, I thought, *ya never do. . . .*

I tightened my grip on the railing, the Atlantic wind whipping into my face, my eyes fixed on my destination.

We approached from the Statue's back. (Lady Liberty, incidentally, has no ass.) I made my way to the disembarkation point while the vessel was still in motion and so was among the first passengers off. And then, as before . . . I ran.

I ran by the people sprawled under the shade trees. I ran into the snack bar, shouting "Stefanie?" at the closed women's room door. I ran across the plaza, around the lawn and onto the brick pedway that encircles the park along the water's edge. Then I took a deep breath, picked up my pace and commenced my orbit of Liberty Island.

Families; couples; lots of little kids. Not many teens, but—wait! Just ahead, four girls were clustered around the long-range binocular machine. I scanned the group: no, no, no, *maybe*—a girl Stef's height was looking through the viewer, surveying the Manhattan skyline. Slender; leggy; chestnut hair . . . she lifted her head, and *no*. Pretty, but not Stefanie.

Vexed yet resolute, I kept running. I ran, in fact, all the way around the island, detecting and rejecting several other "maybe-girls" along the way. Finally I reached my starting point behind the Statue, near the walkway into the great pedestal on which Liberty stands. I slowed, stopped, caught my breath. Peered up and saw the lookout decks at the pedestal's top and bottom, the people milling about at both levels. Maybe . . . maybe she was there.

I charged into Fort Wood, the structure's base, then up the stairway to the lower promenade. I cased the area—families, oldsters, two black girls, a blonde—then shot back inside and resumed my ascent. A series of staircases led me one way, then the other, then back again en route to the next deck. Of course, as I ascended, other visitors were heading down; I surveyed them as we passed, seeking, seeking.

Soon I arrived at the balcony atop the pedestal, just under Liberty's feet. I shot out into the open air, turning, stooping, searching: no. I craned my neck up toward the massive copper Lady, then sagged a bit as it hit me. There was but one place left to look.

I stepped back inside and began clambering up the iron steps: 354 in all, spiraling through the Statue's core from the base all the way to the crown. Here, I couldn't have run if I'd tried; the passage was narrow and the visitors, of necessity, proceeding single-file. In order to prevent collisions, the lone staircase was bisected by a wire fence separating goers-up from comers-down, the former routinely asking through the mesh, "Are we close?" and the latter responding, "Almost there!" If I wasn't careful, Stef might zip right by, going in the other direction. So as I climbed, I looked to my side, squinting through the darkness at each descending face, searching, ever searching for the high-placed eyebrows and the lips I had kissed, for the singular features of the girl I loved.

And what if I *were* to spot her bounding down, so carefree and unaware? I could call out and astound her, watch those eyebrows re-ascend the stairs without her. But we couldn't stop and talk . . . not without causing a traffic jam on par with the one I'd earlier fled. "Philip?" she would cry—with delight, I hoped. "What are you doing here?"

"Wait for me at the bottom!"

"That'll work!"

Then I'd climb to the crown, turn and head back down. Good, then: I had my plan. All I needed to complete it was her.

Thung, thung, thung, the steps rung out with my every footfall. My heart pounded; my legs ached; the canvas straps dug into my shoulders. The book in my backpack felt as heavy as the gigantic one in the Statue's left hand. My girlfriend had mailed me a wonderful gift, but at that moment, I wished she'd sent a pamphlet.

A shaft of light above: the entryway to the crown. "Please," I murmured, as one in prayer: to God, to Love, to Liberty. "Please let me find her." The raised arm and torch had long been off limits, so this lookout atop the head was the terminal point. This was the highest the public could climb, my last shot at finding Stef in the Statue.

She wasn't there.

I stood, palms on the rail, and looked up. I saw the mighty arm, the colossal hand, the great flame of freedom thrust high into the sky. And, by God, it gave me hope. I would find her yet.

What if I'd *beaten* her group to the island, and they were just arriving now?

Then I recalled the announcement at the harbor: ". . . our final outbound of the day."

Hold on, I told myself. *Wait.* Couldn't Stef have been on the same ferry I was on, somewhere behind me in line? Fool that I was, I hadn't thought to check amongst my fellow passengers. *She could be entering the Statue right now!* I turned on my heel and began dashing down.

"Is it close?" someone asked from below.

"Almost there!" My voice was downright jubilant. It was as if finding Stefanie were now a foregone conclusion, and only the minor detail of its occurrence remained. The climb down was, of course, easier and faster than the climb up, a fact that further lifted my spirits. And throughout my descent, I kept an eye on the ascenders, even calling out "Stef?" during the occasional slender-young-brunette sighting. But no one answered back.

Upper balcony: no sign.

Lower promenade: zilch.

Returning to ground level, I departed from Fort Wood—the exit led visitors out in *front* of the Statue—and made my way back to the pedway. Behind Lady Liberty, the sun was starting to set. Soon, the rangers would clear the island; the last ferry would head back to Battery Park. Feet dragging, I began to repeat my orbital tour . . . then stopped.

I turned and looked behind me. The passageway through which I'd emerged was the only public exit. If Stef were inside the Statue at this moment, she'd *have* to come out there.

I stepped over the short wall just beyond the pedway and sat on top of it, facing in. I wriggled out of my backpack, my torn and sweaty T-shirt peeling right off with it. I dropped the bag between my throbbing feet, then removed my sneakers and pulled off my socks. Wearing nothing now but my ever-more-ragged tan shorts—little more, at this point, than a loincloth—I sat keeping vigil as, 20-some yards in front of me, an endless procession of bleary-eyed tourists emerged from Fort Wood.

It felt good, at last, to sit still in one place. Besides, I rather liked Liberty Island—or would have, under other circumstances—though New York itself boggled my mind. Undoubtedly there were a million things to do there at any given moment . . . but what good was that, really, when you could only do one at a time? The city was impressive, but it was no Milwaukee.

Rubbing the soles of my aching feet, I pondered the past 12 hours. It had been one bizarre birthday, with a cast of characters to match—a nearly all-female cast, at that. I'd crossed paths with so many members of the opposite sex, though not yet with the one that I sought. In no particular order, these others now drifted to mind: the sick girl at Acting Camp, the cabbie at La Guardia, Cassie at the bank, the nurse in the Blood Center van, the clowning Jamaican guitarist, the unflappable flight attendant, the smug woman at the arts alliance, the Stef look-alike behind the long-range binocs . . . not to mention Lady Liberty herself.

And kicking things off, of course, was Cheryl Jantz. Again, I heard her open the garage door, then the quick *tik-tik-tik* as she headed home. Would she return tomorrow, hoping to hang out, mess around, kill a little time? Probably. But she'd find an empty house—nor would there be room for her in "Philsville" after I returned. There couldn't be.

I felt badly for Cheryl. Especially considering what she'd done—the "birthday present" she'd given me. True, she'd hightailed it out of there afterward. But did that mean she didn't care about me? Couldn't it mean the opposite: that Cheryl *did* care, but those feelings made her . . . afraid? It was a hell of a thing: letting her blow me . . . then blowing her off. Ditching her for good may have been what I'd had to do. But it wasn't very nice.

Suddenly, emerging from the Statue's base was a familiar face. No, not Stefanie; not a girl but a woman of 50 or so, slight of build and short of stature, wearing a green skirt and blouse. Wasn't that. . . ? Yes: Kim Hunter! Star of stage and screen, "Dr. Zira" from the *Planet of the Apes* movies, "Stella" in *A Streetcar Named Desire*—and crucially, as Stef had written to me, Visiting Artist at Northeast Youth Acting Camp during the final week of its run. She must have been sightseeing with the kids. And if Kim Hunter was there, then Stef had to be close by!

Several teens followed Hunter out—a promising sign. I got to my feet, but with difficulty; my body felt heavier than ever before. I seemed saddled with the weight of that extraordinary day, burdened with the heft of history. All at once, it felt as if the entire summer had led me to this moment.

I'd just begun stepping forward when out of the exit strode . . . could it be—Stefanie? Stefanie! Stefanie, at last! She was a sight-for-sore-everything in her white halter top and denim shorts, shaking her head and laughing at what the tall, lanky kid behind her said—the boy in the boots and the cowboy hat.

That kid she wrote about in her first letter home?

She turned toward him and took his hand.

The one she'd mocked for wanting to do Westerns?

She watched as he spoke, then pulled him close.

The kid Stef thought was ridiculous?

She pushed up the brim of his Stetson.

But—she never mentioned him again!

She said what looked like two words: "That'll work."

Just as, in my letters, I never mentioned. . . .

She kissed him. She kissed him with ardor, she kissed him with zeal—and the young man returned them in full. They kissed like they meant it; they kissed like lovers.

They kissed like *we* used to kiss.

It's true that my day had been largely male-free. But it only took one.

I should have seen it coming. Stef had mailed me the book two weeks before, and she hadn't written since; at our age, two weeks can be a lifetime—as I surely had learned. I'd assumed she was busy with class work, but the true culprit appeared to be extracurricular. Despite her many glowing assets, Stefanie Slocum had turned out to be a flighty, fickle teen. And why not? Why should I have been the only one driven to juggle a pair of partners—or drawn, at the behest of hot-weather hormones, to an attractive, available Someone quite unlike myself? In retrospect, it makes perfect sense.

But on August 29, 1980, retrospect was light years away. There in Liberty's fast-creeping shadow I fell, near-naked, to my knees. "All along," I managed . . . then trailed into silence as the tears began to swell. I shook my head; I grimaced and squirmed. I was a castaway, a wretched refugee; I was a huddled mass, yearning to breathe free. Behind me, waves lapped at the island's rocky shore, while in front of me towered the great copper Lady who had opened herself and let me inside—as, I now knew, Stef would never do. I pounded my fists into the ground. "God damn," I sobbed from low in my throat—from the lowest point of my soul. "Oh, God damn it all to *hell!*"

Then I lifted my weary head and looked up. Up, past Kim Hunter who, apprehending my anguish, was wringing her tiny hands as she stared down at me from a spot off to the side; up, past Stef and her rodeo Romeo, who were far too engrossed in one another to notice me . . . or anyone else in this upside-down world. Way, way up, past the base and the feet and the voluminous robe, all the way up to the top: the implacable visage; the unforgiving eyes; the seven splayed rays; the up-thrust torch she would carry through the ages.

As I would my own.

Escape from the Planet of the Dates

During the December night that our nation counted down to the primary digit "2"—and the worldwide computer grid did *not* plunge into oblivion, nor talking apes rise up to rule the earth—the rampant galas and ovations, speeches and celebrations held little interest for either my girlfriend or me. Sure, we eyed the live network feeds from New York and D.C.; as an indie-film director (and UW-Milwaukee media instructor), I had some professional curiosity. But far more compelling was the woman watching with me, a social worker turned state-senator-elect who was whip-smart, witty and cute as can be.

We had been going out—and, as often, staying in—for just under a year. Our time together had brought us not only joy but *relief*, for we were sick to death of the singles scene. By 36, we'd both spent two decades dating around (and around, and around), each of us finding various partners from across the country and even the globe . . . and then finding, within those partners, reasons to part.

Or—and this was worse—watching *them* find reasons first.

As for our own pairing, it wasn't perfect. Like any living, breathing couple, we had our issues . . . but usually kept them from turning into subscriptions. And so, with our eyes wide open (and crow's feet soon to come), we now found ourselves stealing hopeful peeks at one another and daring, again, to dream.

As midnight approached in our own time zone, I suggested we turn off the TV and take the "bubbly" to bed.

She agreed.

With the lights down low and Prince on the stereo ("1999"—what else?), we greeted Y2K in the best possible way . . . then pulled up the covers for some pillow talk.

I wound up recounting the same story contained within these pages, albeit with greater economy. Basically, I gave her "Cliff's Notes" on that long-ago summer, covering all the key characters, plot twists and themes—this in response to her request, "Tell me about your first time." Then, my recitation complete, I fell silent.

Lying on her side, she gazed over with wide brown eyes. "Whoa. Who knew you were so impetuous?"

"Well, I was young."

"What happened next? She must've *seen* you there, right?"

"Eventually." I shuddered. "Worst conversation of my life. I told her, well, everything—mainly out of spite. And Stefanie . . . replied in kind." I reached past my lover to the bedside table and grabbed the bottle of champagne. "I spent the night at La Guardia and flew home in tears the next day."

She shook her head—"That's cold"—then held out her glass.

I took it but did nothing with it yet, for August 30, 1980 was flooding back to mind. "My flight was delayed; I landed right before my parents. So I'm standing at their gate all filthy and sniffly and miserable, wearing a shredded T-shirt and my 'Tarzan shorts,' pretending I'm there for *them*. . . ."

She squelched a giggle. "Oh, God!"

"Of course, the Pacer was over in *Long*-Term Parking—for no reason I could come up with at the time. And when we reached it, the back seat and the trunk were still loaded with water jugs from my trip to the lake with Cheryl, so I didn't have room for my folks *or* their luggage. . . ."

Now she was laughing. "Shit! Wha—what'd you do?"

"I played dumb; basically, I convinced them I'd been a ditz. But when they got home—by taxi—my dad went to pour himself a drink. Two bottles of Chianti were missing . . . along with some whiskey Jantz had lifted on the sly." Thus reminded, I finally filled the glass in my hand.

She took it. "I'm guessing you were grounded."

I nodded. "For a month. Funny thing is, they never did find out about New York. They still don't know."

She perused the ascending bubbles in her glass, then raised it and took a sip. "Did you ever try to patch things up with Stef?"

"Yeah. We even went out a couple of times. But, well, her heart wasn't in it . . . and the voodoo charms my mom had brought back didn't seem to help."

She handed my own glass to me. "I really hope that's a joke."

"The trust was gone, for both of us." I poured. "It takes two to reconcile, and I guess we had a total of one between us: half of Stefanie and half of me. Still"—I set down the bottle—"she was my first love. It was hard to let go. I ended up lugging that torch around for years."

"I know *that* song"—a reference, I gathered, to her ex. Scooting back, she half-sat up in bed. "All I kept hearing was, 'I'll clean up my act; this time, baby, I'm really gonna try.' I didn't see through it; I . . . didn't want to. I'd lost myself by then. I was nobody's daughter, nobody's friend. . . .'"

"Not true," I said. "You were always my friend."

"You're right—and you were always mine."

I leaned over and kissed her cheek, collecting for my efforts a winsome grin. *Beautiful woman*, I thought, and rested my hand on her hip. "The guy was clueless."

"Pretty much. But mainly, he was selfish."

"Yeah," I said, "it always comes down to that, doesn't it? I mean, isn't that where Stef and I screwed up, too? My God, we were so perfectly matched, especially for a couple of kids; we were so lucky to have found each other. But then we got greedy—both of us. We wanted it all." I shook my head. "How '80s of us."

She laughed. "You two were ahead of the curve!"

"Her dad's the one who called it. 'Each for himself,' he used to say. 'Screw them before they screw you.'"

She turned to me—"I think we can do better"—and raised her glass.

I raised my own. "I think we can, too."

And so it happened that, in the first hour of the 21st Century, my beloved and I drank to a brighter future.

She reached toward the table and set down her glass; I leaned past her to do the same. Since I was there, I ran my fingers through her dense black hair . . . but already, her ever-roving mind was elsewhere. "Y'know," she began, "when I asked about your 'first time,' I didn't mean your first time doing, uh, what you and Cheryl—well . . . really, what she did to you. I meant. . . ."

I found it endearing that, after all *we* had done not an hour before, she could still get a bit flustered alluding to oral sex. I bailed her out: "But my real 'first time' was with Cheryl, too—halfway through senior year."

"Then why," she asked, settling back, "didn't you tell me about *that*?"

"It's not nearly as good a story."

She looked perplexed. "So, for a while there, you two were a couple? 'Cause I sure don't remember. . . ."

"We weren't—not really. In her own way, Cheryl was ahead of the curve, too. Kids today have a term for it: 'friends with benefits.' But that was never enough for me. Even then, I needed a real connection. I guess I . . . always wanted love."

"Mmmm." She pulled me close, her voice low and silky-smooth. "Still want it?"

"Like you wouldn't believe."

We kissed, then, slow and long and deep. "Man," I murmured after a while. "You've sure addressed the needs of this constituent."

She laughed quickly, then shook her head.

"What. . . .?"

"It's crazy, isn't it? I mean, after all the twists and turns that both our lives have taken, who knew you and I would wind up like this?"

"Well, I did use to fantasize about us getting together. I pictured us making love on the beach . . . tried to imagine"—I grabbed her plump little butt—"how you'd feel."

"Yeah"—she batted my hand away—"I remember you makin' your play: 'I find *you* attractive. . . .'"

"Well, maybe you should've 'played' along."

She poked a finger between my ribs. "But you were so skinny!"

"Seriously," I said, "if you had let me *try* to be your boyfriend. . . ."

"Child, after hearing that story of yours. . . ?"

"Nah, it would've been different with us."

She sighed. "I wasn't ready then. This country wasn't ready; Lord knows, my family wasn't ready!"

I touched my thumb to her dear little chin. "And now?"

"And now, what?"

I traced her collarbone with my fingertip. "Well, it's 20 years later."

"So?"

I lowered my hand, placed my palm on her heart. "So, you think they're ready now?"

She started to answer, then stopped. "Wait. Are you. . . ?"

"We can't have it on Mars, but what the hell."

She sat up straight. "For real?"

"For real."

She grabbed her glass and threw back the rest of her drink. She reached out with both hands and took hold of my shoulders, a sly little smile flitting over her lips. Then she tilted her head down in that way she's always done and, peering up, looked me dead in the eye. "Corky," she asked, "what is it you're proposing?"

"Gee, Dee," I answered, "it ain't a date."

YOU'VE READ THE BOOK;
NOW, BUY THE MOVIES—FOR CHARITY!

This book is a work of fiction . . . but "P.C. Productions" are real: the films of "Philip Corcoran" are based on actual sci-fi and monster movies made by Paul "P.C." McComas in his boyhood, from 1973–79. Now, you can purchase your own 90-minute compendium of these ridiculously ambitious, utterly sincere, oft-hilarious little films—with all profits going to charity.

Included are *Beyond the Planet of the Apes*, *Blood of the Wolfman*, *Box* (a *Logan's Run* prequel), *House of Usher*, *The Tale of Captain Shaw* (a Loch Ness opus), *The Twilight Zone: "Reactionary,"* and the *Star Wars* sequel *Vader*. These movies look and sound better than ever, as they've been re-edited (and stellar sound added to them) over the past three years by Paul in collaboration with ace producers Brian Cox (Two Worlds Productions), Mark Mallchok (Brella Productions) and Henry McComas (Crooked Lake Productions) and audio maven Joshua Avila (Dub Vox Studio Services). Added bonus film: Paul & Brian's award-winning 2004 creature-feature homage, *Shock Theatre*!

Paul—a longtime blood donor (90 pints and counting)—and his partners-in-cinematic-crime will contribute *all* profits from sales of this collection to blood-donation services like the one depicted in Chapter 15 of this novel. (The author also encourages all *Planet of the Dates* readers to visit their *own* local blood centers and "give from the heart"—i.e., from the arm.)

For each copy of *No-Budget Theatre: The Best (?) of P.C. Productions*, specify DVD or VHS and send $16 (postage included) to Paul at 909 Greenwood St. 3D, Evanston, IL 60201-4390.

Thank you!

* * *

For more info on Paul and his work, visit www.paulmccomas.com.